But it's amazing how fast even a slow, bulky, elderly detective superintendent can move if he has to. As Donovan watched in astonishment he launched himself up the steps like the demon king in a pantomime.

He was still watching, startled speechless, when he saw the back of Shapiro's coat open like a flower, a red flower blooming in a desert of herringbone tweed.

Time slowed right down. Donovan felt himself rooted to the spot, trying to move and not succeeding. He heard a sort of surprised grunt from Shapiro and a thin cry from the man on the steps above him, slowly, slowly turning to see what had happened. He saw Shapiro falling toward the steps, and though there was all the time in the world he couldn't get his arms forward to break his fall. He crashed facedown on the concrete, and time resumed normal speed.

———————— ★ ————————

Previously published Worldwide Mystery titles by
JO BANNISTER

A BLEEDING OF INNOCENTS
CHARISMA
A TASTE FOR BURNING
NO BIRDS SING
THE LAZARUS HOTEL
BROKEN LINES

JO BANNISTER

THE HIRELING'S TALE

M
BANN

W✷RLDWIDE.

TORONTO • NEW YORK • LONDON
AMSTERDAM • PARIS • SYDNEY • HAMBURG
STOCKHOLM • ATHENS • TOKYO • MILAN
MADRID • WARSAW • BUDAPEST • AUCKLAND

THE HIRELING'S TALE

A Worldwide Mystery/March 2001

First published by St. Martin's Press, Incorporated.

ISBN 0-373-26377-5

PART ONE

PART ONE

ONE

IT HAD BEEN A BUSY weekend for all of them, long periods of serious concentration interspersed by sudden, intense bouts of bargaining. Tempers had frayed and accusations had been hurled in a wide variety of languages—so many, fortunately, that almost nobody knew what he'd been accused of, which speeded the mending of both fences and friendships.

Now the work was over, the deals were done, and almost sixty customers and potential customers for custom engineering products were unwinding in the convivial atmosphere created by a free bar. In the noise and the chaos and the babble, only half of it in English, someone with the inclination could have led a herd of pygmy elephants through the hotel lobby and over to the lifts without being noticed.

The Romanian delegate was on top of a table, reenacting with an imaginary Sten gun his finest hour defending the family factory during the insurgence. Sober he spoke good English, but for a while now he'd been reduced to communication by gesture. It detracted hardly if at all from the story he was telling. He enjoyed the gypsy good looks of many of his kin, and though the glamour was wasted on most of his fellow revellers there were enough women present to egg him on with glances of smouldering admiration. At least, that's what he thought it was. An unbiased observer might have said they were laughing at him.

'Young Nicu's in good form tonight,' observed the Saudi delegate tolerantly.

Philip Kendall chuckled. 'I don't think there must be anyone left in Bucharest who hasn't heard the story. Here he's got a whole new audience. He's like a dog with two tails, isn't he? I should have a last crack at him, see if I can get him to up his order while he's still trying to impress us all.'

Kendall was enjoying himself too. As sales director for Bespoke Engineering, this conference was his biggest budget commitment, and therefore his biggest gamble, of the year. In their own lands these people were hard-headed, successful businessmen like himself, or government officials who'd achieved high rank in similar ways, and they were no pushover. For the first day of the conference, and for a month before, he'd been desperately anxious that the gamble wouldn't pay off. When he started to see interest behind the professional reserve, and they started to discuss their own needs and the cost of meeting them, he was so relieved he could have kissed them. Except possibly the Belgian delegate, who just might have enjoyed it.

A Mexican fishing magnate orbited by, a girl on each arm. In a largely male gathering this could have been considered greedy, but even Nicu Sibiu wasn't drunk enough yet to tell him so. Ian Selkirk was built a little like the champion caber-tossers he was descended from, and a little like the Old Man of Hoy. 'Great party, Phil.' The accent was like the man himself, part Scots, part Latin American.

'Should be.' Kendall waved a canapé. 'These are your shrimps we're eating.'

The big man laughed and lurched away. 'That explains it.'

Ibn al Siddiq sighed. 'There are times,' he confided, 'when forswearing alcohol on religious grounds seems a considerable sacrifice. Then I see what a deeply unattractive spectacle drunken people make of themselves and I think perhaps Allah had the right idea after all.'

Kendall laughed. 'Is it the Spanish who say, God never shuts a door without opening a window? You forget, I've been to your parties. They might be dry but they're not unstimulating.'

'True,' conceded Siddiq, amusement twitching one corner

of his mouth. He was a man in his thirties, dressed fault-lessly and expensively in the western taste to go with his flawless English. 'I hope now we'll see a bit more of you in Dhahran.' His head rose as he spotted someone across the tossing sea of bodies. 'I think that's your date for the evening, Philip.'

Kendall looked round, saw the plump middle-aged woman in the sequinned blouse and, beaming, waved her over. 'Grace, will you have a drink before we leave? You know Prince Ibn al Siddiq, of course.'

'Of course.' Grace Atwood acknowledged him with a smile, but she wasn't sure of the correct form of address for royalty, even minor foreign royalty, and she didn't know him well enough to call him by his given name. 'I hope you're enjoying your visit to Britain.'

'Oh yes, Mrs Atwood,' Siddiq assured her, 'I always do.'

'You're in oil, aren't you?' With a name like that it was a safe bet.

Siddiq gave a little pretend scowl. 'But oil is such a bore. I much prefer to spend my time here in pursuit of fast young fillies.'

Mrs Atwood raised an eyebrow. Kendall stepped in quickly. 'Prince Ibn is one of the leading racehorse owners in Saudi Arabia. Whenever he's here he visits the local studs to see if they have anything promising.'

Grace smiled again. 'Well, I wish you every success.' She turned her attention to Kendall. 'Philip, are you sure it's all right to leave your guests here alone?'

Kendall looked out across the room. 'As long as the bar stays open, one in ten of them will notice I've gone, and not even they will miss me. They've spent three long days listening to me bang on about precision engineering: I'm the last person they need here tonight.'

'So really I'm performing a public service.' They were old colleagues, old friends, and their insults carried no sting.

Kendall shook his head. 'Grace, I haven't seen you prop-erly for years. And though you've been here for three days,

I haven't talked to you properly since you arrived. I'm damned if I'm waving you off back to Ipswich until I have, and since conditions here are not exactly conducive to a good natter we're going out for supper. If anybody misses me I'll be flattered, and very surprised, and I'll see them before they leave in the morning. Now: have you got your coat?'

She had. His car was waiting. 'Where are we going?'

He smiled. 'Wait and see.'

'CAPTAIN BLIGH IS ALIVE and well,' hissed the girl in the matelot shirt, 'and navigating the lesser-known reaches of the Castlemere Canal.'

Her name was Emma Lacey, she was sixteen, she'd spent half her summer clothing allowance on this trip, and already she was regretting it. And the more bitterly because she'd had a choice. No one made her come. She could have gone with her mother on a painting holiday in the Cotswolds. But taking a barge—sorry, a narrowboat—round the Castlemere Ring with her father and brother had sounded...well, cool. She'd imagined sprawling on the sunny foredeck in not much more than suntan oil while local swains hung, salivating, over the lock gates. She'd imagined tying up at night under shady stands of willow, a picturesque stroll from the nearest pub.

She had not thought that May was a little early for a boating holiday in Britain. She had not realized that, in the rain, a canal is the most desolate spot on earth. She had not realized how cold it would be at night, or how the damp would pervade everything she owned. The shady willows dripped, not only water but bugs, and the country pubs were an average of three miles up a muddy track.

Emma Lacey was not having a good time.

Her brother Tom grinned with that *schadenfreude* sympathy that siblings reserve for one another's misfortunes. He wasn't having good time either, but at least he hadn't spent good money on clothes he was never going to wear again.

He said, 'So what made you think he'd be any different on holiday?'

Emma shrugged. 'I don't know. It sounded like fun. I thought we could all relax, drift along, just generally have a good time. It never occurred to me he'd want to go for the Olympic canal-cruising record.'

'Quit slacking, you two,' shouted Barry Lacey from the sternsheets. 'Are the bunks made? You could get lunch started. There isn't a lock for miles, this'd be a good chance to get some of the mud off the decks. Come on, look lively!'

'If he tells me to polish the portholes,' murmured Emma, 'that's it, we set him adrift in the inflatable.' She went below.

Tom looked round for the scrubbing brush. For some reason his father referred to it as a swab; mainly to annoy him Tom called it the mop. He dunked it in the canal, noting with satisfaction that the water it brought on board was hardly less muddy than the deck. 'I'll start at the front end.'

'The bows!' yelled Barry Lacey.

'Whatever.'

When he saw the damage to the canvas stretched across the front hatch, for a moment Tom debated with himself whether it would be more amusing to draw his father's attention to it now or wait for him to discover it himself. He decided that, since he might miss the best part if he was working a lock when the discovery was made, he'd better break the bad news. 'Er, Dad—?'

'*Now* what?'

'Did you tear this tarpaulin thing?'

'*What?* What tarpaulin? What tear? Here, take the tiller. And *don't* steer us into the bank...'

Someone else might have assumed the hire boat had been damaged on an earlier trip. But Barry Lacey inspected it from stem to stern before taking delivery on Saturday morning, so he knew the canvas was intact two days ago. Already he was calculating how much this was going to cost him. Any moment now he'd get round to whose fault it was.

It appeared to have been cut with a knife. Well, he knew *he'd* been nowhere near it with a knife, and though he didn't put much past his children he didn't think deliberate vandalism was their style. That dock where they moored last night, in the heart of Castlemere—that seemed the sort of place where people with knives might hang out.

The council had painted the bollards in jolly primary colours and hung bits of white rope between the stanchions, but the effect was like hanging bunting on a workhouse. It wasn't a jolly place. It was a grim place, built of brutal hard work in grinding poverty. Mere Basin itself was almost subterranean, tall buildings looming above it, all but shutting out the sky. Now they were flats and offices, but they were redeveloped from early Victorian warehouses and the black bricks remembered the lives of those who laid them. There was a pub by the waterside, but Barry had taken one look inside and backed away, shuddering. The last time he saw anywhere like The Fen Tiger it was run by Peter Lorre as a front for white slaving.

He'd locked up the boat before taking the children up the access ramp into town for some supper. It was a recommended mooring, he thought it would be safe enough. It never occurred to him someone might cut their way in through the forward hatch. It should have been timber. If it had been timber no one could have cut their way in with a knife.

They'd had a couple of hours to strip the boat of anything saleable. Barry Lacey frowned. He hadn't missed a thing. The television was still in the saloon, he'd used his binoculars this morning, and his camera... What sort of thieves were they, who cut their way into a boat but left valuables aboard untouched?

Then, as he scowled at the rent canvas, it occurred to him that the tough fabric had not been cut but rather torn. Perhaps it hadn't been deliberate vandalism so much as horseplay—local youngsters taking advantage of their absence to mess about, until one of them jumped on the canvas and it split. Barry sniffed. He suspected he'd still have to pay. But it could have been worse. If whoever split that cover had gone straight through he'd have dropped four feet into the chain locker—could have broken his leg, his neck, anything.

He froze. Picking glumly at the torn canvas, wondering how much it was going to cost him, he saw something that had no business being in a chain locker—not his, not anyone's. A bare arm.

He straightened up, his brain working furiously. Whoever tore the canvas *did* go straight through, and what's more he was still there. He must have been there for fourteen hours.

Barry Lacey walked carefully back to the stern. 'Emma, come up here a moment and give Tom a hand.' His voice sounded odd to himself—and obviously did to Emma, because curiosity made her do as he asked—but probably the interloper would not notice. When he had the children back by the tiller he poked a stern finger at them. 'Stay here. Right here.'

The boat-hook was too long and unwieldy. Instead he armed himself with the biggest wrench in the tool kit before creeping forward again.

The teenagers exchanged bewildered glances. 'Alzheimer's?' hazarded Tom.

The canvas cover was stretched over a wooden frame. One-handed, the other clutching the wrench, Barry winkled out the split pins that held it in place and then threw it back on its hinges. 'All right,' he said authoritatively as it fell, 'let's be having you...'

Then his hand and the heavy wrench slowly fell. He wouldn't be needing either of them. The bare arm in the chain locker belonged not to a burly local tearaway, caged long enough to be dangerous, but to a girl. She was lying face up among the warps, the punctured fenders, the old mouldy life jackets and the other detritus of a thousand tiny voyages. She was naked, and she was dead.

TWO

THE FORENSIC MEDICAL EXAMINER took a little longer over his examination but then he confirmed Barry Lacey's diagnosis. The girl was undoubtedly dead, and had been for several hours.

'How many?'

Dr Crowe shook his head. 'Ask me after the post mortem.'

Detective Superintendent Shapiro smiled tolerantly. He knew the man wasn't being deliberately difficult, it was just that all his kind really hated being asked this particular question. Whatever he said, sooner or later he would be proved wrong. 'I will. But if you can give me even a rough idea now we'll know where to start our enquiries. Less than three hours and she was alive when the boat left Castlemere. Between three and fifteen hours and she came aboard at Mere Basin. More than fifteen hours and she was on the boat when it arrived in Castlemere.'

The FME frowned. But he knew that, this early in the game, even a ball-park guess was more help than no guess at all. So he did what he always did: swallowed his professional pride and gave it his best shot.

'I think it's your problem, Superintendent. She's certainly been dead longer than three hours. Best guess?—twelve to fifteen. I'll be surprised if we find anything to put it outside that range.'

'So around nine last night would be a reasonable time for it to have happened.'

Crowe nodded, warily. He was a large young man, and people still sometimes took him for a medical student. In fact that cherubic face hid a sharp, enquiring intellect. 'It would. But why do you think it was?'

Barry Lacey was sitting in Shapiro's car where they'd been talking a few minutes before. He wasn't under arrest, he just hadn't got enough of a grip on himself to get up yet. 'They arrived in Mere Basin about eight-thirty last night, moored the boat and went into town for some supper. They got back about eleven. The two hours they were missing would be the easiest time for her to get on board.'

'Unless they know more than they're telling.'

Shapiro arched a sceptic eyebrow. 'You mean, they did her in, hid her in their boat, brought her out here, and *then* called us?'

Put like that, it didn't seem very likely. Crowe sniffed. 'You're the detective—I'm only an old-fashioned pathologist with a posh new title.'

Shapiro grinned. 'Well, Donovan'll be pleased anyway.'

The FME puzzled over that but still didn't understand. '*Why?*'

'A corpse on a canal boat and it turns out to be somebody else's case? He'd be heartbroken.'

Detective Sergeant Donovan lived on a narrowboat. He was widely believed to have canal water running through his veins.

'All right, next question,' said Shapiro. 'How did she die?'

That really was beyond the pale. Crowe stared at him indignantly. 'Oh, come on...!'

'I know, I know—that's what the post mortem's for. But I need some idea now. Are we talking murder? Could it have been an accident?'

The FME thought for a moment before replying. 'She fell. I don't know why she fell, that's your job, but it was the fall that killed her. See the blood-flow from her nose and ear?—that says she landed there on her back, lived just long enough to bleed a little and then died. There's blood on the things she's lying on that matches exactly, and the back of

her skull is comminuted in relation to the surface under her.
I'm pretty sure she hasn't been moved since the time of
death.

'But dying wasn't the first thing to go wrong with her
evening. Somebody beat seven bells out of her. Those
bruises on her face and body, she didn't get them falling
into the hold. They didn't have long to develop but they
were certainly caused prior to death. The fall finished her
off, but she wasn't having a good time when it happened.'

'Chain locker,' said a disembodied voice with an Irish
accent.

Dr Crowe looked around in surprise, but there were still
only the two of them standing on the deck. 'Donovan?'

'Down here.' He'd commandeered a dinghy and was
groping his way round the outside of the narrowboat, looking for evidence. Evidence of what it was hard to say: Shapiro suspected he'd just seen the chance to get into a boat
for ten minutes. The dinghy's owner, a boy of about twelve,
was standing in rapt fascination on the bank. 'It's not a hold,
it's a chain locker.'

'I see,' nodded Crowe. 'Well, I suppose I'll have to revise
my entire diagnosis in the light of that.' He winked at Shapiro and clambered up the gangway on to the bank.

The hire boat *Guelder Rose* was tied up at the first waterside cottage she'd come to after Barry Lacey's discovery.
This was some five miles east of Castlemere, a bit past
Chevening. Shapiro had been in his office when the call
came in, three minutes later he was on his way. Lacey was
too shocked to make perfect sense, but it was hard to see
how the body of a naked girl on a boat where she had no
right to be could be other than a suspicious death.

Donovan was actually off duty today. No one had called
him, although his expertise would be valuable to the investigation. Shapiro knew he'd appear by a process similar to
magnetism when rumour of a corpse on a boat reached up
the canal as far as Broad Wharf. In fact, the waterfront version of Jungle Telegraph must have been operating at peak

efficiency, because Donovan's bike gunned to a halt outside the cottage while Shapiro was still talking to the Scenes of Crime Officer.

'Found anything?' asked Shapiro. He couldn't be more specific because he didn't know what Donovan was looking for.

Donovan hauled himself up on to the short foredeck of the *Guelder Rose*. It was raining again: he looked as if he'd been in the canal. When he shook his head the water flew off the black rat-tails of his hair. 'No sign of a boat coming alongside. No scratches, no mud, not even a rub-mark from the fenders. More likely she was boarded from the port side.'

Shapiro was puzzled. In more than thirty years on the job he'd seen dead bodies in odder places than this. He'd seen naked dead bodies before, too. But he couldn't construct a sequence of events that put a naked dead body in the hold—sorry, the chain locker—of the *Guelder Rose*. It wasn't an excess of party spirit that led this girl to streak through Mere Basin at nine o'clock at night: she'd been beaten up, the last thing she'd have felt like was playing games. She might have been looking for help, she might have been looking for somewhere to hide. Maybe in the end it was a simple mistake—taking the canvas cover for a solid surface—that killed her. But if she was wandering round naked on a dock full of people, why did nobody help her? Or failing that, complain?

'How did she get there?'

Donovan shrugged. He was a tall man, stick-thin, with bony shoulders made for the job. 'She fell through the hatch.'

'With no clothes on?'

'I doubt anybody went down to undress her afterwards. For one thing, they couldn't have got out again without ripping away more of the canvas.'

'All right. So why did no one notice? Not the Laceys, they were in town, but the Basin's full of people up to midnight and later. If she walked up the wharf with no clothes on around nine o'clock at night, climbed on to a boat and then fell through a hatch, why did nobody see her?'

'Maybe she wasn't naked then.'

Shapiro considered that. 'So she climbed on to the boat, did a strip act and then fell through the hatch. You think that would go unnoticed?'

'Maybe she didn't walk. Maybe she was helped, or carried. Maybe someone wrapped her in a coat or a blanket, carried her on board and dropped her through the hatch. Then he took his blanket away with him.'

'Why tear the canvas? Why not just lift the hatch? It wasn't locked, there were only a couple of split pins securing it. Lacey got it open easily enough. If somebody wanted to hide her, that was the thing to do. She could have been down there for days before anybody—er—smelled a rat. I'm right, aren't I?—a boating party would have no reason to go in there?'

'Wouldn't think so,' said Donovan. 'I don't use mine much, except as a dog-kennel. Mostly you keep your fenders over the side and your warps coiled on deck, ready for use.'

'So, apart from the torn canvas, it would have been a good way to dispose of a body. By the time she started to smell there'd have been no way to establish when and where she came aboard.'

'But the canvas *was* torn,' objected Donovan. 'Someone was bound to notice, sooner rather than later.'

'Exactly. So he was more concerned with getting her off his hands than with concealing her long-term. He was in a hurry. He was afraid of being seen; or of being missed; or maybe it wasn't him who killed her, he was just helping out, if he could get her off his hands he didn't care how quickly she was found.'

'You reckon it's murder then.'

Shapiro scratched his eyebrow with a thumbnail. He was fifty-six, a solidly-built man with a slightly rumpled, lived-in face indistinguishable from a thousand others except by a particularly sharp pair of clear grey eyes. 'The fall that killed her may have been an accident, but according to Crowe she was beaten before she died. It may or may not be murder, but it's certainly one for us.'

'So she was hurting, maybe she was concussed. Maybe she wandered on to the boat looking for somewhere to hide and fell through the hatch.'

'Then what became of the blanket? If she came on board alone she was already naked, in which case someone would have seen. If she was wrapped up enough to pass unnoticed, somebody took the blanket away afterwards.' Shapiro squatted beside the open hatch. SOCO and the FME had been down there with her, they couldn't do their jobs at arm's length, but there was nothing Shapiro could learn from such close examination. He'd leave her in peace until the paramedics removed her.

He found himself trying to estimate her age. Twenty-four, twenty-six? Under the bruises and the blood she was a pretty woman. Her hair was dyed blonde, the bubbly perm a recent investment, and enough of her make-up had survived the assaults on her to show that she'd taken some trouble with it. She'd made an effort to look good for whoever had done this to her.

He felt a surge of anger under his breastbone. People assumed that policemen became hardened to the aftermath of human tragedy, but Shapiro never had. He'd learned how to deal with it, both practically and emotionally, and that made it easier to see what he had to see and still somehow get on with the job. But every time he took a phonecall that led him here, that left him looking at the lifeless wreckage of a human being who'd begun their last day full of the same hopes, fears, concerns and things to do as everyone else and ended it on a slab, the long experience that stopped him throwing up was no protection against this burgeoning anger. At the waste of a life; at the sheer impertinence of whoever presumed to take it.

He gritted his teeth to keep his voice low. 'One way or

another, someone's responsible for this girl's death. Someone beat her black and blue, then he brought her to this boat
and pushed her out of sight to die alone in the darkness.
Then he folded up his blanket and went home. I want the
bastard, Donovan.

'Ask round in the Basin, see if anyone saw anything. It
might not have looked like a man carrying a woman—it
could have looked like a couple of drunks leaning on one
another, or somebody delivering equipment to the boat. He
may have had a van; he may not have been alone. But he
must have been there. Find someone who saw him.'

'Where will you be?'

'I'll be trying to find out why she's been dead for fifteen
hours and still nobody's reported her missing.'

PART OF THE ANSWER came from the autopsy. Shapiro attended in person. It wasn't strictly necessary—a police officer had to be present but it didn't have to be him—but he
worked on the basis that the cadaver was the only witness
to the murder that he presently knew of and the post mortem
was her only chance to speak. If he wanted to hear what
she had to say first-hand, rather than through the filter of a
formal report, he had to be there, ready to ask questions,
when the FME was giving his running commentary to the
tape.

When she heard his heavy step pass her door, Detective
Inspector Liz Graham put aside what she was doing and
followed her chief to his office. He had a spare chair for
visitors but Liz took Donovan's favourite spot, on the windowsill overlooking the canal. 'So do we know anything
more about our Jane Doe now?'

Shapiro nodded and lowered himself behind his desk. He
looked glum, his broad lived-in face falling into dejected
creases. This stage of an investigation was often depressing.
You had a corpse, and no killer, and not enough facts to
think you'd ever find one. Over the hours and days ahead
they started trickling in, one at a time, building up a picture

of the victim and how she spent her last hours that by degrees focused suspicion on a particular individual—usually someone she knew, very often someone *you* knew. But this first day, unless there were eyewitnesses or real smoking-gun evidence, the task could look impossible.

'Two things,' he said. 'How she died, and how she lived.'

She died, as Crowe had predicted, of falling through the canvas hatch and smashing her head on the steel plates below. But if she hadn't collided with the bottom of the *Guelder Rose* she still wouldn't have been in the peak of health. There was enough cocaine in her system to drop a donkey.

'Which perhaps explains why she was naked,' said Liz. 'And why she didn't see the hatch. But if she'd taken that much, how come she was still on her feet and clambering over boats? Shouldn't she have been curled up somewhere snoring?'

'Donovan thinks she had help—that someone wrapped a coat or a blanket or something round her and took her there. Which sounded reasonable enough until we got the blood-work. You're right, she shouldn't have been able to walk, even with help. And a man carrying a woman's body through Mere Basin would have been as conspicuous as a naked girl.'

'Maybe someone did see them. This is the Basin we're talking about, the crowd that hangs out down there in the evening wouldn't rush to call us if they saw something suspicious. Hell, if they saw a naked girl staggering about they'd give her some music and take up a collection.' Barry Lacey had been right to back away from The Fen Tiger: it wasn't his sort of pub at all.

Shapiro rocked his head non-committally. 'Apparently it was quite a fall. I know, you can break your neck tripping over a kerb-stone; but she didn't break her neck, she smashed her skull. Crowe thinks she fell further than four feet into the bottom of the boat.' He was too old to undergo metrication now. 'Actually, a lot further.'

Liz frowned. 'This is a canal boat we're talking about, not a square-rigger. I mean, she didn't fall from the yard-arm.'

'The highest point on the *Guelder Rose* is the top of the cabin roof, about four feet above the deck. If she'd fallen from there she could have managed about eight feet. It still isn't enough. And how did she get there? She was too tripped out to walk; and if someone was trying to kill her, why risk being seen with her in a public place?'

'Could she have fallen off something else? It's a boat, it passes under bridges—could she have come off a bridge? If Lacey was busy steering he might not have noticed. Even if he felt the bump he might have thought he'd brushed against something: he's a novice at this, after all, he can't be too familiar with the boat.'

It sounded plausible, and there was room in the time envelope. Time of death had been narrowed to between seven and ten p.m.; the *Guelder Rose* arrived in Mere Basin after eight; if you could accept that a man busy steering a large unfamiliar boat through a narrow bridge could fail to notice someone falling on to his foredeck she might have come aboard up to six miles short of Castlemere. Shapiro could believe that, but other parts of the theory still gave him problems. 'If you're trying to commit suicide you don't wait till there's a boat underneath you! Besides, we hit the same snag: she had too much cocaine in her to be doing more than crawling round the bedroom floor. Someone must have helped her. And if he helped her off a bridge that's still murder.'

'You said you'd learned something about how she lived as well,' Liz reminded him. 'Do you know who she is?'

Shapiro shook his head. 'But I know what she is: a prostitute. Well, probably. Crowe said there was enough wear and tear, inside and out, that if she wasn't being paid for it she should have been.'

Liz wasn't surprised. Violent death takes people on the fringe of society much more often than it ambushes those at its cosy heart. And people who turn up naked anywhere but their own beds tend to be burning the candle at both ends. 'Working as in, that's how she made her living? Or working as in, that's what she was doing when she died?'

'Both, apparently. Read the report if you want the gory details.'

'Then somebody'd better talk to the Toms' Union.' Queen's Street, like most police stations, had an ambivalent relationship with the local prostitutes. The girls were committing an offence, and at intervals there would be prosecutions, fines and short, pointless prison sentences. But between times hookers and coppers were a fact of one another's lives, and there were benefits to be gained by keeping the relationship amicable. Sometimes the girls needed protecting, sometimes the police needed the sort of information picked up by women who made their living on the street. 'Donovan's off today, isn't he?—shall I go?'

With his chin in his chest Shapiro smiled a secret smile. 'Yes and no. Donovan *was* off; Donovan then heard about a body on a boat and all but beat me to the scene of crime; now he's down at the Basin looking for someone who saw something.'

Liz elevated a surprised eyebrow. She was a good-looking woman rather than a beautiful one, tall and athletic, with strong features and a clear intelligence in her hazel-green eyes. She was forty-one: when she released her curly fair hair from its businesslike pleat and swapped her tailored clothes for a checked shirt and riding breeches she could pass for ten years younger. 'Was that a good idea? He isn't exactly Flavour of the Month at The Fen Tiger.'

Despite its prestigious location The Fen Tiger was a villains' pub. It had been there since Mere Basin was a stinking sink, nine-tenths derelict, subterranean and all but forgotten between Castle Place and Brick Lane. Ten years earlier a go-ahead council with its eye on a European grant had restored the Basin, turning the warehouses into valuable canalside properties and opening up the inland waterway to hol-

iday mariners. For years before that the only people using
it had been commercial carriers who travelled in convoy
with someone riding shotgun on the first boat. It had been
a massive undertaking and, but for the occasional excess
with the gold paint, a successful one. Castlemere had been
built to serve the canal; now the canal served the shopkeep-
ers and restaurateurs of Castlemere. It would never be a
tourist magnet in the way that Cambridge and Norwich
were, but a fair bit of money came through Mere Basin
during the summer months.

And a fair bit of it got as far as The Fen Tiger and no
further. The place was full of thieves, professional and casual, conmen, cloners of phones, hackers of hole-in-the-wall
cash machines and dealers in outboard engines which had
fallen off the back of a barge. Shapiro would have been
glad to shut it down, but naive magistrates kept believing
the proprietor's protestations, that the nefarious activities of
some of his clientele were not his responsibility, and renew-
ing his licence.

Shapiro shrugged. 'I'm not sure they hate Donovan any
more than they do you and me. Anyway, the wharf's his
backyard—at least they'll be talking the same language.
Anyone else'd need an interpreter.'

'So, shall I do the toms? Have we got a photo yet?'

'Should be ready now,' said Shapiro. He blew out his
cheeks. 'You'd better warn them this may not be an isolated
incident. However she got on to the boat, she was beaten
black and blue first. A man who hires a prostitute and keeps
her quiet with cocaine while he beats the living daylights
out of her does it because that's how he gets his kicks. He
doesn't ever do it just once.'

THREE

THE FACT THAT A PLACE like The Fen Tiger went quiet when
he walked inside concerned Donovan not at all. He was a
CID officer, and at any given time about half the Tiger's
clientele were wanted for something. He was quite pleased
they considered him enough of a threat to fall silent as he
passed: sometimes he felt that the best efforts of all Queen's
Street were as a flea-bite on the hide of Castlemere's criminal fraternity.

What bothered him more was that perfectly respectable
people, nice decent law-abiding citizens who were more
likely to have a sixth finger than a criminal record, also went
quiet as he passed. They'd done this since he was about
fifteen. At the time, with the cocky innocence of youth, he'd
taken it as a compliment, that they recognized him as an
individual not to be trifled with. Later he began to wonder
what it was they saw that made them mark him and stand
back. He wasn't a dangerous man. He wasn't violent, or
unhinged, or prone to sudden bursts of embarrassing eccen-
tricity. He thought himself a pretty ordinary man on the
whole: a bit of a loner, a bit of an outsider, but still an
ordinary decent citizen doing an honourable job. And yet
other decent citizens looked at him and moved aside, and
he didn't know why.

But he didn't spend much time thinking about it in a place
where, on the law of averages, every tenth man would like
to put a baling hook in his back.

Fortunately, with the lunchtime rush yet to start, there
were only nine people in the bar. One was the potman
Donny Toomes. Donovan didn't have any friends in The

Fen Tiger, but on the long list of his enemies Toomes would have figured somewhere near the bottom.

He didn't order a drink. He had no wish to appear part of this company; besides, mostly what he drank was non-alcoholic and he didn't particularly want Toomes to know that. 'Were you on last night?'

Toomes shrugged: a can't-remember, don't-care, wouldn't-tell-you-if-I-was sort of shrug. Donovan rolled his eyes but hung on to his patience. It was a necessary preamble: Toomes would answer his questions eventually, but it was vital to his own credibility that he shouldn't make it too easy.

'Simple enough question, Donny: were you working here last night? Say, between eight and closing time—or midnight, whichever came first.'

Toomes sniffed. He was a sturdy middle-aged individual with the beer belly that's an occupational hazard. Apart from the people he worked for and the company he kept, Donovan didn't have much on him. A bit of handling, a bit of aiding and abetting, it was probably better not to enquire where the venison sandwiches came from, but nothing that entitled the man to wear the hunt button of the Castlemere Mafia. Only habit kept him from answering fully and frankly.

'If you've any complaints about us not closing on time, Mr Donovan,' he said stolidly, 'you'd better take them up with the management.'

'Give me any of your nonsense,' growled Donovan, 'and I'll sick the VAT inspectors on them.' With the end of transportation and public flogging, this was about the direst threat that a public servant could legally issue.

Donny Toomes recognized the fact. He had nothing to hide, and knew he wouldn't be thanked for holding out any longer. 'OK, OK,' he grumbled. 'Yes, I was here. What do you want to know?'

'There was an incident on the dock. Did anybody see anything?'

'What sort of an incident?'

Donovan bared his teeth in a feral grin. 'The sort of incident where somebody ends up dead, Donny. A girl—blonde, about twenty-five, not wearing a lot in the way of clothes. Anybody see her?'

Toomes began to look interested. '*How* little in the way of clothes?'

'To the nearest round figure?—none. So if you saw her you'd tend to remember. I take it you didn't?'

'I don't think anyone did,' said Toomes regretfully. 'They'd have mentioned it if they had. Where was all this going on, then?' He craned his neck, looking out of the window as if there was a chance of a repeat performance.

The Fen Tiger enjoyed perhaps the best location in Castlemere, with a street entrance just off Castle Place and a rear entrance, one storey down, on to Mere Basin. The lounge bar was upstairs; down here was where the hard cases drank. It wasn't the view that attracted them so much as the fact that if someone you didn't want to meet came in one way you could always leave by the other.

Hire boats mostly moored on the north side of the basin. Donovan pointed with his nose. 'Over there somewhere. On a boat—the *Guelder Rose,* black hull, blue and cream upperworks. Did you see *her?*'

Toomes nodded. 'I saw them tying up—about eight, eight-thirty? Man and a couple of kids. Didn't see no twenty-five-year-old blonde.'

'Did you see anyone else on the boat, a bit later? A couple of drunks, maybe—one wrapped up in a coat or something?'

But if Toomes had missed a naked twenty-five-year-old blonde he wasn't much interested in anything else he might have seen. He shook his head glumly.

Donovan turned to face the room, meaning to repeat the question for general consumption. But the bar was empty. He gave a snort of scornful amusement. 'Jesus, Donny, your customers are a shy lot. Anybody'd think they'd been up to no good.'

Toomes sighed. 'Listen, Mr Donovan, don't take this the wrong way but... You come swanning in here with your threats and your questions, you'd be sensible to bring somebody with you. To watch your back.'

Donovan's dark eyes rounded in astonished indignation. 'Are you telling me I'm not safe in here? Are you telling me this dive is some sort of a no-go area?'

'I'm not telling you any such thing,' said Toomes wearily. 'These are properly conducted licensed premises: you're welcome to drink here, or to ask questions. You're as safe here as anywhere in Castlemere. What I can't vouch for is what happens after you leave. I wouldn't like to think of you turning up face-down in the canal one night.'

'Your concern's downright touching,' sneered Donovan. 'This place has obviously changed since Jack Carney went down.' The Fen Tiger never officially belonged to the old thug: it was held in his wife's name. These days it officially belonged to the wife of a second cousin of Carney's; but the only thing that had actually changed was the name above the door.

Toomes sniffed and said no more. His concern was genuine but not altogether altruistic. Odd jobs were always the preserve of the potman, and getting blood off wrought-iron railings was a bugger.

Donovan had one last question before he left. 'So where did they tie up the *Guelder Rose?*'

Toomes stumped to the door and pointed. 'There, in front of The Lock & Quay.' It used to be Gossick's Chandlers: folksy names came in with the redevelopment and the toytown paintwork.

An arched ironwork bridge spanned the basin: Donovan preferred its old livery of black and rust to the council's colour scheme of dark green and gold. But time heals all ills: he noted with satisfaction that the rust was beginning to make a comeback.

Tonight there would be another hire boat tied inexpertly to the bollards outside The Lock & Quay, but for the moment the bit of dockside where the Laceys spent last night was vacant. Donovan took his time looking round but although it was now midday and the spring sunlight was pouring through the well of the buildings he could see nothing suggestive of a struggle, of an accident, of anything out of the ordinary. There was nothing that looked like blood, and no one had tossed a blanket into the deep shadows of the car park between the stilts of The Barbican.

When he had done with looking around, he went back to the quayside and looked up.

'SHE DIDN'T FALL THROUGH the hatch of the *Guelder Rose*,' he explained, a thread of electric satisfaction running through his voice. 'At least she did, but she wasn't on the boat at the time. She fell off the roof of the Barbican.'

'The roof?' echoed Liz faintly.

'Six storeys up,' nodded Donovan. 'She didn't fall eight feet, she fell about eighty—of course she smashed her skull.'

'Have you been up there?' asked Shapiro.

'Yeah, just to make sure. Then I called for a PC to preserve the scene. Immediately above where the boat was tied up, something's been rested on the parapet. There's a load of junk up there—dirt, bird shit, the lot. But not right there. SOCO's on his way up there, but I'll stake my reputation that's where she came from.'

'Then it really was murder,' said Shapiro pensively. 'She didn't get herself up there, not in that state. Someone took her and threw her. She was meant to die.' He stood up and reached for his coat. 'I'd better get down there. Come with me, Donovan, show me what you found. What about you, Liz?'

She shook her head. 'I'm seeing the toms.' Castlemere didn't have a red-light district as such: they'd arranged to meet, somewhat incongruously, in the Tudor Tea-rooms.

The three of them went downstairs together. When they

parted at the top of Queen's Street Liz murmured after Donovan, 'You haven't got a reputation *to* stake.'

He looked back with a grin. They'd known each other long enough to enjoy the privilege of a friendly insult. 'Then I'll stake your reputation,' he said.

THE LOCAL PROSTITUTES may not have had a trade union as such, but they certainly had a self-help network. Girls who got little support from anyone else had to be able to depend on each other. So while Dawn and Zara avoided contact with the police in most circumstances, to help find the killer of a fellow working-girl they were prepared to break the habit of a lifetime.

If she was a fellow-worker. The two women pored over the photograph Liz put on the table, took the time to picture her alive, and in the end were sure they'd never seen her before.

Liz frowned. 'She isn't a local girl? The pathologist who did the post mortem reckoned she was on the game.'

Dawn, who was the older of the two, shrugged. 'I'm telling you what I know. She doesn't work in this town.'

'Could she be—I don't know—an enthusiastic amateur?'

Dawn shook her head, a mass of coal-black curls dancing on her shoulders. 'If she was enthusiastic enough for it to show up at the autopsy, we'd know her. I'm telling you: that's not a local girl. She was brought in. Maybe for a special. They do that sometimes, if there's a big conference or something.'

'Conference?' The Barbican Hotel was big enough for the conference trade.

Zara sniffed. 'Think themselves a bit sophisticated, the conference trade do. A cut above the local talent. They come down from London in a coach.'

Liz blinked. But the principles of business are much the same whatever business you're in: if you want work you have to put yourself in its way. 'Are they in town at the moment?'

Dawn shook her head again. 'We'd know if they were. There was some sort of a gathering at The Barbican this weekend—a few of us met up with guys there—but there wasn't anything laid on in the way of entertainment. People were making their own arrangements.'

'Maybe she knew one of the guests personally,' Liz speculated. 'Does that happen—a man calls a particular girl to meet him somewhere?'

'Honey,' said Dawn heavily, 'in this business *everything* happens. Sure he could have called her. He'd got away from the wife for a long weekend, he had his own little friend, he told her where to come and they spent a few days together instead of the usual hour-and-a-bit. That way we wouldn't even have known she was in town.'

'He went to that much trouble so he could kill her?' said Zara doubtfully. She had warm *café-au-lait* skin and blonde streaks dyed through her dark hair.

'Maybe she threatened to tell his wife,' hazarded Liz.

But Dawn wasn't buying that. 'No way. Not if she was a pro—it's the one thing you never do. For one thing, you don't *want* them to leave their wives. You don't want to live with them, for Chrissake!—you want them safe at home, just restless enough to pick up the phone from time to time. If the wife chucked them out, they might shack up with someone who'd keep them happy, and that's bad for business.'

Liz thanked them for their time and paid the bill. She didn't envy these women their lifestyle but she didn't condemn it either. She wished there was a way of keeping them safer, but suspected that, however liberal the law became, a working prostitute would always find herself beyond its protection. Not because she wanted it that way but because the clients did.

'OK. Well, thanks for your help. And go carefully, won't you?—till either we've got this man or we're sure he's left town. Just in case it wasn't personal, and beating up on girls is how he gets his kicks.'

'Wouldn't be the first one,' grunted Dawn. With a hand decorated with blood-red talons she waved a cheery farewell to an outraged waitress as they left.

THE *GUELDER ROSE* had been tied along the north wharf, under the angle of the northern and eastern blocks of The Barbican. The four buildings framed a great atrium with Mere Basin in the well, springing across the four canals on massive brick arches. They were built as warehouses when this was a main commercial artery: now they were shops and restaurants at ground level, businesses above, flats above that.

And The Barbican Hotel, which occupied the eastern block. Anyone staying in the hotel would have access to the roof. Shapiro filed that interesting fact away for further consideration.

Donovan took him to the spot he'd found where years of airborne pollution had been swept from the parapet. The roofs ran together in a continuous concrete span, so the fact that the girl had gone off the northern building didn't mean that's where she'd come from. The spot was chosen simply because there was a kind of concrete step against the wall which would have made it easier to lift someone over.

'I wonder if he knew there was a boat there,' said Shapiro. 'Maybe he meant her to go in the canal.'

'Better for him if she landed on something solid,' grunted Donovan. 'He may have thought her injuries would cover up the beating he'd given her.'

The superintendent nodded slowly. 'I suppose it was meant to look like suicide. Or an accident. If he'd fed her a bit less cocaine it might have done. She got high, she was prancing around up here in the buff, she lost her balance and fell. Only we know she wasn't prancing anywhere. She couldn't have walked, let alone climbed the parapet.'

'At least we know now why nobody saw anything. Unless you were looking at precisely the right moment, there was nothing to see. First she was up here, out of sight; five seconds later she was dead in the bottom of the boat. Doped up like that she wouldn't even have yelled.'

Shapiro looked around. The concrete desert was interrupted by various outcrops: water-tanks, gear-houses for the lifts, doors that led by way of stairs into the buildings below. When The Barbican was redeveloped from the old warehouses the architects had it in mind that a very pleasant roof-garden could have been created up here. But somehow roof-gardens weren't very Castlemere. Even after the council had done its best it remained a working town rather than a bastion of middle-class gentility. If they'd done the redevelopment ten years earlier people would have strung washing-lines up here.

'Has anybody tried the doors?' he said. 'To see which open and which are locked?'

Donovan tried them now. There were eight in all, two on each building. Only two opened from the outside: one each on the north and east wings. 'Doesn't mean they won't open from the inside. They might have to, as part of the fire regulations.'

So it proved. Shapiro sighed. 'So he could have come from any door in any building, walked round till he found a handy spot and pushed the poor girl over, and unless he was unlucky enough to bump into a late-patrolling caretaker there was next to no chance of him being seen. Get hold of the caretakers, make sure they really didn't see anyone at the top of the stairs, then meet me in the hotel foyer.'

'They could as easily have come from one of the flats,' objected Donovan.

'Of course they could,' agreed Shapiro. 'But the hotel will have a much bigger turnover. Plus, if you were planning on killing a girl you probably wouldn't want to chuck her off your own roof and have her found still pointing an accusing finger at your bedroom window. It's different for hotel guests: they could be miles away before she was found.'

'But she died last night,' said Donovan. 'Whoever killed her was here last night.'

'So our prime suspect is someone who was staying in the hotel but left last night or first thing this morning.'

That narrowed it down, but not very much. When he went down to The Barbican Hotel Shapiro discovered what Liz had just learned: that a conference booking had occupied some forty rooms, some of them doubles, from Friday evening until Monday morning. Of the sixty-three delegates, forty-eight were men. None had their wives with them. Most had left before Tom Lacey noticed the split in the canvas.

'I'm going to need names and addresses for all of them,' said Shapiro wearily. 'And since crime is an equal opportunities employer, you'd better give me the women as well.'

'We have the names, of course,' said the manager. 'But you might get a more comprehensive list from Mr Kendall. He organized the conference and he made a block booking for rooms and other facilities.'

Shapiro raised an eyebrow and the manager replied with an angry blush. 'I didn't mean girls. I meant the Jacuzzi.'

'Where would I find Mr Kendall?'

'As a matter of fact he's here at the moment, settling the bill.'

Shapiro joined him in the manager's office. It was by no means clear that the dead girl was ever in the hotel, and even if she was neither her activities in life nor the manner of her death could fairly be blamed on the management. He saw no need to conduct his investigation publicly in the foyer.

He'd met Philip Kendall before, at Chamber of Commerce dinners or the Civic Ball. He was senior sales executive at Bespoke Engineering, one of Castlemere's major employers. They custom-made machinery for clients throughout the world in a high-tech plant with a lot of smoked glass off the ring road.

He was a man in his mid-forties, strong open face, hair on the cusp of going grey. He looked up as Shapiro entered, surprised but not initially troubled. Then the awareness of something wrong—the knowledge that senior detectives don't walk in on you for no particular reason—grew in his eyes and his brows gathered uneasily. 'Superintendent. Is something wrong?'

Shapiro nodded soberly. 'I'm afraid so, Mr Kendall. A girl died here last night. We think she was a prostitute, we think she may have been visiting one of your delegates.'

He had a photograph of the girl in his pocketbook. Mr Coren, the hotel manager, didn't remember seeing her, neither did Kendall. Coren took the photo out to reception but none of his staff had seen her either.

He returned it with an apologetic shake of the head. 'I don't think she was staying here. She just might have been visiting a guest. Unless he brought her through the foyer wearing thigh-boots and carrying a cash-box, I couldn't guarantee we'd have spotted them.'

That was realistic. No respectable hotel likes its guests bringing in prostitutes; most of them accept that they can't prevent it.

'We don't know how she was dressed,' said Shapiro. 'That's something you might look out for: a bundle of women's clothes. In the meantime, Mr Kendall, I'm going to need a full list of the names and addresses of your conference delegates.'

Mechanical engineering is a precise business: not very much happens that's seriously unexpected. Shock had run like a wave through Kendall's expression: when it reached his knees they went weak and he'd sat down abruptly. He was still struggling to come to terms with this. 'My God. You think one of my delegates...?'

Shapiro was not an unkind man. 'We don't know. But it's a possibility we have to look into. Fifty strange men in town and a prostitute ends up dead?—we can't assume that's a coincidence.'

As the first horror passed, so Kendall's concern became focused on his own interests. 'You're going to contact my customers and ask if they had a prostitute in their hotel room? Superintendent, I brought them here to try and sell our services to them. This was our major marketing ploy for the year. And you're going to tell them they're suspects in a murder investigation? What's that going to do for our sales figures?'

Shapiro breathed heavily and hung on to his patience. Shock took people different ways: you couldn't hold them responsible for the first thing they thought of in its aftermath. 'Mr Kendall, your sales figures are not my prime concern. I have a dead girl to worry about. I have to find out why she died and who was involved. Until I get something concrete to go on, the only way I can do that is by speaking to everyone who could conceivably have been involved and start eliminating those who probably weren't. I'm sorry if that's going to knock the bottom out of the grommets market for a while, but I expect your cooperation.'

Philip Kendall was getting control of himself already. He sucked in a deep breath and nodded. 'Yes. Yes, of course. I'm sorry. Of course we'll cooperate any way we can. But I feel I should warn you, you may have trouble contacting some of the people who were here. It's an international business, we have clients all around the world. Some of them have a rather—casual—attitude to their own law enforcement agencies, I'm not sure how quickly they'll respond to enquiries from ours.'

Shapiro knew what he was saying. He knew what it meant. He just felt he had to have Kendall say it before he could believe his bad luck. 'You mean, they've already left the country?'

'Not all of them,' said Kendall hastily. 'But yes, a lot. Some of them left after breakfast this morning; some of them left to catch flights last night.' He brightened a little. 'There are a few people left in the hotel. Would you like to talk to them?'

'Yes: thank you.' But if Shapiro was sure of nothing else, he was confident that whoever was responsible for this had fled the scene soon afterwards. 'And could I ask you to separate the ones who've gone into two lists—those who went last night and those who had breakfast here this morning?'

While Kendall and Coren were working out who left when, Shapiro addressed the stragglers in a small room off the lobby. There were less than a dozen of them. Three were catching later trains back to London, one was waiting for a train to Manchester. Four were British nationals and were making a leisurely start before driving home. One had slept in and missed his flight—Shapiro mentally ruled him out there and then—and two more wanted to round off their visit to Castlemere with a bit of sightseeing. Try as he might, Shapiro couldn't imagine what they thought there was to see.

'Some of you may already have heard,' he said, 'but for those who haven't these are the facts. There was an incident here last night, in the hotel or one of the adjoining buildings, and a girl fell from the roof.' He passed round the photograph, watching faces as he did. 'Did anyone see her, either in the lobby or upstairs in the corridors? Did anyone hear a disturbance?'

A small man with a Zapata moustache gave a Latin shrug. 'There was a great deal of disturbance here last night, Superintendent,' he said, half apologetic, half amused. 'Unfortunately, we were responsible for most of it. I think you could have fired a cannon upstairs and no one would have heard.'

'I see. Mr—?'

'Eduardo da Costa,' the man introduced himself with a small bow. 'I am here representing the government of Brazil.'

'Mr da Costa. So there was a bit of a party down here?' The Brazilian nodded. 'To put it mildly.'

'And I assume that meant girls? Girls, I mean, rather than female delegates?'

He shrugged again. 'I was dancing with women who seemed to know very little about engineering.'

'What about this girl?'

'No.'

'You're sure?'

'Yes.'

A woman who knew a great deal abut engineering raised her voice. 'Grace Atwood, Superintendent. Are you going to want us to stay here indefinitely? I'd like to phone home, tell them not to expect me if you do.'

The vague mental picture which Shapiro had of the culprit in this case matched in no particular the squat, middle-aged woman with the round intelligent face who addressed him. But bitter experience had taught him to assume very little. 'Where is home, Mrs Atwood?'

'Ipswich. I'm not saying it'll be difficult for me to stay, Superintendent, just that I don't want my husband worrying where I've got to.'

Shapiro nodded. 'I'd like a brief statement from each of you at this point. Those of you who live in Britain will then be free tó return home. Those from overseas, I'm afraid I'll have to ask you to stay a little longer. Hopefully we'll have this sorted out in a day or two.' And indeed that was what he hoped, even if he didn't expect it. 'I'm sorry for the inconvenience, but you'll appreciate this is a murder investigation: while there's any chance you may have seen something that could help I need you to be available.'

There was a certain amount of muttering, a few startled looks, but nobody raised any objection. Da Costa said, 'In that case I'll go back to my room and unpack again.'

'I appreciate your cooperation,' said Shapiro, almost without irony.

He knew, of course, that these eleven people were the least likely of the entire conference to be involved. If one of Bespoke Engineering's customers had thrown a girl off the roof, it was a pound to a penny that he checked out immediately afterwards and was on the first flight going anywhere without an extradition treaty. That was why he didn't take too much trouble hiding the body. He just needed two or three hours to escape the jurisdiction of British courts. He couldn't leave her in his room: as soon as he checked out a maid would go in to change the linen. Dropping her in the canal would serve his purpose: even if she was spotted right away it would have taken time to establish where she'd come from and prevent anyone from leaving. That she went undiscovered for fourteen hours was a bonus.

He went back to the manager's office. 'How's that list of names and addresses coming? Mr Coren, I'll need you to match them up with room numbers. Then I'll get my people to check all the rooms that were occupied last night—not just for the conference, any others as well. If we're lucky there'll be bloodstains or clothing left behind to tell us who she was visiting.'

'The maids have already cleared the rooms booked by Mr Kendall,' said the manager. 'They didn't report anything out of the ordinary.'

'But they didn't know then what we know now,' said Shapiro grimly. 'Believe me; you beat someone the way that girl was beaten, it takes more than a quick tidy-up to remove all the evidence.'

He used Mr Coren's phone to call Superintendent Giles. 'You heard about the girl on the boat?' Castlemere's senior police officer had. There was, in fact, very little that escaped his notice. 'I've got forty hotel rooms, and after that maybe twenty flats, to search and right now there's five of us to do it. Any chance of a bit of help?'

FOUR

LATE MONDAY AFTERNOON, just when Shapiro was convinced that whatever evidence there was would be found in the room vacated by the Korean delegate Kim Il Muk—so that even sending him a postcard asking 'Did you murder someone in Castlemere? Tick box A for Yes, box B for No' would strain Queen's Street's budget—signs of a bloody struggle were found in the unlikeliest of places.

The major breakthrough in police detection of the twentieth century was the discovery of how much physical evidence was created by an act of violence, and how much of it could survive a rigorous clean-up and still be read if you turned the microscope up high enough. A spot of blood in the crevice between the wall and the skirting board would elude all but the most professional search but could contain enough information to jail someone for life.

The maid who cleaned the room had noticed nothing amiss. But Detective Constable Dick Morgan saw what both she and the departing occupant had missed: that one of the roses on the wallpaper behind the headboard was a deeper, richer red than the others. He called the Scenes of Crime Officer, and when Sergeant Tripp looked closely he saw more spots of rusty pigment in places where they were even less obvious—on the underside of the window ledge, in the hinge of the bedside cabinet. When he looked very closely there were also traces of blood in the grain of the wallpaper around the bed. A damp rag had removed the surface spotting but left a residue in the tiny canyons of the texturing.

'There must have been enough of it,' said Tripp; and two things all Queen's Street knew about SOCO, that he knew his blood and that he never exaggerated. He looked round the room. 'She was probably on the bed when he was hitting her. No knife wounds on the body?—so he did the damage with his fists. Her nose or maybe her lip was pouring blood, and she was turning her head to try and avoid him. Going off what's left, this whole wall must have been spattered.'

Morgan shook his head in a kind of brooding wonder. Like Tripp he was a Fenman born and bred, not given to emotional outbursts. Inside he was seething. Someone had pinned this girl to the bed and pounded her face until it ran with blood. Why?—because that was how he got his kicks? Because he only enjoyed sex with women he'd first beaten senseless? Toms made their living fulfilling some pretty odd male fantasies, but they didn't sign up for something like this. Which was why when he'd finished with her he killed her. By the time she knew what he was capable of, he had to.

Morgan pulled himself together and called Superintendent Shapiro, and Shapiro opined that the discovery would probably earn Morgan a promotion. Since DC Morgan had spent the last ten years avoiding promotions—a canny, intelligent man who already had all the responsibility he sought—this was not what he wanted to hear.

But Dick Morgan's discomfort was soon forgotten when Mr Coren's list put a name to the last occupant of room 411.

'Can't be,' said Morgan with certainty.

'Wouldn't have thought so,' agreed Donovan.

'Stranger things have happened,' observed SOCO gravely.

Room 411 had been occupied by Mrs Grace Atwood.

A straw poll of everyone who knew her would have voted Mrs Atwood the last person in England to be involved in a suspicious death. Shapiro remembered her from his meeting with the remaining delegates: a sturdy, shrewd woman of about fifty with a regrettable penchant for floral chiffon. She'd left Castlemere after giving her statement, but she hadn't gone far. Ipswich, wasn't it?

Philip Kendall confirmed that. He'd known her for years, they'd worked for the same firm once. Until this weekend he hadn't seen her for a while, but he'd be astonished to learn she was involved in a murder. She surprised people quite enough by hiding behind that plain apple-cheeked face one of the keenest brains in the machine tool business. Surely to God she wasn't also concealing a fondness for beating and murdering young prostitutes?

But Shapiro had spent over thirty years learning to take nothing on trust. Not long after Mrs Atwood arrived back in Ipswich, Liz set off to follow her. It was clearly necessary to talk to her again; but she didn't expect to return with the murder solved and the murderer in handcuffs.

Mrs Atwood had hardly finished telling her husband and the two of her four children who were at home about the appalling events in the hotel in Castlemere when a Detective Inspector arrived on her doorstep with more, and yet more disturbing, news. They talked in the kitchen, alone.

'We think we've established where the initial assault on the girl took place. Room 411.'

Mrs Atwood blinked. That sounded familiar, but it took her several seconds to realize why. When she did her jaw dropped. 'But—that isn't possible.'

'We have forensic evidence,' Liz said quietly. 'Laboratory analysis will give us positive confirmation, but I can't think of any other reason why there would be traces of blood on your walls. Can you?'

Innocent or guilty, Mrs Atwood wasn't the type to babble. When she got her voice back she said, quite firmly, 'Nothing happened during my occupancy of room 411 that would leave traces of blood anywhere.'

'Nevertheless, that's what we found.'

'Could it pre-date the conference?'

Liz was impressed. Not many people could think that clearly in a state of shock. 'That's something we'll check, of course. But it would be the hell of a coincidence, wouldn't it?'

Grace Atwood thought so too. But she was no closer to understanding. 'So what are you saying? That someone let himself into my room in order to meet a prostitute there? That they used my bed?' She shook that thought out of her head, but not before it had left its impression in her eyes. 'And then he killed her?'

'Probably not in the room,' said Liz. She thought that might matter to Mrs Atwood. 'But he certainly gave her a bloody nose there—he cleaned up afterwards but we found traces that he missed. They must have been there half an hour or more, probably between nine and eleven. I take it you weren't in the room at that time?'

Mrs Atwood shook her head. 'I don't believe I'd have missed all that going on. No, we had drinks in the bar about eight-thirty, then I went for a bite of supper with'—the pause as she thought through her next words was brief but significant—'one of the other delegates. I got back to the room a little before midnight. There was nothing obviously wrong at that point—it never occurred to me that someone had been there.'

'You weren't supposed to know,' said Liz. 'He tried very hard to leave it as he found it. Who was it you had supper with?'

There was a sharp, machine-tool-specialist glint in her eye. 'It was only supper with an old friend. But I'd just as soon my husband didn't know, and I imagine my companion would feel the same way about his wife.'

Liz had no problem with that. 'There's no reason they should know. But you're one another's alibis: it's important that we know who you were with during the relevant period.'

After another moment's thought Mrs Atwood nodded. 'Of course. As I say, it was perfectly innocent. But we were catching up on one another's gossip, and it got late, and... Well. It was Philip Kendall, the sales director at Bespoke. He organized the conference. We used to work together, we had a lot of news to swap, and it was so noisy in the bar he suggested we go out for some supper. And there was no reason not to, except that I try not to do things I'll have difficulty explaining to my husband afterwards. I work in a man's world, Inspector Graham, there are myriad opportunities for misunderstandings. I usually try to avoid them.'

'I know about that,' Liz assured her. 'It's no different in police work. As I say, this should be the end of it. I now know where both you and Mr Kendall were at the critical time. That narrows the list of suspects down'—to a mere sixty or so; assuming it was someone staying in the hotel and not just hijacking the room for an hour. 'Thank you for your help. Unless the timing becomes an issue, I don't expect I'll need to trouble you again. The best thing you can do is forget about it.'

'Forget that I slept last night in a bed where a prostitute entertained a client and he beat her so badly that he needed to clean the blood up afterwards?' Mrs Atwood's voice soared incredulously.

Liz gave a rueful shrug. 'I said it would be the best thing. I didn't say it would be easy.'

AT CLOSE OF PLAY on the first day Shapiro still didn't know who the dead girl was. He knew roughly when she died, but he didn't know when she entered The Barbican Hotel or who she went there to meet. He accepted Liz's judgement that the registered occupant of the room knew nothing about the incident, but if she wasn't involved then the field was wide open again. A hotel room is not like a bank vault, it doesn't take much in the way of specialist skills to get inside. Despite the best efforts of Mr Coren's staff to run a safe and efficient establishment, anyone with a little nerve and ingenuity could have walked in off the street, found an empty room and called a prostitute to meet him there.

Except that she wasn't a local prostitute, and if he'd picked a room at random—even if he'd assumed the conference group would be in the bar until late—he couldn't waste time waiting for her to travel here. She must have been nearby. Maybe they arrived together. But if they'd been staying here someone would have seen her, and no one did. Maybe no one saw him either. The invisible woman had been drugged, beaten and then murdered by the invisible man, and CID had somehow to bring in a prosecution. Thanks a bunch. Shapiro took his coat off the stand and went home.

FIVE

As soon as Tuesday's sun was up Donovan took his dog for a walk. Even before he had the dog he'd enjoyed walking at quiet times of the day, late at night or soon after dawn. He wasn't a sociable man, preferred his own company to that of people he cared nothing about, whose only topics of conversation were the weather and the government. He had a few close friends, almost no casual ones.

Dawn and dusk suited Brian Boru as well. He was no more into small talk than Donovan was. Also although he definitely wasn't a pit bull terrier, he wasn't the sort of dog you could walk in the park in the middle of the day. The ducks, and indeed the poodles, were just too damned tempting.

They set off along the towpath and went as far as Cornmarket before heading back along Brick Lane. It was a clear morning, full of promise for the day, the pale early sunshine glinting off the water and illuminating a faint haze over the distant fields of The Levels.

Halfway along Brick Lane someone fell into step behind them.

Donovan broke his stride and looked back. It was a woman; more than that, it was someone he knew. The red satin blouson, the short skirt, lighter streaks running through the dark mass of hair: subtlety isn't much use to a streetwalker. 'Zara?'

'Keep your voice down,' she hissed. 'I don't want people to know I'm talking to you.'

He blinked. Being accosted by a prostitute wasn't something he'd boast about either. 'So...?'

'I'm worried,' she said. 'I think he may have done it again.'

Donovan didn't need her to draw him a diagram: he knew exactly what she meant. His attention sharpened like wind catching a sail. 'What makes you think so?'

She shrugged awkwardly. She'd more or less caught up with him now: in an empty street you couldn't be close enough to talk to somebody and still look as if you were nothing to do with each other. 'Somebody's missing. One of the girls. I asked Dawn if we should report it, and she said we could get her in trouble. You know what it's like in this business: you get a good offer, you can disappear for a few days and all it means is you had a profitable weekend. Only, with what happened at the Basin...'

'My word any good to you?' asked Donovan. 'Because if it turns out to be a false alarm, I promise we won't make life difficult for either of you. Tell me who she is and where she lives. If she is in trouble, the sooner we know about it the less chance we'll find her with her skull smashed somewhere.'

'And if she comes back with a john and finds you crawling all over her house?'

'Then somebody smelled a leak and we're from the Gas Board! Zara, we're talking about somebody's life here. You've heard of people dying from embarrassment?—well, this is how it happens. Tell me what you know.'

She wouldn't have stayed out watching for him if she hadn't meant to do exactly that. Her mind was made up before the sun rose, it was only cold feet that made her hesitate now. 'All right. Her name's Maddie Cotterick. That's her real name—her working name's Shawna. She has a house in Viaduct Lane; I don't know the number, it's a yellow door. Since what happened yesterday we've been checking round—calling the register, if you like. Anyone who hadn't been seen, somebody called on her. I called on Maddie, but she wasn't there. But she hadn't cancelled the milk.'

It could mean nothing at all and they both knew it. But if it did mean something it probably meant something bad. 'OK, Zara, I'll get round there. She's probably got an address book or something: I'll call her friends, see if she's with any of them.'

'Jesus, Mr Donovan,' exclaimed the girl, 'you can't work your way through her book like that! Nearly everyone in it'll be...you know.'

He did know. He gave a saturnine grin. 'Credit me with a little tact. I wasn't planning on starting the conversation with: "Hello, this is the police, do you know a tom called Shawna?"'

He took the dog home and fed it before heading to Viaduct Lane. Castlemere didn't really have a Nob Hill, but it did have a scabrous underside and this was it. Even the viaduct was defunct: it used to carry the railway line from the shunting yard at Cornmarket, but that closed a generation ago. There was just a passenger halt now on the other side of town: nothing had rattled over the viaduct in the time Donovan had been in Castlemere.

And except for the bright yellow door halfway along, nobody had painted any of the little houses here for at least that long. Castlemere's only surviving length of cobble-stones was in Viaduct Lane: not preserved, merely forgotten about. There was dirt in the gutters, weeds growing in the rain-damaged brickwork.

He rang at the yellow door, but no one came and he heard no movement. He waited a moment, but he wasn't about to walk away. 'Goodness,' he said aloud to himself, 'is that gas I smell?' With the aplomb of someone who'd done this before he put his elbow through the little glass pane in the front door and groped around for the latch.

From the street this looked like the last stop on the high-way to hell. No one who could beg, borrow or steal anything better lived in Viaduct Lane. People in The Jubilee looked down on Viaduct Lane. So Donovan was startled by what he found inside. It was a proper, even a nice little house.

Tiny: two up and two down, and even then the rooms were smaller than he had aboard *Tara*. But nice. She kept it clean and decorated, with lots of primary colours and Walt Disney curtains. There were patchwork cushions and soft toys lying around. Maddie Cotterick might have to live in Viaduct Lane, but she didn't let it past that yellow front door.

There was no one here. The house felt too still even to have someone sleeping upstairs. Donovan checked the ground floor for signs of a struggle and found none; then he went upstairs. The house was too small to have a hall: the stairs were boxed into a little alcove off the living-room.

There were two bedrooms, as different as chalk and cheese. His first thought was that two people lived here, and whoever decorated the rest of the house slept in the front bedroom. It was sunny and cheerful, with a toy clown hanging from a balloon as a lamp-shade and more of the soft toys lying around: a sheep, a lion, an Old English Sheepdog with a zip down its middle for pyjamas. The smaller back bedroom was decorated all in reds: scarlet and crimson and dark blood-red, with vivid slashes of cerise; the sort of colour-scheme that provoked migraines. Donovan nodded to himself, thinking he understood. This was Shauna's room, all right. The other must belong to...

And then he realized that he hadn't understood at all; and though he was alone and his mistake a private one, still his lack of insight made him flush darkly. This was certainly Shawna's room; and the rest of the house belonged to Maddie Cotterick. This was her place of business; the rest of the house was her home.

As a policeman Donovan had known his fair share of prostitutes. On the whole he'd found them a tough, coarse, resilient, humorous bunch of women who had mostly fallen into the life as a result of some personal disaster but had a talent for making the best of a bad job. They had swum and not sunk. They talked about what they would do when they'd made enough money to retire, but Donovan got the impression that by the time they'd made the streets their own they were reluctant to abandon them in favour of a more genteel but less familiar way of life. He'd heard it said so often it was less a truism than a cliché: You can take the girl out of the business but you can't take the business out of the girl...

But he'd never considered the likelihood that, when they got home from work, they'd change out of their business clothes and catch up on a bit of reading or knitting, or painting the kitchen units. He hadn't thought of them as having a life much beyond the realm of rubber and zips. He knew it was absurd: that's why he blushed. He'd thought of them as a problem, he'd thought of them as an information resource, he'd thought of them as part of the street-furniture, but until now he'd never thought of them as people.

As far as he knew he'd never met Maddie Cotterick, and now it might be too late. But she'd taught him something just by the way she decorated her house.

There was no sign of trouble up here either, and no reason for anyone to have cleaned up as they did at the hotel. So probably she left willingly, just didn't come back. That didn't mean she was dead. Perhaps she was scared, thought now was a good time to take that holiday she'd been promising herself. He looked in the wardrobes—both wardrobes, in both rooms. The rail in the front room had a gap along its length, as if she'd grabbed a handful of clothes at random. So she'd left in a hurry. Oh yes, she was scared. The question was, had she any particular reason to be? Not uneasy, not on her guard, but scared.

He found her address book, and checked that it contained personal friends as well as clients. Then he found a bit of sturdy board to nail over the hole he'd made in her door, and left, closing the little house up behind him.

IT WAS STILL EARLY, so Donovan was surprised to be hailed as he rode his bike through Castle Place in the direction of Queen's Street. Not a tom this time: he recognized the big green 4 × 4 as belonging to one of the local vets. He pulled up and took off his helmet, and his whole expression said *Now* what?

Keith Baker backed his jeep and rolled down the window. He was a solidly built individual of about thirty with a thatch of straw-coloured hair and the ruddy outdoor complexion of a man who wrestles bullocks for a living. 'Got a dead sheep in the back,' he said by way of greeting.

Donovan considered for a moment. 'Well, keep your voice down or everybody'll want one.'

Baker grinned. 'I'm going to do an autopsy to confirm the cause of death. There's a lot of things that kill sheep. Diseases that have no real equivalent in us or any other species. And dogs, and crows, and getting stuck on their backs, and falling off cliffs, and sometimes just having nothing better to do. You find them lying in the field with their legs stuck up in the air, and it can be a right bugger, sometimes, working out what killed them. But I've got a fair idea this time, right enough.'

Donovan felt the day slowly passing. 'Good. Fine. You must be sure and let me know.' He went to put his helmet back on.

Baker was still grinning. 'You think this is nothing to do with you, don't you? You think I'm just gossiping to pass the time. What if I told you that sheep was shot?'

Donovan shrugged. 'Maybe it was rabid.'

'Oh yeah,' nodded Baker ironically. 'And maybe it was flitting from tree to tree and got mistaken for a pheasant. I don't mean the farmer shot it. I mean, he found it dying in the field and called me. He thought a dog must have had it. But you get more damage with dogs, to the fleece and to the carcass. The only thing I can think of would make three neat holes like that would be a gun. Not a shotgun, a rifle.'

'Three holes? It was shot three times?'

'Reckon so. If I'm right I'll let you have the bullets. Bloody kids, I expect. Got hold of a gun, can't wait to try it out on something, not good enough to hit rabbits so they look for something bigger and slower. Thought I'd better let you know. Anybody that stupid with guns, sooner or later it's a person gets hurt.'

Donovan nodded. 'Whose sheep was it?' Baker gave him a name and the address of a farm out on The Levels. 'OK. If I get the chance I'll take a run out there later, see if he can tell me any more. But we're up to our eyes right now, it might be tomorrow.' Or sometime next week, he added privately; or perhaps that quiet time we get in the middle of August. 'Most useful thing you can do is put the word around. If it is kids, it could be farm kids—you know as well as I do what passes for security with most farm guns.'

'Most farmers have shotguns,' said the vet. 'I don't know how many would have a rifle.'

Neither did Donovan: dead sheep weren't really his field of expertise. 'Leave it with me, I'll see what I can find out.' But he wasn't planning on giving a shot ewe much priority at the present time.

He wasn't expecting that someone would have walked into Queen's Street in the middle of the night and confessed to throwing a girl off the top of The Barbican Hotel, thus freeing him for other enquiries, and so it turned out. In fact, far from getting lighter, the workload had increased. There'd been an incident at Cornmarket.

'Cornmarket? I've just come from there. Everything was quiet forty minutes ago.'

'Well, it's not quiet now,' rumbled the Station Sergeant. 'The chief's on his way over, he said would you meet him there? He tried to phone you but you must have been on your way in.'

'Chief' was no longer an appropriate form of address for Shapiro, but he seemed to be stuck with it. It didn't matter to Sergeant Bolsover, who'd known him since he arrived in Castlemere, that he'd been promoted from Detective Chief Inspector to Detective Superintendent, or even that he was still not the senior officer at the station. (That honour fell to Superintendent Giles, and his soubriquet was The Son of

God.) By the time you've called a man Chief for ten years you can hardly start calling him something else.

'What sort of incident?' said Donovan.

Sergeant Bolsover gave the sort of grim facial shrug his jowly fenland face had been designed for. 'Messy,' he said succinctly. 'Is there another kind?' It was an exaggeration, but though they dealt with an awful lot of stolen cars and break-ins and closing-time punch-ups for every murder that came along, some weeks it didn't feel like that.

Concerned for his springs, Shapiro had left his car at the end of Brick Lane and picked his way on foot across the urban wasteland that was Cornmarket. But this was Donovan's backyard, he knew his way round in the dark. He rode surely across the broken ground towards the knot of people gathered in the far corner where the northern spur joined the main Castlemere Canal.

Shapiro was one of them. He looked up at the sound of the bike. 'Come over here and tell me who this is.'

Donovan parked well away from the tapes, for fear of obscuring signs of an earlier vehicle. Immediately he was mobbed by the small community of homeless people who lived at Cornmarket and were among his nearest neighbours. Desmond Jannery was in a state of shock and couldn't explain what was happening. Sophie was in tears. He gestured them to stay where they were and ducked under the tape.

'That's Wicksy.' He must have had another name but Donovan had never known it. He was about thirty-five, bone-thin and slightly mad. In an earlier, uncivilized age he'd have been locked up in an institution and fed three times a day. But Wicksy had been lucky enough to qualify for Care in the Community, which meant that he got all the freedom he could use including the freedom to go hungry. He only owned one coat so he wore it winter and summer. Now he'd died in it. The hole drilled in the centre of his chest had spilled just a teaspoon of blood before his heart stopped pumping.

'Somebody *shot* him?' Donovan hadn't supposed that

Wicksy, or any of them, mattered enough to get shot. Being homeless was the next best thing to being invisible.

'That,' grunted Shapiro, 'or he stood still long enough for someone to take a Black & Decker to him.' It wasn't disrespect: bad jokes are sometimes the best way for police officers to deal with tragedy.

Donovan didn't understand. *'Why?'*

'We'll find the man who did it and ask him,' promised Shapiro. 'Right now I'd settle for knowing where from.'

Wicksy had taken the bullet high enough to pitch him on to his back, pretty much where he stood. He'd been standing on the edge of the canal because he'd been using it as a urinal. His friends had seen him fall and, imagining he'd been taken ill, had hurried over to help. He was dead by the time they reached him.

So he'd been shot from across the canal. But this far out there were only fields. The nearest road, just visible as an embankment rising through the green corn, was quarter of a mile away.

'Is there an easier way to get there?'

Donovan shook his head. 'The towpath's on this side; the nearest bridge is at Mere Basin, but you can't get here from there—you couldn't get through the tunnel under The Barbican. Going out into The Levels, the next bridge is about two miles from here. No, the road's your best bet.'

'So somebody walked or drove out by River Road, stopped right about there, waded through quarter of a mile of growing corn—with a rifle held above his head like a Green Beret crossing a Vietnamese swamp—all in order to shoot Wicksy?' More than perplexed, Shapiro sounded indignant. It defied logic, and above all he was a logical man.

Donovan gave an apologetic shrug. 'Looks a bit like it.'

'Then why didn't he leave a track through the corn?' It was standing a foot high, it should have been perfectly obvious if it had been trampled, but neither man could see any indication of it.

'Maybe he came by boat?' hazarded Donovan. It wasn't that wild a guess: it had happened before.

'Same question,' said Shapiro. '*Why?* You don't have to kill people like Wicksy, you just have to wait for the next hard winter.'

'Could he have seen something he wasn't supposed to?'

'Oh yes,' agreed Shapiro, heavily ironic. 'As I recall, Wicksy's the one who sees spaceships. Damn sure you'd have to silence a witness as reliable as that!'

'The man who shot him may not have known him that well,' said Donovan reasonably. 'He might not know that Wicksy spent most of his life on a different planet. If he saw something, and if it mattered enough, he was killed because whoever did it couldn't count on us not believing him.'

It was speculation but it made sense. 'All right,' said Shapiro. 'What did he see?'

Donovan's eyes rounded. 'I'm supposed to know that?'

'Actually, yes. He was shot about twenty minutes ago. According to Desmond, you passed through about twenty minutes before that. So what did Wicksy see in those twenty minutes that got him killed? What did he see that you didn't?'

Donovan cast his mind back until Zara caught up with him on his way back along Brick Lane there had been nothing memorable about his walk. There had been nothing for Wicksy to see.

He shook his head. 'Beats me, chief.'

'Call yourself a detective,' grunted Shapiro.

They were back at Queen's Street, trying to organize two parallel murder inquiries, when—almost simultaneously—Shapiro received one phonecall and Donovan received another that cast a new and still more disturbing light on the death of the man known as Wicksy.

Shapiro's call was from Dr Crowe. The FME had begun a special post mortem; he'd broken off mid-scalpel, as it

were, because he'd found something he believed the superintendent would want to know right away.

'The bullet I took out of him. It's a rifle bullet, right
enough; well, we knew that. But it's not common-or-garden
rifle ammunition. I'm no expert, I've passed it on to Ballistics for a full assessment, but the last time I saw anything
like that it came out of a South American diplomat who was
assassinated on the steps of their London embassy.'

'Assassinated?' exclaimed Shapiro, startled. 'You think
Wicksy was killed by a hit man? A South American hit
man?'

'Well, that's a fair bit of ground to cover in one stride,'
said Crowe. 'But it was a professional job. That bullet, the
sniper rifle that fired it, and the precise positioning of the
wound make it highly professional. A job like that costs
serious money.'

Shapiro didn't ask how an old-fashioned pathologist with
a fancy new title came to know a thing like that. Conver-
sations with Dr Crowe could always turn up surprises: the
man was a sponge for arcane bits of information. 'A sniper
rifle?'

'Get the authoritative word from Ballistics,' said Crowe.
'But yes, that's what it was. In the right hands—which it
was—a gun like that would be accurate at very long range.'

'Quarter of a mile?'

'Quarter of a mile would be nothing to a gun like that.'

Which left Shapiro more confused than ever. So now he
was supposed to believe that Wicksy saw something in the
twenty minutes after Donovan left Cornmarket that not only
meant he had to be killed, but that whoever needed him
dead had immediate access to a hired assassin, possibly from
South America, who was accurate with a sniper rifle at a
range of quarter of a mile or more. He thought he'd go back
to believing in the Golem before he'd believe that.

Then Donovan came in, knocking as an afterthought, and
though he didn't know it he had the answer. 'I just had the
funniest phonecall.'

Shapiro sniffed. 'And you think that makes you someone special?'

Donovan gave his saturnine grin before continuing. 'Keith Baker. You know, the vet? He stopped me this morning, he had a dead sheep, apparently it had been shot—by kids, he reckoned. Except when he opened it up and recovered the bullets, they didn't come from any kid's gun, or any farmer's gun either.'

Shapiro felt the creeping unease of *déjà vu*. 'Let me guess. It was a sniper rifle? Fired from anything up to quarter of a mile away?'

Donovan had long suspected Shapiro of having extrasensory perception. It was the only explanation for some of the leaps of intuition he'd made over the years. But even that didn't explain this. 'Have you bugged my phone?' he asked suspiciously.

Shapiro shook his head. 'I've just heard from Crowe. Wicksy was shot with the same gun.' He sucked in a deep breath. 'You know what this means, don't you?'

Donovan was good at his job, but as a philosopher he wasn't in Shapiro's class. 'That the sheep saw the same thing Wicksy did?'

But Shapiro was too worried to be amused. He shook his head. 'Wicksy didn't see anything. The man who killed him didn't know him, had nothing to gain from his death. But he sure as hell means to shoot someone, and he wants to be sure of a clean kill. It's going to be a long shot, so he needs to get the gun sighted in—is that what you call it?—adjust the sights so that he hits what he's aiming at even at long range.

'Donovan, the bastard was practising. First on the sheep; and when he was happy with that, just to make sure, he practised over the same distance with a human being.'

SIX

'THE CONFERENCE,' said Liz. 'Where's that list of delegates?'

He wasn't sure whether he was getting old or she was getting sneaky, but increasingly these days Shapiro found himself having to work to keep up with her. He found the list but still hadn't worked out why she wanted it. 'You think the two things are connected? You think that whoever killed the girl... Or rather, you think the man who killed the girl is the target? Or maybe...' He gave up. 'What do you think?'

Liz looked taken aback. Nothing so sophisticated: it had only occurred to her that, with so many foreigners in town over the weekend, anything smacking of international intrigue might involve one of them. 'Dr Crowe mentioned South America. I wondered if any of Mr Kendall's delegates came from there.'

Two Brazilians representing a company in São Paulo had shared one room, a third representing the government occupied another. 'He's still there,' said Shapiro. 'Eduardo da Costa. I met him: small man, sharp dresser.'

'It's hardly a reason to assassinate him.'

'Maybe he's the assassin.'

Liz thought about it, then shook her head. 'That hotel's at the centre of a murder inquiry: it's the last place a mechanic would stay. And da Costa's been here for five days, which is four days too long. Whatever the mechanic's here for, he'll do it today. He arrived overnight, he sighted his gun in first thing this morning, he'll do the job today and be gone by the time we hear about it. No one in The Barbican Hotel is a mechanic; but one of them may be the target.'

Also on the list were a Uruguayan from Montevideo and a Mexican with a Scottish name. Most of them checked out after breakfast on Monday, long before Wicksy or even the sheep got shot. It was hard to see why anyone who wished them ill would be sighting in his gun twenty-four hours after they left town. Which suggested the target was one of the eleven delegates left at The Barbican. Two of them were from South America: da Costa and Selkirk.

'Don't get hung up on the South American angle,' advised Shapiro. 'A professional mechanic will work for anyone who can afford him, the politics are irrelevant. Even if it is the same man, he won't confine himself to people from one part of the world.'

It was never more than a shot in the dark. Liz was just looking desperately for somewhere to start: somewhere to begin chipping at the monolith. Someone they didn't know was going to kill someone else they didn't know for some reason beyond their ken. It was like looking at a black glass pyramid, there was no way of getting hold of it and no way of getting inside. Somehow they had to chip a hole in the façade to see what was happening behind it, and all they had was the list.

Everything had happened so quickly there'd been no time to register the astonishment that events common enough in Colombia, in New York and Moscow and Naples, and not totally unheard of in London, had found their way to Castlemere. Dull, grey, work-a-day Castlemere. When she had a moment the fact that they were up against a hired killer would leave her breathless, even more amazed than appalled. But right now she needed to concentrate on the practicalities, and nothing was more practical, more concrete, than two corpses in the morgue. 'All right. But the target's on this list somewhere. And so, probably, is whoever killed the girl.'

Shapiro couldn't argue with that. 'The same man?'

She considered. 'No. It doesn't work. Nobody hires a top-class assassin to avenge a hooker. Even if they did, it wouldn't happen here. Whoever killed the girl is long gone. If someone was after him, he'd have followed.'

Shapiro closed one eye in a pensive squint. 'So if the mechanic's here the target's still here; so whoever he is he didn't kill the girl.'

'That's how I see it. The target is probably one of the eleven men still in the hotel. The man who killed the girl is probably one of the thirty-seven who've already left.'

Shapiro nodded. 'Get over to the hotel, get those eleven together and tell them what we suspect: that a hired killer is after one of them. That should loosen somebody's tongue. I'll see Kendall, have him flesh out the list with a bit of background information. Once we identify the target we can do something about protecting him.'

'What do you want me to do about Maddie Cotterick?' asked Donovan gruffly. He'd been sitting on the windowsill, contributing nothing until now.

'I'm not sure what you can do. You could leave messages with some friends, so if it's a coincidence and she's safe enough she can let us know. Unless she turns up dead, she probably just went off on holiday without telling anyone.'

'She didn't pack for a holiday,' objected Donovan. 'She grabbed things in a hurry and got out. She was scared.'

'If she'd heard about the girl on the boat she had good reason to be scared,' said Liz. 'If I was a tom, I'd think this was a good time to be out of town too.'

It was a fair comment, but somehow Donovan didn't think they were taking Maddie Cotterick's disappearance as seriously as they might. As seriously as they would have if she'd been, say, the local librarian, she hadn't turned up for work one day and her house looked as if she'd left in a hurry. Perhaps it was natural, even inevitable. If he challenged them they'd say, reasonably enough, that people with regular jobs keep regular hours and acting out of character is less likely to be significant in those without much character in the first place. Yesterday he'd have agreed with them. But now he'd been in her house, he'd got some kind of a handle on Maddie Cotterick, and he thought she was entitled to more from them than she was getting.

He went back to his office and started leafing through her address book. One of the few advantages of converting a private house into a police station was that everyone above bog-standard constable got their own office. Donovan's had originally been a maid's bedroom. Shapiro's, as befitted his status, had been the butler's.

'Did you sense a certain chill in the air just then?' asked Shapiro after he'd gone.

Liz nodded. 'He thinks we'd be doing more if the victims had been People Like Us.'

'Maybe he's right. We've got two bodies, a prostitute and a wino, but what we're actually talking about is who the next victim might be. Because if somebody's brought in a professional mechanic, a man who's such a perfectionist that he practises on real people, his target is someone important.'

'More to the point,' said Liz, 'his target is still alive. If we find him quickly enough we may be able to keep him that way. Wicksy and the girl on the boat are a lower priority not because they're less important but because things can't get any worse for them. We have to protect the living before we can spare time for the dead.'

'But you don't think the two cases are connected.'

She'd already said so, and given her reasons. If he was asking again it was because he was unconvinced. She thought some more but didn't change her mind. 'I can't see how. There's a mechanic in town, and he killed Wicksy for target practice. That's seriously scary. He's going to kill someone else—but it won't be the man who pushed a prostitute off a roof. Who'd have paid him—her friends? He earns big, big money. Whoever the girl was, if she mattered to someone with that deep a pocket she wouldn't have been on the game.'

'So we've got two killers to find, and one of them we

have to find before he kills someone else. All we know about him is that he's an expert with a sniper rifle.' Shapiro shook his head, defeated. 'Our only chance is finding the target. Go talk to the people at The Barbican.'

Liz was halfway to the door when her step slowed and she turned back, her expression troubled. 'Damn it, Frank, have we got this wrong? It would almost make more sense if he's not one of the delegates at all. If he was, the mechanic should have been here earlier. It's only a fluke that any of them are still in town. What if it's a local man he's after?'

Shapiro scowled at her. 'You're supposed to be narrowing the field. Now you tell me it could be anyone in a population of about sixty thousand.'

Liz twitched him a little smile. 'Not just anyone. Someone wealthy and well-connected. Whoever wants him dead certainly is, but he wouldn't have to spend this kind of money stepping on some little person who annoyed him. If he's hired a real pro it's because the target's going to be hard to reach. He may have permanent protection, or he may know he's in danger. That's why it has to be a long-range hit.'

Shapiro thought, She's getting good at this. 'So on a list of council-tax payers he should be in the top band.'

'Along with an awful lot of others,' Liz admitted ruefully. 'We can't protect them all. We can't even warn them all: ten per cent would have heart attacks, forty per cent would grab the nearest gun—to the immediate danger of themselves, their families, their neighbours and their milkmen— and the rest would end up in hospital with perforated ulcers. If we do nothing, someone's going to die. If we do too much, half a dozen people could.'

That was when the phonecall came in. Shapiro took it; Liz went to leave but he waved her back to her seat. 'Mr Kendall—Mr Kendall, calm down. Tell me what's happened.'

DONOVAN WENT WITH HIM. Shapiro explained while he drove. It would have been normal practice for the sergeant to drive while the superintendent sat in state beside him, but motorcyclists don't make good chauffeurs. They lean into the corners, and forget that they need more space on the road than the width of their knees.

'Well, now we know what our assassin's here for,' he said. 'He's here for Philip Kendall. How the sales director of a custom engineering company comes to make the sort of enemies who send round a professional hit man is something else.'

'He wouldn't tell you?'

'He said he didn't know. He sounded panicky enough for it to be the truth.'

'What happened?'

Philip Kendall took a leisurely breakfast, as he always did, with his wife and the *Financial Times*. Before leaving for work he took his geriatric Labrador for a stroll round the garden of his house at Cambridge Road. Once they used to walk as far as the Chevening Moss Road; but Rosie was getting old seven times faster than her master, a gentle inspection of the shrubbery suited her better now.

They were returning to the house. Kendall was actually climbing the steps to the back door, when a brick in the wall beside him exploded. There was no noise except a sort of clipped pfutt as a shower of masonry fragments erupted from the hole. They stung his hand; it was almost more that than the sound that drew his attention.

When he looked at the hole in the wall, his first absurd thought was, You'd almost think a bullet did that. His second was, A bullet did do that! He left his third thought out on the step with the surprised dog while he raced inside, locking everything that would lock, curtaining everything that would curtain, grabbing for the phone.

'Is he all right?'

'He says so. He doesn't think there was a second shot. Of course, by then he was under the sofa.'

Shapiro's car wasn't the only one heading for the scene. Access to the back gardens in the smart part of Cambridge Road was by a green lane running behind the houses. An Armed Response Unit was on its way to intercept anyone leaving that way, though in all likelihood it was already too late. The moment Kendall disappeared into his house a professional assassin would evacuate the area. He wouldn't get another chance in the immediate future, and any delay increased the risk that he wouldn't be able to return. A man got to be a top-class mechanic partly by being good with a gun but mainly by being good at risk assessment. A hit man who doesn't know when to leave and come back later is going to figure in a lot of photographs with numbers on them.

But a top-class mechanic would always come back. He would always complete the job. Nothing, including threats to his freedom or his life, would make him abandon a job. It was part of the credo. You decide whether the money's worth the risk before you take it. Because in this line, commitment has to be absolute.

Another police car was heading for the motorway interchange. But with no description the chances of spotting something suspicious were right around zero. People like this man didn't get careless and leave their telescopic sight on the car's parcel shelf beside the nodding Alsatian. They wore suits and had a briefcase on the back seat, and if stopped their credentials were faultless. If the papers in the briefcase were about critical path analysis, they could talk critical path analysis with the best.

All of which was bad news for the man on whom a professional hit had been ordered. If he ran he'd be followed; if he hid he'd be found; if the attempt was unsuccessful it would be repeated, as often as necessary. The assassin couldn't be found by assiduous detective work among the target's circle of acquaintance. Even the person who hired him may never have met him, and might be in no position to stop him even if—by dint of detective brilliance or great good fortune—CID managed to track him down. A mechanic on your case was a little like having Creutzfeldt-Jakob disease: it mightn't show right away, but ultimately the results would be devastating.

'Bespoke Engineering,' ruminated Donovan. 'These guys make bits of machinery for individual customers?'

'As I understand it.'

'Remember the Iraqi gun fiasco?'

Shapiro did. A British company was commissioned to manufacture some piping to an Iraqi design. The end use was uncertain: something for the oil industry was a good guess, and one expert positively identified the finished product as part of a condenser. Only it turned out to be part of an artillery piece designed to hurl shells at Israel. Export was blocked, but it took a court case to exonerate the manufacturers.

'You think Kendall's sold his firm's services to—what? An unfriendly government? A terrorist organization?'

Donovan shrugged. 'Maybe he didn't know. Maybe he's found out and they want to shut him up.'

It made sense. It belonged to a different world, but it did make sense. The sort of organization or individual who could commission that sort of job could afford the most expensive hit available.

'Then perhaps the best way to protect Kendall is to find out what he's sold to whom and make it public,' said Shapiro. 'If it's no longer a secret his clients might as well call off the dogs. It'll be hard enough to explain placing an illegal order; if it turns out they were willing to assassinate the salesman as well, they may find it pretty hard to do business in future.'

'Will Kendall talk? A deal like that, confidentiality will be built in.'

'The way he sounded on the phone, he'll tell us everything he knows, everything he suspects and everything his wife's mother saw in the tea leaves. He's a frightened man, Sergeant, and frightened men rethink their priorities. Besides, whatever confidentiality he signed up to, it didn't include this. They lied to him; now they're trying to kill him. He'll talk faster than you can write it down.'

Understandably, Philip Kendall didn't meet them at his front gate. The area car was there and PC Stark checked the occupants of Shapiro's Jaguar before admitting them. WPC Wilson answered the door.

'They're in the morning-room, sir.' It was at the side of the house; only a sniper perched in the cherry tree outside would have been able to shoot through its one window.

But Kendall was still nervous. Half an hour ago someone tried to kill him. If he'd been six inches to the right as he came up those steps it wouldn't have mattered how many policemen had been distributed around the house and grounds.

Shapiro tried to reassure him. 'He'll have gone by now, Mr Kendall. The moment you slammed the back door he'd have been on his way.'

'But I don't understand!' The man's voice rose towards a wail; Mrs Kendall, by contrast, sat beside him on the sofa like a statue, rigid and silent, a handkerchief balled in one fist so tightly she'd probably never get the creases out. 'Somebody shot at me. Somebody tried to kill me! Who? And why?'

'I think, when we talk about it calmly, you'll be able to tell us that,' said Shapiro. 'You must know something about somebody that would be damaging if it got out. You may not even realize its significance. Something someone said in an unguarded moment; something you saw in someone's office. I presume you visit your clients' offices?' Kendall nodded, shakily. 'Then it could be something that happened while you were abroad, that you haven't yet recognized the importance of but which you would come to understand with time. Does that make any sense to you?'

This time, shakily, Kendall shook his head.

Shapiro sighed. 'All right. Can you tell me who you've had dealings with that just might try to forestall a scandal this way? Governments with iffy human-rights records, say, and the more ruthless kind of private company.'

In the end, the list of Kendall's clients was not very different from the list of his conference delegates, and he found it hard to say which of them might indulge in this kind of cover-up without knowing what it was they were covering up.

Shapiro hoped he might be thinking clearer by tomorrow, suggested they talk again then.

Kendall looked alarmed. 'But—if you don't find him, I could be *dead* by tomorrow!'

'We'll try and prevent that,' said Shapiro solemnly. It was about as far as he could honestly go. 'I'll leave officers here round the clock, at least until we figure out what's going on. Alternatively, you might feel safer moving into an hotel.'

'What—like The Barbican?'

Shapiro understood his misgivings. 'I'm not sure what more I can say, Mr Kendall. You need to be careful. We'll do our best to sort this out, but I don't want to mislead you, it won't be overnight. In the short term I suggest you stay indoors as much as possible. Oh—except that it would be helpful if you could come outside and show me where you were standing when the shot was fired.'

Even that was enough to make Kendall uneasy. 'You're sure he's gone?'

He was afraid for his life: Shapiro wasn't going to mock him. 'I'll check with the ARU before we go out.'

But they'd had time now to walk the back lane from end to end and there was no one there.

They went into the garden. It was entirely ringed by high hedges: unless he brought a stepladder with him, the sniper must have made a hole to shoot through. The only problem with that was...

Donovan was behind him as they headed back to the house. Shapiro turned to him and frowned. 'It's too close.'

Like a chain reaction, like dominoes falling, what that

meant tumbled through his brain and landed in his eyes. Donovan saw comprehension widen them; he saw them flick up, above the hedge to the gently rising ground beyond. Then Shapiro spun back towards Kendall, ahead of him on the steps, and his arms spread as he went to cover the man's back.

It was a year or two now since Frank Shapiro had felt justified in considering himself middle-aged. Many policemen of his age were retired, or had moved on to second careers. Since Shapiro had no wish to do anything else, and no wish to do nothing, he stayed where he was and did what he was good at. The increasing creakiness in his knees didn't much affect his abilities as a detective: in his midtwenties he realized he'd have to catch criminals with his brain because it was the only agile part of him. Since then his brain had got smarter and quicker, and his body had got bulkier and slower.

But it's amazing how fast even a slow, bulky, elderly detective superintendent can move if he has to. As Donovan watched in astonishment he launched himself up the steps like the demon king in a pantomime.

He was still watching, startled speechless, when he saw the back of Shapiro's coat open like a flower, a red flower blooming in a desert of herringbone tweed.

Time slowed right down. Donovan felt himself rooted to the spot, trying to move and not succeeding. He heard a sort of surprised grunt from Shapiro and a thin cry from the man on the steps above him, slowly, slowly turning to see what had happened. He saw Shapiro falling towards the steps, and though there was all the time in the world he couldn't get his arms forward to break his fall. He crashed face-down on the concrete, and time resumed normal speed.

Donovan unglued his limbs and flung himself to cover Shapiro's body with his own. But there were no more shots, and after a moment, still keeping between his chief and the lane, he pushed himself up on his knees and looked around. WPC Wilson was coming at a run. He waved her back with an urgent sweep of his arm. 'Get on the radio,' he roared. 'Ambulance first, then the DI. You'—he meant Kendall—'inside. Lock the door. Don't worry about me,' he added fiercely as the man went to argue, 'it's not *me* he's shooting at!' Then, and only then, did he dare look at Shapiro.

And he thought Shapiro was dead; or if by sheer bloody-mindedness some spark of life persisted within him, it couldn't possibly last long enough for the miracle-workers at Castle General to get their hands on him. There was a hole in the middle of his back Donovan could have sunk his fingers in, and enough blood had come out of it to baptize them both.

Someone was cursing: not inventively, just the same obscenity endlessly repeated in a high thin whine of a voice laced through with shock and an agony of rage. Donovan looked up, wondering who it was. But there was only Shapiro—white-faced and deeply unconscious—and him, so he supposed it was him.

PART TWO

ONE

SUPERINTENDENT GILES wasn't really a copper's copper. He was a highly intelligent man, and a dedicated police officer. He was a graduate, and a Bramshill Flier, and the likelihood was that he would make Assistant Chief Constable. No one at Queen's Street had a bad word to say about him. At the same time, he knew that if he stayed in Castlemere for the next ten years still no one here would feel about him the way they felt about Frank Shapiro. He commanded respect, he didn't inspire affection. He was sorry about that, but doubted there was anything he could do about it. He wasn't one to court popularity, and not only because he knew it didn't work.

In the sixteen months he'd been here he'd developed a regard for Queen's Street that he hadn't felt at every station where he'd served, and he would have liked to feel accepted as one of the team. He knew how the computers worked; he knew how to get the best out of Interpol. Men like Sergeant Bolsover, and Shapiro himself, who'd spent thirty years doing this job and knew it back to front and inside out could never wholly empathize with a man to whom crime statistics seemed important.

He was the new generation, the new face of policing. The nearest thing he had to a contemporary was Liz Graham, who had also done her stint at Divisional HQ and never hit 'Cancel' on the keyboard when she meant to hit 'Save'. But bizarrely enough, the one he felt to have most in common with was Donovan. They were both outsiders, for reasons that were beyond their powers to amend.

What Superintendent Giles may not have known, and what somebody really should have told him, was that—on top of and apart from the considerable respect he enjoyed here—every so often he did something that genuinely touched the people working under him and made them wish they knew him better. He did something like that today. He didn't go straight to the hospital when he heard about Shapiro. He went to the house in Cambridge Road where it had happened, to take over the inquiry so that Liz could go to the hospital instead.

She found Donovan prowling the corridors like a caged tiger, oblivious of the blood on his shirt. A couple of months ago it wouldn't have been so obvious, but in deference to the improving weather he'd switched his usual black for a stonewashed denim that now looked as if he'd salvaged it from an abattoir.

Liz had spoken to Mary Wilson so she knew how he got so much of Shapiro's blood on him. He'd used his own body to protect the injured man from further gunfire. It was what she would have expected; still, it was not a small thing. The shot that felled Shapiro could have been the first of many: it would have been hard to blame anyone whose natural human instinct led him to dive behind the nearest wall.

'Any word yet?' she asked.

Donovan shook his head. The savagery of the movement told Liz all she needed to know about the turmoil raging in his breast.

'No news is good news,' she said tritely; and felt moved to justify that against the contempt in his eyes, flicking at her like a whip, by adding, 'If he'd died they'd have come out and said so. While they're too busy to talk there's still a chance.'

'He was shot in the back,' snarled Donovan. 'The bastard took out his spine. If he lives he'll be in a wheelchair.'

'You can't know that!' Liz flashed back angrily. 'People who spend their whole lives dealing with back injuries can't predict which ones are going to be devastating and which will mend. Millimetres count: a fraction one way and your spinal cord's gone, a fraction the other and all you lose is a chip of bone. Don't tell me he's going to be a cripple when you don't know that!'

'You're right, I don't. He probably won't live that long.'

She wanted to slap his face. But a calmer voice inside her head reminded her that neither of them was wholly in command right now, neither should be held accountable for everything they said or did. She only had to look at Donovan to know he was in shock, and she didn't expect she looked much better. She spread her hands, palms down, in a pacifying gesture. 'All right,' she said, a shade unsteadily; 'all right. Don't let's bite one another's heads off. Are *you* all right—you weren't hurt?'

Donovan shook his head again. 'I was too far away. I couldn't get to them...' That bothered him. He wasn't paid as a bodyguard any more than Shapiro was, but the deal had always been that Shapiro did the thinking, Donovan did the gymnastics. But when it mattered most he'd been too far away to help. A man he cared about more than any of the family that remained to him had dropped at his feet with a crater gouged out of his back because he'd thought quicker than Donovan could react.

'He wasn't in the lane. The bastard. The mechanic.' He wasn't an articulate man at the best of times. Under stress his Ulster accent thickened and the words came out disjointed, not in sentences but pushed out as they occurred to him. The Irish are a nation of poets, but that particular gene seemed to have passed Donovan by. 'We checked the lane and the lane was clear, but he was never in the lane. He was where he'd been all along—quarter of a mile away across the fields. That's what he was saying. The chief. He said, ''It's too close.'' Then he moved to get Kendall inside, and while I was still trying to work out what he meant the bastard shot him.'

His head rocked back: if he'd been a dog he'd have howled. 'If he'd thought of it sooner he could've hustled Kendall inside and nobody'd have been hurt. If he'd left it a bit longer, at least the man would've stopped his own bullet. As it is, he's thrown away all of his life that's worth the name, and for nothing. Kendall will still get his, as soon as the mechanic gets himself organized.'

'God damn it, Donovan,' snapped Liz, 'don't say that! The man has a killer on his tail, and you're telling me there's nothing we can do about it? What the hell's he been paying his taxes for all these years?'

Donovan shoved his hands deep in his pockets. 'Be realistic. This guy's a pro. World class. He's killed a lot of people, a lot of them had people trying to protect them, and every time a police force somewhere has had catching him as its top priority. But he's still free, and still making a living. We don't know his name, we don't know what he looks like, his age, nationality or colour. We don't even *know* that he's a man. I don't think we can stop him.'

'Well, fortunately for Mr Kendall,' retorted Liz, 'it doesn't come down to what you think. However difficult the job, he's entitled to our best efforts to protect him. And more, not less, because of what the chief's already sacrificed. Don't you dare tell me that the man who put Frank Shapiro in this hospital is beyond our ability to make him pay!'

Dead on cue a door opened and a man in surgical greens came out. Liz caught his eye and saw weariness and the worst possible news there. But it wasn't her he was looking for: he gave a little nod of acknowledgement before seeking out the people who were waiting for news of another patient. Liz let out a ragged sigh and looked for somewhere to sit down.

She found herself puzzling over something Donovan had said earlier. '"It's too close"? What *did* he mean?'

'You don't need a sniper rifle to shoot somebody over his own back hedge, and you sure as hell don't have to tweak your sights by practising on live targets. Wicksy was shot at long distance—probably from River Road quarter of a mile away. If he was practising at quarter of a mile, quarter of a mile was his intended range. Not fifty metres from the lane at the back of the house.'

Her eyes shut, Liz nodded slowly. 'We should have known that. The information was there, if we'd only made use of it.'

'There wasn't much time for thinking.' Talking about it was calming Donovan as nursing his rage had not. 'We knew about the lane behind the houses, it seemed obvious that was where the gunman was. Even the chief only realized when he saw the layout, and by then it was too late.'

'That depends on your point of view,' Liz observed tiredly. 'From where Kendall's sitting it was just in time.'

'Will you leave him in the house?'

She shook her head. 'It's too open. If this man really can hit a moving target from quarter of a mile away, our only chance of protecting him is to send Kendall into hiding.'

'Where can you put him that a good mechanic won't find him?'

She had no personal experience, but as she understood it there was nowhere that a good enough mechanic wouldn't find his target eventually. That was the key word: eventually. 'I can't; but I can make him waste a lot of time looking. We can use that time to find out what the hell's going on.'

'Did Kendall come up with anything useful?' Donovan had left the house with the ambulance, he'd had no time to talk to the man after the shooting. He was having to fight the notion that Kendall was to blame for what had happened. He knew it was unfair—he knew that a man who'd been shot at in his own back garden was entitled to ask for help—but at gut level, which was where he did a lot of his thinking, Donovan still held him responsible.

Liz elevated an eyebrow. 'Have you ever tried to conduct an interview in a broom cupboard? Maybe the Son of God's had more luck. Or maybe he really doesn't know who's trying to kill him. Bullets coming over your back fence concentrate the mind wonderfully: if he still can't say why, maybe he's being targeted because of something he might have seen but actually didn't.'

'A mechanic as good as this guy's been sent on the off chance?'

'The best mechanic in the world could be hired for the small change in the back pockets of some of the people Philip Kendall deals with. And the more you've got, the more you have to lose, the more you're prepared to do to protect it.'

There was a long pause then. Donovan was clearly thinking about something and wondering whether to speak. When he caught Liz waiting with increasing impatience he shrugged. 'I was just wondering when we can expect the visiting fireman.'

Liz frowned. If there was one thing more impenetrable than Donovan keeping secrets, it was Donovan thinking aloud. 'Visiting fireman?'

'Serious Crime Squad,' he said, as if the words tasted bad. 'They're not going to leave it to us, are they? With the chief out of action, the senior detective in Castlemere is now an inspector; and if you trip on a kerbstone it'll be a sergeant. We get left to our own devices as much as we do because they've no one can hold a candle to the chief. Now it's just us Indians, we're going to get a visitation.'

Liz hadn't given it a thought. Now she realized he was right. For a second it knocked the wind out of her. They could use all the help they could get, but the idea of someone coming in over her head was disturbing. They were a small team at Queen's Street, they worked well because they knew each other intimately, read each other's minds and covered each other's backs. Extra bodies and fresh ideas would be welcome, but they would also be disruptive. A peripatetic superintendent would have his own way of doing things, and though it mightn't be too different from hers it would be diametrically opposed to Donovan's. Just when they needed to be at their best, their strongest, they were going to find themselves on the defensive, sidetracked and marginalized. The king-pin of their success was fighting for his life, and if they wanted any part in the hunt for his assailant they were going to have to play by somebody else's rules. It was hard to swallow. And if it was hard for her, it would be nigh impossible for Donovan.

But it wouldn't be today. If they could get a grip on this thing in the next twenty-four hours, perhaps whoever came would pick it up and run with it instead of trying to dazzle them with his superiority.

'All right.' She stood up. 'Look, I can't stay here, I've got to get things moving. Get Kendall somewhere safe. Then pick his head apart for whatever it is that's in there that makes him worth assassinating.'

'Do you need me?'

'Yes,' she admitted, 'but to be honest I'd sooner you stayed here. It's stupid, but I just feel that while one of us is here the chief's not going to slip out the back door. Call me as soon as there's any news. If I have something for you to do, I'll call you.'

'I'll be here.'

THERE ARE PROPERTIES for use by the police in circumstances like these. Liz fast-tracked the application and got approval within half an hour, which must have been close to the national record. Taking Kendall to an hotel was no longer an option. When the mechanic came back, as come back he would, it was enough that there would be police officers between him and his target. She didn't want members of the public there as well.

When it was arranged she went to the Kendalls' house in Cambridge Road. 'Pack a bag each, I'm taking you somewhere safe.'

Kendall just nodded. Mrs Kendall said, 'What about the children?'

Children. Of course there were children. They'd left for school before all this started, but around four o'clock this afternoon they'd return to an empty house. 'Where are they? I'll pick them up.'

They were at the Rosedale Academy. The boy was eleven, the girl thirteen. 'We'll pick them up right away and bring them to the house where you'll be staying.'

Mrs Kendall frowned. She was a small, dark woman, and though she'd been shocked to the core by what had happened there was a steely resilience underneath. 'I don't want them missing school. Could they go to my mother's?'

Liz didn't know how to put this without upsetting them further. 'We can do a better job of protecting you if we keep you all together.'

Iris Kendall wasn't a stupid woman. The import of that sank through her eyes. 'You mean, the children could be used against us?' The pitch of her voice rose in fear and horror.

'We'll prevent that happening,' Liz said, with as much conviction as she could muster. 'But I don't want to make the mistake of underestimating this man.'

While they were packing Superintendent Giles said, 'Will you stay with them?'

Liz shook her head. 'I can't, sir, there's too much to do. I'll leave Morgan and, if you can spare her, WPC Wilson. They're a couple of cool heads.'

'Neither of them is an Authorized Firearms Officer.'

'I doubt we can stop this man with guns, sir. Our best chance is to out-think him. If he finds Kendall, filling the house with Coldstream Guards won't save him.'

Giles nodded. 'All right. Er—' He hesitated.

Liz smiled. 'I know: you've been on to Division and they're going to send someone to take over. I've been expecting it. You hadn't much option: it's too big a mess to leave to a DI. We'll give him all the help we can.'

Giles looked relieved; more than that, he looked impressed. 'It's a real pleasure working with professionals.'

'There is that,' she said; and added a little impishly, 'Plus, if it all goes pear-shaped, it'll be on someone else's record. Do you know who they're sending?'

'Hm. Detective Superintendent Hilton.'

It was the 'Hm' that alerted her, that made her search her memory. 'Oh yes. Little chap—well, for a policeman. Little moustache. Takes himself a bit seriously.'

Giles nodded. 'Do you know what his people call him—his own team, the people he's worked with for years? Not to his face, I mean, but when they're talking about him?'

Liz thought then shook her head. 'Hitler' came to mind, but if they did she didn't think Giles would be telling her. 'No.'

'They call him Sir,' said Superintendent Giles quietly, and with that simple, accurate and perfectly inoffensive sentence conveyed everything that Liz needed to know.

ANOTHER HOUR PASSED and still no one came near Donovan. He didn't know what to do. He was wasting time, and time was of the essence. They had a dead prostitute and a missing one to worry about. They had a dosser in the morgue, a Detective Superintendent in surgery and a local businessman in hiding. They had not one but two killers currently at large in Castlemere—unless whoever was responsible for the girl's death had already left, in which case the chances of making him amenable were already small and diminishing by the hour. On top of all that, they had someone on his way over from Head Office to mind the shop. The last thing Donovan had time for was kicking his heels in a hospital waiting area in case sometime someone felt a sudden urge to tell him what was happening.

And yet he couldn't bring himself to leave. Clearly DI Graham had felt the same way. She needed him at Queen's Street, but she wanted him here. If Shapiro was going to die, he shouldn't have to do it surrounded only by strangers in masks. One of the two of them should be here for him.

So should his family. With all that was going on, it seemed likely that no one had thought to call them—none of them lived locally any more, the closest was probably his ex-wife who now lived in Bedford. He was about to call Sergeant Bolsover to organize it when a woman he recognized only from the photograph on Shapiro's windowsill came through the swing doors from reception and stood looking round as if she wasn't sure what to do next.

She was older than in the photograph, of course—ten years older. It was taken in Jerusalem, on the last family holiday before the Shapiros first started taking separate holidays and then living in separate houses. It wasn't, of course, the holiday that split them up. But it had been a mistake to try to push five people who'd been growing steadily apart back into close proximity in what was after all a foreign land. It was something they'd all looked forward to, and it had been a disaster. The strain was already showing in the photograph in Shapiro's office. David had taken it. Shapiro looked as if he was telling him how to do it—though David had gone on to make photography his career and his father's excursions into the medium were marked by thumbs and left-on lens caps. Angela looked as if she wanted to bang their heads together. Rachael and Sally looked as if they wished they were somewhere else—better still, two somewhere-elses.

And ten years later Angela Shapiro was again somewhere she didn't want to be, in a hospital in a town where she used to live, looking for news of a man she'd given up trying to live with but still cared for enough to rush to his side when he was hurt.

She'd never met Donovan, had no way of recognizing him. He took a deep breath and went over to her. In the second before he opened his mouth to introduce himself he remembered that his shirt was decorated with her husband's blood. He stammered, 'Er—Mrs Shapiro? I'm the chief's— I'm with...I'm Donovan.'

She looked at him in some puzzlement. 'Yes? You, er'— she nodded at his shirt—'were operating on Mr Shapiro?'

He laughed. He always laughed at inappropriate times.

'Jesus, it looks like it, doesn't it? No. Detective Sergeant Donovan: I work for your husband.' He wondered for a second if he should amend that; but 'ex-husband' sounded too much as if the man had died already.

Angela Shapiro was still staring at his shirt. 'You were with him when it happened?'

'Yes.' He didn't know what to do. It wasn't coat weather, he had nothing he could button up to hide the blood. In desperation, yet with a kind of panache, he whipped off the offending garment—standing momently bare-chested in the middle of the waiting area—and pulled the sleeves through before putting it on again inside out. It was an improvement, just; mostly, it was a distraction.

Mrs Shapiro blinked. 'Frank's told me about you. I believe the expression he used was, Full of surprises.'

'Yeah? One of my better weeks, obviously.'

It seemed to strike both of them at the same moment that they weren't here for this. Angela said, 'How is he?' and Donovan said, 'There's nothing much I can tell you...' in about the same breath.

Angela smiled wanly. 'You first.'

'I don't know anything,' said Donovan plaintively. 'I've been here a couple of hours now and nobody's been anywhere near me. My inspector insists that's a good sign. Me, I'd rather know what's happening.'

As if he'd said the magic words, a door opened and another man in those ubiquitous green pyjamas emerged, wiping his glasses on a corner of his smock. 'Detective Sergeant Donovan?'

'Yes! This is Mrs Shapiro.'

Glen Turner replaced his glasses and then blinked, wondering if the policeman knew he had his shirt on inside out. He decided it was none of his business. 'Well, the superintendent. It's too soon to say he's out of the woods, but he coped well with the surgery, he's stable and his vital signs are encouraging. He lost a lot of blood, but we sorted that out as soon as we got him into theatre. In fact, for a man who's been shot in the back he's not in bad shape. He'll be waking up before long; you can probably talk to him this evening.

'As to the injury itself, well, it's nasty enough. But it could have been worse. The bullet glanced off the side of his spine, there's some damage to the bony structures there and the plumbing to his right kidney's been disrupted. It'll be a few days before we know if that's going to mend or if he'd be better off without it. Of course, if we have to remove it he'll manage perfectly well on one.'

He looked between them with a sombre smile. 'You want to know if he'll be able to walk. The simple answer is, it's too soon to tell. When he wakes up he's probably not going to have much feeling below the waist, but there's a chance that'll pass. What happens is that the tissues around the injury swell, and that can cut off the messages travelling up the spinal cord. But if the cord itself isn't damaged, sensation will return when the swelling goes down.

'We can't be sure from the X-rays that that's what's happened. But there's no obvious damage to the vertebrae that would mean the cord itself had to be involved. You see what I'm saying?—I can't swear that the central nervous system isn't compromised, but if it was I'd expect to be able to see where. There's a good chance that a bit of time and physiotherapy will get him on his feet again.

'But I know, what you want from me is a promise, and it wouldn't be fair to any of us to make it. We have to wait and see.'

'How long?' asked Angela faintly.

Mr Turner shook his head apologetically. 'Even that's more than I know right now.'

TWO

LIZ COLLECTED THE Kendall children from school and took them to the safe house in Northampton. Castlemere didn't have one of its own: it wasn't big enough and there'd never been the need before. Besides, it made sense to get the family out of town. It wouldn't make their pursuer throw up his hands in despair and go home, but it would make his job harder. Unless and until Liz could find out what this was all about and stop it at source, buying time was not only the best option, it was the only one.

She fetched the children herself because she didn't want more people than necessary to know where the Kendalls were. Not because there were those at Queen's Street whose discretion couldn't be trusted, but because this man would go through anyone to get at Kendall and the fewer who knew, the fewer were in danger from him. For the same reason she stopped Iris Kendall giving the address or even the phone number to her mother. 'We'll keep an eye on her, but the best protection is that she doesn't know anything.'

Now he'd got over the shock of seeing a man dropped by a bullet meant for him, Philip Kendall was coping well. He understood the need for absolute discretion, didn't think he could continue going to work through the crisis. He used Liz's mobile to phone his secretary and put his appointments on hold. He didn't offer much of an explanation, but there wasn't much need. Anyone with a television would know exactly why he was keeping his head down as soon as the evening news went out.

'Feeling any better?' asked Liz when Mrs Kendall took the children upstairs to work out the sleeping arrangements. Kendall made a non-committal rocking movement with his hand. 'I'm not sure how I feel. I've never seen anyone shot before. Is there any news—is he going to be all right?'

Liz could only shrug. 'Nothing yet. But that means he's still hanging in there. Take it from me: he's tougher than he looks.'

'But it's my fault, isn't it? That other man, and now Superintendent Shapiro—it's my fault they were shot. I don't know why, I don't think it's anything I've done, but they were shot because of me.'

Liz shook her head. 'They were shot because someone with a lot of money and no conscience decided murder was the answer to a problem he had. You can blame the gunman, you can blame the man who sent him, but I honestly don't see how you can blame yourself.'

He smiled gratefully. He had noticeably bright-blue eyes that he'd passed on to both his children. Her first thought when the school principal gave them into her keeping was, No blaming these on the milkman! 'I appreciate everything you're doing for us,' he said. 'I only wish I could offer a proper explanation.'

'You still can't think who's behind this?'

'I've no idea. But look.' He produced a dog-eared copy of the same list of delegates she'd already seen. This one had notes jotted on it. 'I've been going through my diary. The names I've underlined are foreign clients that I've visited in their own cities in the last four months. The dates are beside them. I've also put down the sort of business each is in. Those marked with asterisks are in what you might call sensitive areas, either in terms of what they do or where they are. Don't take that as a suggestion that I know or suspect anything discreditable about any of them: I don't. But if we're into speculation, and we start by assuming that the man behind this is more likely to be an ex-Warsaw Pact arms manufacturer than a Swedish bicycle magnate, the asterisks are the arms manufacturers.'

Liz took the list with an appreciative nod. 'I'll get someone with a knowledge of international affairs to look at this.

Maybe one of the names will ring a bell. In the meantime, I know it's not much comfort but we'll be doing everything we can think of to keep you and your family safe. Don't go outside. Don't use the phone—if you need to contact someone, Detective Constable Morgan will do it for you, untraceably. Try not to worry. This could all finish as quickly as it started.'

'You're very kind, Inspector.' There was something vastly attractive about those blue eyes. Liz had to remind herself that Brian had things going for him too: one, that he was her husband, and two, he'd probably still be alive at the end of the week. 'You're all putting yourselves at risk to protect us, and I can't even tell you who we need protecting from. You will let me know if there's any news about Superintendent Shapiro?'

'Of course. Now, I'd better get back. Is there anything more you're likely to need from home?'

Kendall shook his head. 'I think we've got everything— right down to the kids' favourite toys.' They were spilling out of a hold-all on the sofa: electronic games, a plush kangaroo, a straw donkey, a racing car half-metamorphosed into a robot. He saw her expression and gave a shame-faced grin. 'I take it you don't have children, Inspector Graham. If you had you'd know that there's nothing in the entire house as important to our peace of mind as having the right toy— *this* week's right toy, not last week's! If we'd brought the camel instead of the kangaroo, by the end of a week we'd be ready to take our chances with the gunman.'

LIZ HAD SOME DIFFICULTY finding a financial expert. In view of the fact that more crimes are committed for money than any other motive, there are surprisingly few police officers who are thoroughly at home with the genre. Someone at Divisional HQ suggested a DI Colwyn and she left a message for him to call her. But by close of play on Tuesday she still hadn't heard from him. Tomorrow she'd have to try someone else. Maybe Scotland Yard could come up with a name.

Meanwhile there was still the poor girl from the boat. A day and a half had passed since she was found, and Liz was no closer to knowing who she was or who killed her. He was probably on Kendall's list, but so were almost fifty others. He wouldn't have to be particularly rich or particularly powerful, but if he'd thought sufficiently far ahead to meet her in someone else's room he was particularly clever and he'd have covered his tracks with the same aplomb.

As evidenced by how he disposed of the girl's clothes and the bloodied sheets off Mrs Atwood's bed. Sergeant Tripp, who was also quite astute, found them at the bottom of the linen cupboard down the hall. Despite everything the killer had had the presence of mind to fold them neatly, with nothing untoward showing, and conceal them under a stack of identical sheets.

Sooner or later, if SOCO hadn't found them first, the housekeeper would have got a nasty shock, but by then the man would have been safely home. Replacing the bloody linens with a clean set bought him some time. Even if the body had been found earlier, no one would have looked for evidence in Grace Atwood's room if Mrs Atwood herself was unaware of anything amiss.

At three o'clock the phone rang. It was Donovan. 'Update on the chief.'

Liz steeled herself. 'Go on.'

'Without staking his pension on it, the surgeon reckons he's out of danger. He just might lose a kidney, they're going to wait and see. There's some paralysis but it may not be permanent. It'll be a while before they can be sure.'

'But we're not going to lose him.'

'Doesn't look like it.'

For a minute she just breathed. Right now that was all that mattered. Later she'd start worrying how good a recovery Shapiro would make, how mobile he was going to be, whether he'd get back to work or if he'd have to take that early retirement he'd managed to fend off so far. At fifty-six he had another four years in the job—if he wanted, and if he was fit to do them. After a shave as close as this one, he might be ready to call it a day.

But that could wait. He could take his decision in the light of his recovery over the next weeks. Right now Liz was too relieved that his life was out of danger to worry that he might be in a wheelchair and she might have to break in a new superior.

Donovan was speaking again. 'His wife's here.'

'Mr Giles called her. I'm afraid I didn't think of it.'

'I thought I'd take her over to the chief's house. He had his keys on him, so I can let her in. Then I'll go home and get cleaned up. I'll see you in about an hour.'

DONOVAN GOT A TAXI to take them back into town. He didn't have it wait: from Shapiro's little stone house in Castle Mews it was only a ten-minute walk to Mere Basin and up Broad Wharf to where *Tara* was moored.

He found the key on Shapiro's ring and opened the door. Angela Shapiro stood in the hall, looking round her as if she'd never been there before. Donovan said awkwardly, 'I think there's a spare bedroom on the left, at the top of the stairs.'

She smiled at him. At fifty she was still a notably attractive woman. Too damned attractive, people had said, to be snared by the man she married: a wry twenty-six-year-old Detective Sergeant built like a brick privy, with a crumpled face and an odd way of looking at things. It was by no means certain then that this last feature would help him to a good career in CID. It might equally well have led to his being labelled a maverick, someone who didn't do things the establishment way. Someone who got results his own way often enough that the job he had was safe but it was as high as he'd ever go. Someone like Donovan, in fact. Angela became Mrs Frank Shapiro knowing he might be a DS to the end of his career.

And left him when he was a Chief Inspector. Where was the sense in that? Only that they'd been in love when they were younger and somehow, between the work and the hours, that love had shrunk first to a simple fondness, then to indifference, finally to irritation. They had different priorities. Angela grew tired of the things that mattered to her, that mattered to the family, always having to play second fiddle to the victims and criminals who seemed to matter to him more.

'Can I make you some tea?' she asked. 'Or at least find you a clean shirt?'

Donovan shook his head abruptly, startled out of a kind of reverie of contemplation. Of course, he was tired. 'I'm only a step from home. I'll get over there and get cleaned up. Is there anything you need?'

'I don't expect so. If there is I can pop down to the shops. I lived in this town for three years, you know, I still remember my way round.'

He left his number anyway. 'We'll be at Queen's Street till late, but call me anytime if there's any problems.' It wasn't grammatical but it was kindly meant.

There was a way in which this dour, awkward man reminded her of her son. It wasn't physical. They were both dark, but where David was small and compact, Donovan was long and thin as string. So it went deeper than that. It was something in the eyes, in the way they looked at the world—wary, intense, committed, like explorers in an alien environment. She'd long suspected that David was a changeling, a fairy child left to be raised by humans and somehow—change of policy or a new filing system at Fairy HQ—never collected. Perhaps the same administrative cock-up had abandoned DS Donovan in a world for which his genes, his racial memory, did not prepare him.

'I'll phone the hospital later. When Frank's awake I'll go in and see him. I'll let you know how he is.'

Donovan nodded and left. Attracting strange looks as he

crossed Castle Place, he remembered he was still wearing his shirt inside out.

'YOU WERE RIGHT about the visiting fireman,' said Liz when he got in about four o'clock. 'The Son of God knows him; I've met him a time or two. Detective Superintendent Hilton. He'll be here tomorrow morning.'

Donovan's eyes widened in recognition. 'Hilton? I had him when I was a DC in Kilburn. He hates me!'

'It's not *just* you he hates,' said Liz comfortingly. 'General consensus is, he hates the whole human race.' She gave it a little more thought. 'Still, knowing him, and knowing you, it is possible he hates you more than most. What can I say?—keep out of his way as much as you can.'

'How am I supposed to do that?' demanded Donovan indignantly. 'I think he'll notice if I hide in the bog every time he calls a briefing.'

They turned on the television for the six o'clock news. As expected, the shooting of a Detective Superintendent while protecting a Castlemere businessman headed the run-list. The item had Shapiro's photograph and another of Kendall's house. Liz had agonized with Superintendent Giles over how much detail they should give out with the press release, but they needn't have bothered. The reporters had got hold of everything they left out anyway. It didn't matter. The mechanic obviously knew who his target was so there was no point making a great secret of it. As long as nobody knew where he was, and so far even the BBC had failed to discover that.

'I wonder if Frank was watching,' said Liz pensively. 'He'd have liked that bit about "brave and self-sacrificing".'

'He'd have liked the bit about "swift and agile" even better,' said Donovan with a grin.

The girl in the boat got a one-line mention, mostly because of the curiosity of another serious crime in the same small town in the same brief space of time. Wicksy didn't get even that.

A little after eight WPC Flynn rang up from the switchboard. 'I've got a caller wanting to talk to someone about Mr Shapiro. She won't give her name. She sounds drunk to me. I think it's probably a crank, but I thought you'd want to talk to her anyway.'

'Yes, Cathy, thanks. I better had.'

Cathy Flynn was a good enough officer, but she wasn't in Mary Wilson's class. Wilson wouldn't have thought the woman on the phone was drunk. She'd have known she was hysterical with fear.

'Try and calm down,' said Liz. 'I can't understand what you're telling me until you calm down. Now, can you give me your name?'

'Later,' said the woman jerkily. 'Maybe. If it's safe. If you can help me.'

'Help you with what? What's happened?'

But she slid away at a tangent without answering. 'I don't know who I can trust. You think you know what's going on, but you're wrong. You don't understand. Where it started. Who's involved.'

Liz was making nothing of this. 'I'm sorry, I'm probably being very dim, but I'm not following what you're saying. You know something about the shooting of Detective Superintendent Shapiro?—or have I got that wrong too?'

'No,' said the woman, 'that's right. At least, I think so. The girl in the boat—I know who she was. I know who killed her.'

'Wait a minute,' said Liz, her brows bent, 'let me get this straight. Are you saying there's a connection? Between the girl who was killed and the attempt on Mr Kendall's life that put Mr Shapiro in the hospital?'

That drew Donovan back. He was only next door in his own office: with both doors open he could hear what she said. He came and stood in her doorway, his eyes puzzled and suspicious. His thin lips made a kind of silent question mark.

'Yes!' exclaimed the woman. 'That's what I'm telling you. I know who she was and I know who killed her. He killed her so she couldn't identify him, and then he tried to kill Kendall so *he* couldn't identify him. And now he's going to kill me so *I* can't identify him, and I want protection or I'm putting this phone down and you'll never know who I am and what I know.'

But Liz had been doing this job for a while now, and she'd got quite good at it. She beckoned to Donovan, and said softly into the phone, 'It's Maddie Cotterick, isn't it?'

THREE

THERE WAS A GASP at the other end of the line, and after that a silence so long that Liz began to think the other woman had dropped the phone and gone. 'Maddie? Are you there? Talk to me, tell me what you want me to do.'

At length she heard Maddie Cotterick suck in an unsteady breath and knew she was still there. So she wanted to talk, to sort something out. She'd just been startled speechless by how little her anonymity had protected her. She didn't know what it meant. Were the police looking for her? Did they already have the information she'd hoped to buy her safety with?

Finally she managed, 'How do you know my name?'

'We've been worried about you,' said Liz. 'One of your friends reported you missing. Someone went to your house and it looked like you'd left in a hurry. We were afraid something had happened to you.'

'Something happened to me, all right,' blurted the woman; it sounded as if she was choking off a sob. 'I watched a man use my best friend's face as a punchbag. Even when I knew he was going to kill her I was too scared to help. I pretended I was out cold. I just lay in a corner with my eyes shut, and when he took her outside I grabbed my clothes and ran.'

She was crying now, shame and grief distorting her face. 'I could have saved her. Even then: if I'd gone for help, maybe there was time to stop him. At least I could have made him pay. But I was afraid, so I ran. And now my friend's dead, and the man who killed her is going to kill me too.'

That was, had to be, the important point. What Liz wanted

to hear was how all this fitted in with the shootings, but what she had to sort out first was where Maddie Cotterick was and how she could be protected. Except to dismiss it, they hadn't even considered a connection between the two episodes. But Maddie said there was one. It was her bargaining point, the thing she was offering in return for help.

Liz didn't need a bribe. If the girl was in danger she'd help even if she didn't know next week from Wednesday. But if she could cast light on the attempts on Philip Kendall's life that had put Frank Shapiro in the hospital and perhaps ended his career, that was a huge bonus. 'Maddie,' she said, trying to instil calm with her voice. 'Does he know where you are now? The man who killed your friend?'

'I—don't think so. I don't see how. But—you don't know these people, you don't know what they're like. They buy what they want. He'll have people looking for me. I don't know if there's anywhere I can be safe!'

'You can be safe here,' said Liz firmly. 'No, listen to me. He wants to kill you because of what you know. Share that information with me and you're safe. Tell me what happened, who was involved. Tell me now. Then tell me where you are and I'll send someone for you. No one'll harm you in the police station, and by the time you leave there'll be no point in trying to. Do you understand?'

She understood, she just didn't believe. 'Not a chance. I'll talk to you, I'll tell you everything, but not now—not while I'm out here on my own. What's to stop you leaving me here? While I have information you need, you have to keep me safe. Once you have that information, some of the urgency goes. I don't want anybody thinking time doesn't matter when my life's on the line!'

Liz saw no point in arguing. The woman was frightened, beyond being convinced. Nor were her fears absurd. Police work is full of prioritizing: she couldn't guarantee, particularly when tomorrow the decision would be someone else's, that collecting Maddie Cotterick from whatever sanc-

tuary she had fled to would still be a priority when they
knew what she had to say.

But from what she'd said so far there seemed a good
chance that Maddie held the key to understanding and then
cracking a difficult, dangerous case. Liz had got it wrong
once already: she'd thought these were two separate events.
But Maddie said she could connect them. Unless she'd
sought sanctuary in Nova Scotia, it was worth parting with
someone for long enough to bring her in.

And particularly since there was someone she wanted to
keep away from Queen's Street until Superintendent Hilton
was firmly in the saddle and had taken up the reins.

'All right, Maddie. Tell me where you are. I'll send my
sergeant to fetch you.'

Even that didn't reassure the woman. 'I'm not telling you
where I'm staying. Inspector, it's not that I don't trust you.
But these are powerful people. They can get things done.
The man who wants me dead, he isn't wandering round East
Anglia with a sawn-off shotgun. He picked up the phone
and made a cash transfer, and now someone who's made a
career of finding and killing people who've seen things they
shouldn't have is looking for me. I'm not saying you'll sell
me out. I'm saying if you know where I am you could let
slip the least fragment of information that's all someone like
him needs. I don't want your sergeant getting here and finding only a nasty stain on the carpet!'

'What do you suggest?'

The woman had clearly thought this out before ringing.
'I'm in King's Lynn, in a call box. That's all I'm telling
you. I'll meet him in the town centre. There's a café in King
Street, near the market place. The Wherry Café. Tell him to
go inside and wait. I'll join him when I'm sure he hasn't
been followed. When can he be there?'

Liz thought. 'Are you safe where you are tonight?'

'Yes.'

It was a sixty-mile drive, it would take maybe ninety
minutes each way. The earliest she could be here was ap-

proaching midnight, and Castlemere wasn't the kind of party
town where you could drive around at midnight without
been conspicuous. If someone was looking for her, it would
be safer to wait until the roads were busier. 'Then first thing
tomorrow morning. He could be there by—what?—eight-
thirty if you're ready then.'

'Say nine o'clock, then the traffic'll be thinning out.' Liz
was impressed. The woman had thought this through. If a
marksman was on her trail, she didn't want to be in the only
car on the road but she also didn't want to be sitting in a
traffic jam like a duck at a rifle range. 'Tell him to be in
the Wherry Café by nine, and I'll join him some time after
that. What does he look like, how do I recognize him?'

With Donovan standing there Liz hesitated to answer.
Donovan frowned at her, not understanding the little smile
playing over her lips. She could have said, 'Tall, thin, thirty;
dark hair, dark eyes, dark clothes; face like a vulture whose
last gazelle disagreed with him.' Instead she said, 'Darth
Vader on a diet.'

Maddie got the idea. 'All right, I'll know him when I see
him. Tell him to wait. I won't show myself until I know
it's safe.'

Privately, Liz thought the woman had been watching too
many movies, but if that was what it took to keep her happy
it could be coped with. 'All right. He'll wait for an hour. If
you can't get there in that time, call me again and we'll fix
a new rendezvous.'

When it was settled and Maddie Cotterick had gone back
to her secret sanctuary, Liz realized Donovan was still looking at her suspiciously. 'Darth Vader?'

She thought quickly. 'We had to agree on a password.
When she approaches you, you introduce yourself as Darth
Vader.' She told him where and when they were to meet.

'And how am I supposed to get there?'

'Ah.' His bike was not the ideal transport for collecting
a valuable witness, and a squad car would probably send
the woman back into hiding. Reluctant to commit a CID car

for most of the morning, she was about to offer him her
own when a better thought occurred. 'Take the chief's. It's
in the yard—I had it brought from Cambridge Road.'

Donovan raised an eyebrow. 'Won't he mind?'

'That you're using his car to fetch a woman who says
she knows who shot him? Would you?'

'He never lets me drive it normally.'

'He isn't normally lying in a hospital bed with a bullet
hole in his back! Needs must when the devil drives, Sergeant.'

'I don't think it's the devil's driving he's worried about,'
muttered Donovan.

Liz passed him the bunch of keys. 'Just don't scratch it,
that's all.'

IT HAD BEEN A LONG DAY, she was tired; she'd need an early
start in the morning—as early as Donovan's—if she wasn't
going to be caught on the hop by the arrival of Superintendent Hilton; still there was one thing more she needed to
do tonight. She got in her own car and drove the thirty-five
miles to Northampton.

It was ten-thirty before she got there; the Kendalls were
in bed. It had been a long day for them too. Philip Kendall
put on his dressing-gown to come down and talk to her.

'We've been contacted by someone who says she knows
what happened in the hotel,' said Liz. 'She thinks the shootings at your house are part of the same thing. Can we go
over it again in the light of that and see if we can work out
who's behind it?'

She didn't go into more detail than she needed to. 'Somebody brought in a couple of call-girls, and used Mrs Atwood's room to entertain them while'—the possibility that
they were being overheard occurred to her just in time—
'she was having supper. He gave one of them cocaine. Then
he beat her so badly he thought she'd report him. So he
killed her.

'When the man took her friend to the roof, the other girl

took her chance and got away. She grabbed some clothes from her house and got out of town. Now she's telling me that the murder of her friend and the attempts on your life are connected. She wouldn't explain how—my sergeant's fetching her in the morning, I'm hoping to get a clearer tale then.

'In the meantime, perhaps you can help me make sense of it. If the man who killed the girl also wants you dead, it's because you two can identify him. This isn't because of something you saw on a visit to Outer Mongolia—it's because of what happened in The Barbican Hotel on Sunday night. Whether or not you're aware of it, you know who murdered that girl. He knows you know, and he wants to silence you.'

Philip Kendall was trying desperately to think. She could see the cogs whirring away behind his eyes. His forehead creased in an agony of self-catechism; a couple of times his lips pursed on an answer, but either it was the wrong answer or it danced away before he could grasp it. Finally he shook his head. 'I don't know,' he said helplessly. 'I don't *know*.'

'All right,' said Liz, 'try this. The man we're looking for knew where to find an empty room that he could use. He knew Mrs Atwood wouldn't come in and surprise him. So he knew she'd gone out for the evening—and further than the hotel bar or she could have come back at any moment. Whose idea was supper—yours or hers?'

He spread his hands. 'Mine. We found ourselves together in the bar, the party was too noisy for conversation, it was going to be a while before we met again—I asked if she fancied a bite of supper before we called it a night. I never *thought*—'

'Of course you didn't,' nodded Liz. 'Neither did she. But someone saw you going, or overheard you in the bar, and realized that Mrs Atwood's room was going to be empty for an hour or so.' Was it long enough? He obviously thought so. Long enough for sex with a prostitute; long enough to beat her; even long enough to take her on to the roof and throw her off. But not long enough to start phoning round for a suitable girl. So he had the girls lined up already, the only question was where he took them. He knew he'd find somewhere. Oh yes, he was certainly staying at the hotel. 'Do you remember who was with you, or sitting around you, when you decided to go out to eat?'

He couldn't remember. 'Just about everybody. No, some of them had already left, but everyone else had gathered in the bar.'

'So—what? You made a public announcement?'

Kendall flushed a little. 'Of course not. We weren't particularly looking for company. But we didn't fix it up in a huddle behind the bicycle sheds either. Someone could have overheard. But I honestly can't say who.'

'All the same, maybe that's it,' said Liz. 'If he was sitting beside you at that point, he may think it's only a matter of time before you remember. And of course, if you remember you can tie him to the murder.'

'One of my customers?' Kendall said it as if the idea had only just occurred to him. 'One of my customers is trying to kill me?'

'Tomorrow,' said Liz, 'with any luck, I'll be able to tell you which one.'

IT WAS MIDNIGHT before she got home. That in itself wasn't unusual; but even as long days go, this had been a bad one.

Brian had gone to bed, falling asleep over the book he was reading as he waited for her. The sound of her car woke him. He opened the front door in his pyjamas.

'Any news about Frank?'

Liz shook her head. 'I'll phone the hospital now.'

But nothing had changed since she phoned before. They said he was stable and sleeping comfortably; which seemed a shade unlikely but Liz knew what they meant. If there was no news, at least there was no bad news.

Brian was making some supper. 'Get into bed and I'll bring it up.'

'Have I time for a shower?'

'If you're quick.'

The water pounding down on her, pummelling her, just the cool side of comfortably warm, massaged the exhaustion from her bones and refreshed her skin and her mind. When Liz emerged, wrapped in a towel, to sardines on toast soldiers—Brian was the sort of vegetarian who considers fish an aubergine with fins—the worst of the day was swilling with the sweat and the grime down the plughole.

There's a kind of quiet strength in knowing that the worst has happened and still somehow you've survived. She'd never imagined a day as bad as this one—a hired killer on the loose, two bodies already in the morgue and Shapiro fighting for his life, a family to be protected from a threat with no face, no reason, and tomorrow she was going to have to hand over control to a head-office hero who thought criminal investigation was something you could do by the book.

Liz had worked for superiors with a wide variety of styles, from the imperious to the downright casual, and she'd formulated a rule of thumb. Rank sat most effectively on those who exercised it as little as necessary. Frank Shapiro could go days without issuing a direct order, but only because everyone knew that his suggestions were to be acted upon with despatch. Nobody took liberties with him. He was so clearly on top of the job, so confident in the respect of his colleagues, that there was no need to keep proving it. Calm, thoughtful and dogged, he brought out the best in his officers. Men like Donovan, and to a lesser extent Dick Morgan, who would have been misfits almost anywhere else, had been able to do good and sometimes outstanding work under Superintendent Shapiro. That was his reward, not a quota of 'sirs' added to every conversation.

'They seem to think he's out of danger,' she said through a mouthful of sardine. 'They're not committing themselves on how much damage has been done.'

'You mean, he may not get back to work?'

Liz shrugged. 'The man's fifty-six, he's got to retire in four years anyway. Any injury which sidelines him for more than a few months is bound to be considered a reason for bringing that forward. Outside of Hollywood, you don't find many policemen in wheelchairs.'

Brian shook his head. 'It's funny but I never considered anything like this happening to Frank. Donovan, certainly—it's a minor miracle every time he ends the week with all his bodily parts. And you. I've thought a hundred times I could lose you in something like this. But Frank?—it never seemed a possibility. He's so—solid, so permanent. It's like asking yourself if the Tower of London's really as strong as it looks. I suppose the answer is, nothing is. Nothing's so strong, so enduring, that it can't be destroyed if the will is there.'

'Most things can also be rebuilt if the will is there,' Liz said.

'God, I hope so.' Brian Graham was a sensitive man, he didn't just pity someone facing a life of disability, he felt for him—understood how it would feel from the inside. The despair. The way such a thing washed all the hope out of the future, all the colour, leaving only a burden. A split-second of being in the wrong place leading to a lifetime of sheer drudgery. Having to plan the simplest action like a military campaign. Because it isn't the ability to run Marathons that the paraplegic misses. It's the freedom to nip upstairs for a handkerchief at the first sign of a runny nose.

'But even if he does recover, there's no guarantee he'll want to come back to work. You mustn't underestimate the trauma, Liz—not just physical but mental. It'd take a tough man to put it behind him and go back to doing a job that got him hurt this badly.'

'He *is* a tough man,' insisted Liz. 'Tougher than anyone ever gives him credit for. If he was thin and angular his name would be legendary as someone not to mess with. Since he looks like everybody's favourite uncle people tend to think he's soft and kind and easygoing to match. But he isn't. Inside, where it matters, he's hard, tough, resilient. He's a survivor. People think Donovan's tough—he looks the part—but they're wrong about that too. He's brittle, like glass; if that cracks he's raw flesh all the way down. Frank's like steel: he may bend but he'll never, ever break. Chisel your way through the surface and all you'll find is more steel underneath. Steel isn't dead—warm it up and it can flow—but the toughness is intrinsic. He won't give up. If he can live, he'll live; if he can get back on his feet, he will; and if he's fit enough to come back to work, he'll do that too.'

Brian hoped she wasn't convincing herself it was possible just because she wanted it so much. 'You know him better than anyone so I expect you're right. But what if you're wrong?'

Liz cast hunted eyes at him. 'Then we'll get a replacement. We may even get lumbered with the guy they're sending down tomorrow, in which case I'm very quickly going to run out of excuses to keep Donovan out of his way.'

'Maybe your promotion'll come through. Everyone says it's overdue.'

She squinted. 'It doesn't quite work like that.' She thought about adding that part of the reason it was overdue was that she hadn't pressed for it, but decided against. He'd want to know why. She didn't mind telling him that working with Frank Shapiro, and even with Donovan and the others, was worth more to her than Superintendent on her door and an increment on her salary. She didn't particularly want to tell him the other reason, which was that she wasn't keen for her career to set him back yet again. 'No, I don't think anything now can save us from Detective Superintendent Hilton, Sir to his friends, at least in the short term. I'd better get practising my expressions. Respectful admiration should be about right.'

Brian nodded doubtfully. He'd seen her do Respectful Admiration before. It wasn't as far as it might have been from Downright Incredulity.

FOUR

IT WAS WEDNESDAY, so King's Lynn was less hectic than
it had been the day before. The Tuesday market, much more
than the Saturday one, was the commercial and indeed cul-
tural heart of Lynn, and packed the old streets with locals
and visitors alike.

Donovan knew his way around Lynn. He'd even been to
the Tuesday market before now, arriving the sneaky way—
crossing the Great Ouse from the western bank on the passenger ferry that lands a stone's throw from Tuesday Market
Place. (Other markets might be a moveable feast, but chang-
ing the day of that in King's Lynn would involve reprinting
the street maps.) Of course, what he knew best was the river.
Here in its last reach before dumping its silty contents into
The Wash it was wide and brown, decorated by sailing boats
and swans and oddly green mud.

He parked Shapiro's car, carefully, and walked down
King Street looking for the Wherry Café. There was a
wooden sign above the door like an old inn sign, showing
a great barge with a single vast black sail. The heavy door
with its bull's-eye panes tinkled a little brass bell as he
pushed it open.

He wasn't expecting to find Maddie Cotterick waiting for
him. It had just turned nine o'clock, the café was still serving breakfasts. Donovan sat down and ordered everything
on the menu. He hadn't eaten since yesterday. He wasn't a
great breakfast man normally, though that was more to do
with not wanting to cook than not wanting to eat. Like many
naturally thin men, he could eat until the cows came home,
and then he could eat the cows.

As he ate he studied his fellow diners, paying particular

attention to those who came in after him. He didn't know what Maddie Cotterick looked like—it occurred to him only when he was halfway here that he should have returned to her house and hunted out a photograph—but a tom ugly enough to pass as one of the builders' labourers and cattle-truck drivers who made up the bulk of the café clientele would have had difficulty making a living even in Castle-mere. There were a handful of women in the café but none of them looked promising. One probably *was* a builder's labourer; another was twenty years too old; a third might have been a milliner or a librarian with her chintzy dress and pale shoes. Every time the bell tinkled Donovan waited a moment and then glanced casually over, but he saw no one who seemed to be looking for him.

When the bacon, the sausage, the fried egg, the fried bread and the mushrooms had all gone, and so had the pot of coffee, he checked his watch and found that most of the hour had gone too. She wasn't going to come. He gave a frustrated scowl. But he'd done what she asked: there was nothing more he could do. He waited another five minutes, then got up, paid his bill and left. The little bell tinkled his departure.

Twenty metres up King Street he was aware that he had company. He broke his stride, about to look round, but the woman's voice hissed at him, 'Keep walking. Where's your car?'

He'd been waiting for her so long that finally to be jumped like this, in the street, made him startle. Being star-tled made him ratty. 'Jesus, Maddie, where do you think you are—Checkpoint Charlie?'

'I *think* I'm in danger,' she said tightly. 'I'm your only witness to a murder, and the only one who can connect that with two other shootings. I think shutting me up must be quite high on somebody's wish-list, and I think it's in both our interests to take this seriously.'

She'd succeeded in surprising him. He knew nothing about her, only what she did and where she lived, but still he had clear enough expectations to be taken aback when she confounded them. In his experience prostitutes were earthy, laconic women, often witty in an ironic, self-depracating way. With their clothes on they were good company. But incisive, articulate, focused?—not for the most part. Even under stress, she talked like a woman who'd not only had an education but absorbed some of it. She wasn't intimidated by him, wasn't going to be grateful for whatever crumbs of aid he might condescend to throw her. She'd brought him here, and she was still calling the shots.

He stopped in his tracks and looked at her, and that's when he got his second shock. He recognized her. He'd been sitting a few metres away from her for the last half hour. She was the woman who, with her sprigged cotton dress, white loafers and mousy-fair hair pulled back in a pony-tail, he'd taken for a librarian.

Then he remembered her house—not the room where she worked but the rest of it. Simple and sunny and optimistic: a house where a librarian would feel at home. He was beginning to understand that prostitution was something she did: it was neither who she was nor where she lived.

She slipped a defiant arm through Donovan's. 'I suppose if we're going to walk together we'd better try to look normal.' She thought about that, suspected it was asking too much. 'Who are you, anyway?'

Donovan remembered what Liz had said. He still hadn't realized it was a joke. 'Darth Vader?' he said doubtfully.

Maddie Cotterick began to laugh. It had been a little while since she felt even like smiling, but trying to pass unnoticed in the company of a six-foot Irish detective calling himself Darth Vader did the trick. As a couple they were about as normal as Laurel and Hardy, as Fred Flintstone and Wilma, as Michael Jackson and Bubbles. It was too late to worry about it. She'd watched for an hour and seen no one following him. Besides, she needed a laugh. It released some of the tension that had been building inside her for the last three days. 'No, really.'

'Detective Sergeant Donovan, Castlemere CID. My car's up here. And I am taking it seriously.'

She wasn't convinced. But she'd got what she asked for, an escort back to Castlemere, and she'd had practice at being grateful for small mercies. 'I'm Maddie Cotterick. I imagine you guessed that. Don't you want me to prove what I say?'

Donovan shrugged. 'Not my problem. All I have to do is get you back to Queen's Street. My boss'll figure out if you know anything useful.'

'Was that her I talked to?'

'DI Graham; yes.'

'Have you talked to anyone else?'

Donovan was getting a little irritated by this. He'd had a late night followed by an early start and a long drive, and he didn't need a hooker with a keen sense of her own worth telling him how to do his job. 'No, I haven't. I haven't talked to anyone, I haven't been followed, and in the unlikely event that someone is looking for you he's looking sixty miles away. No way could he have traced you here. Unless you were staying with your mother.'

She shook her head, the pony-tail tossing scornfully. 'An old school friend, from before I moved to Castlemere. No one could have known about her.'

'There you are then. No one knows where to find you.'

'You did. So did your boss.'

In the same way they called Shapiro the Chief, Donovan called Liz the Boss. It was odd to hear someone else call her by the same name. He snorted, half a laugh, half a bark. 'If you think we're in league with a hired killer, maybe you'd best talk to the police here. Or could he have got at them too?'

She knew she sounded neurotic. She believed she had every reason to be cautious. If Detective Sergeant Donovan wasn't exactly Kevin Costner, he was still the best on offer. 'That's all right. I'll trust you.'

'Gee, thanks,' growled Donovan.

LIZ INTENDED TO MAKE an early start too, to have the office ready for Superintendent Hilton. There was important work to do; the sooner they were on the same wavelength the better. She didn't want to spend the first day on the defensive, explaining that in an understaffed department in a crime wave they could go looking for a killer or get on top of the paperwork but not both. If she and Hilton were talking the same language before Donovan got back, he might be willing to believe her when she said that actually he was a seriously good detective.

Her best intentions flew out the window, however, when she phoned Castle General before breakfast and the sister on ICU said Mr Shapiro was awake, making a certain amount of sense and anxious to see her. She made a bacon sandwich while Brian was still laying the table and ate it on the way out to her car.

Taking the lift up to the Intensive Care Unit she tried to imagine what she'd fine. Frank Shapiro much as always, just a little pale from the involuntary blood donation? A shrunken, cadaverous figure held motionless by ironwork? Donovan had warned her there was some paralysis. Would she find him in traction, in a wheelchair, or just propped up on an extra pillow with a bedpan within easy reach?

He looked worse than she hoped, better than she feared. They had him wedged on his side and he looked uncomfortable and disorientated. If Donovan had woken up in ICU he'd have recognized his surroundings as soon as the mists cleared, but Shapiro was unaccustomed to waking in any bed other than his own. When he saw Liz crossing the ward relief softened the corrugations of his brow. 'Over here,' he croaked.

He looked strained and grey, lumpen under the bedclothes, his diamond gaze muddied by confusion and fear, but already he didn't look like a man in danger of dying. That crisis had passed: the next occupied him now. His eyes clung on to her like a child in a room full of strangers attaching itself to its mother's leg.

Liz pulled out a chair and sat down quickly, manoeuvring herself into his limited field of vision. 'Frank. I'm so glad to see you. If it isn't a silly question, how are you feeling?'

It was a silly question, silly enough to get a little enervated chuckle out of him, but it was still the only one that concerned her. 'Pretty rough,' he admitted.

'Do you know what happened?'

He had a memory of having been told, but somehow it hadn't quite sunk in. 'Somebody said I was shot.'

'At Philip Kendall's house. He called in a muck sweat to say somebody was taking pot-shots at his back door, and you went round with Donovan. Apparently he was still there, just further away than anyone had thought to look. As you went to push Kendall inside he fired again.'

It was starting to make sense. He remembered going to Cambridge Road and he didn't remember leaving: presumably this was why. 'It's my back, isn't it? That's why I can't move.'

Her heart twisted. 'Well, that and the sandbags,' she said. 'And there's probably still a load of anaesthetic swilling round in you from the operation.'

'They got the bullet out?'

'Oh yes. According to the surgeon, the damage could have been a lot worse. There's some swelling, but when that starts going down...' She ground to a halt. She couldn't promise him things not in her gift. He wouldn't want her to; he wasn't a child. Even in this state he needed facts more than he needed reassurance. 'Things'll be clearer,' she finished lamely.

She shook her head quickly and clasped his hand, gripping it tightly. 'Frank, I'm not keeping anything from you. Donovan talked to the surgeon as soon as he'd finished, and he said he'd seen nothing to prevent a full recovery. Swelling at the site blocks the normal passage of nerve impulses, but as that reduces you should start getting some feeling back. But it could take a while. You just have to be patient and wait for the healing process to kick in.'

It wasn't the most cheering answer he could have had, but it could have been worse and at least he trusted her to be honest with him. 'All right,' he said, a shade unsteadily, 'I can do that.' He made a deliberate effort to think beyond his own condition. 'Is Kendall all right?'

Liz nodded. 'I've moved the family to a safe house while we try to figure it out. It's beginning to look like there's a connection with the girl on the boat after all.'

He hadn't the energy to elevate both eyebrows, settled for raising one. 'What sort of a connection?'

She told him about Maddie Cotterick. She hadn't come to discuss the case with him, only to see him and reassure him and make sure he wasn't wasting precious strength trying to work out what had happened.

'So Donovan's bringing her in this morning?'

Liz nodded. 'I was glad of the excuse to get him out of the office for a few hours. Superintendent Hilton is taking over.' She said it as evenly as she could, but he'd known her too long: the very absence of inflection told him that she didn't want to cede control to an outsider, and particularly she didn't want to cede it to Superintendent Hilton.

She was anxious not to tire him. He seemed happier for talking to her, but the fact remained he was still wedged immobile in a hospital bed and she had no idea when, or even if, he'd leave it. 'I expect the doctor'll be making his rounds soon. He may be able to tell you something more by now.'

'About the outlook?' Prognosis, he corrected himself; outlook's weather. 'Until you came I wasn't even sure what day it was. The nurses pretend they don't know anything, and the doctors pretend to be busy elsewhere. If somebody doesn't talk to me soon I shall get out of this bed and see if I hit the floor. That'll be a clue.'

'Frank, you mustn't.' But it was a good sign that he was feeling enough like himself to be irritable. 'Listen, I have to get to work now. But I'll come back later, and if you still don't know the score I'll caution your doctor and take him in for questioning. Oh.' She was already on her way when she thought of something else and turned back. 'Angela's here. She stayed at your house last night.'

Shapiro's eyebrow shot up again. 'I didn't know she had a key.'

'Donovan let her in. You had your keys on you when you were shot.' She thought about telling him that Donovan had borrowed his car, decided not to. He'd need to be stronger to cope with that bit of information. 'Is there anything you need?'

He couldn't be bothered thinking. Talking, even to her, had drained him. 'Just the roller skates and a football,' he said sourly.

'Something to read?'

The Walker's Guide to the Peak District?'

Liz gave up. 'If you think of anything, have someone call me. I'll see you later.'

Shapiro just grunted. He knew he wasn't behaving with much fortitude. He was too low to care.

GOING TO THE HOSPITAL had made her late. A message was waiting on her desk to see Superintendent Hilton as soon as she got in.

He'd taken over Shapiro's office. It was the obvious thing to do, the incumbent wasn't going to need it back for a while and Queen's Street wasn't so capacious that spare offices were available on every floor. Still it stung Liz to have to tap on this door and wait for a reply, and then introduce herself to the man inside.

'Detective Inspector Graham, sir. I'm sorry I wasn't here when you arrived. I've been to the hospital.'

Most men get broader, bulkier as they get older. But Hilton was smaller, more compact than she remembered, like a spring packed into an ever tighter space. He still had the moustache—out of sheer stubbornness, she supposed, he must know by now who it reminded people of—and the carborundum eyes. The manner had, if anything, grown more abrasive. Not one of life's charmers, she reflected, so probably he was very good at the job. He hadn't cosied his way up to Superintendent.

'Not feeling well, Inspector?' he said. Almost but not quite snidely.

'To see Superintendent Shapiro, sir,' she said woodenly. But he already knew that: he was baiting her. She wouldn't give him the satisfaction of rising. For that he'd have to try Donovan.

'How is he?'

'Keen to get back in harness, sir.' It wasn't exactly a lie but it certainly inferred something that wasn't the truth. But the less permanent Superintendent Hilton felt in this chair, the better.

'Really?' Hilton sounded surprised. 'At his age?'

They were fencing, testing one another's strengths and weaknesses, keeping just the safe side of objectionable. Liz set her jaw. If there was one thing Castlemere didn't need right now it was a Senior Investigating Officer who felt he had to mark his territory with little wounds.

'I've put Detective Inspector Colwyn in the room at the end of the corridor,' he said. 'I imagine that's all right.' Not hope but imagine: he wasn't seeking approval, just informing her. 'You'll be working closely together.'

The name rang a bell: when she remembered why her heart lifted. Divisional HQ's financial expert. It made her wonder if Hilton might make up in acuity what he lacked in personal charm. 'In that case perhaps he'd like to share my office, next door.' It wasn't really big enough for two, but it was probably better than evicting Donovan to haunt the building like the Ghost of Christmas Past.

But Hilton thought it was a kind gesture and softened slightly. 'Perhaps. Have a word with him. In fact, call him in here while we go over what we've got so far.' He'd been in Queen's Street half an hour and already it was 'what we've got'.

She realized she was being unfair. It was a difficult task,

to take over in the middle of an investigation. It caused resentment, it caused confusion, it meant you never got a chance to learn the significant minutiae of either a town or a police station; but someone had to do it because police officers were as mortal as anyone else and you couldn't put a murder investigation on hold while you invited applications for the post of SIO. Visiting firemen were a necessary evil and deserved a great deal more sympathy than they ever received.

But it was hard to sympathize with someone whose motto appeared to be Divide And Conquer. It was easier to sympathize with the DI who had the task of travelling with him, trying to make the round hole squarer, attracting the same negative feelings without the protection of seniority. She called his name, turned with a smile as DI Colwyn joined them.

Sheer surprise froze it on her face. Detective Inspector James Colwyn, Divisional HQ's idea of a top-flight financial expert, couldn't have been a day over twenty-six. That was in a suit. If he changed into jeans, people would assume he was waiting for an appropriate adult to arrive before he could be interviewed.

Liz blinked quickly and hoped he hadn't noticed. It wasn't his fault he was so young. It almost certainly meant he was gifted at his work and Queen's Street was lucky to get him. She tried to shrug off the feeling that if they were here late tonight she'd start worrying about his bedtime.

She summarized what had happened so far. They'd had the bones from HQ but that was like playing Chinese Whispers: the actual facts always came as a surprise when you'd only had them filtered by Division. Liz concentrated on what had happened and what they knew; she could add in the detail and the suppositions later. She finished with Donovan heading for King's Lynn to collect what might turn out to be a valuable witness and might turn out to be an hysterical self-publicist.

'Donovan,' said Superintendent Hilton thoughtfully. 'Irish?'

'I believe so,' said Liz; which was an idiotic response but the only one which permitted the requisite degree of cool.

'I think I came across him at the Met.' He said to Colwyn, 'The surliest detective constable I ever met.'

'Really?' said Liz. 'Superintendent Shapiro's managed to get some excellent work out of him.'

This was a master stroke: Hilton couldn't pursue his attack now without including Shapiro in it, so he had to leave unchallenged the suggestion that Shapiro had succeeded at something in which he himself had failed. He changed the subject; but Liz saw in his eye that he had recognized the trap she'd laid for him, marked it and wouldn't forget it.

'Meanwhile the Kendall family is at a safe house in Northampton. The address?'

She'd been half-expecting this. She'd hoped he wouldn't ask, or at least not in front of anyone else. She took a deep breath. 'In the circumstances, I'm trying to keep that information to as small a circle as possible. The Kendalls don't know the address. I know, so do the two officers at the house, and that's all. I spoke to Superintendent Giles, and he agreed that he had no overriding need to know, and the fewer people who had the information, the less chance of it accidentally getting out.'

Superintendent Hilton smiled at her, without warmth. 'I think Detective Inspector Colwyn and I can keep a secret.'

'I'm sure you can, sir. I still think it would be safer to leave it with me until you have a need to know. Two people can keep a secret, because if it gets out they both know who was responsible. Any more and only one knows for sure. Right now, I'm the only person in this building who can betray the Kendalls.'

Hilton's smile was a real crocodile job. 'Which is too much of a burden for anyone, so I'm going to take it off your shoulders. The address, Inspector Graham.'

She gave it one last try. In the final analysis, if he wanted the address she couldn't withhold it. But she was right to try, and he was wrong to press. 'Sir, if you insist on having the information I'll give it to you. You can also get it from Divisional records. But it's my urgent recommendation that we leave things as they are. Lives depend on our discretion, and I see no overwhelming benefit to justify the risk of spreading the information further.'

His gaze held her, speculative. 'I presume you are no less mortal than Mr Shapiro, Inspector. Suppose something unfortunate befalls you too?'

'Then I imagine you would inform Division, and get the address of the safe house at the same time. If you're sure I'm wrong about this, sir, make it an order and I'll comply. But those people have already been shot at twice, by a professional killer who's very good and very patient and will exploit the first mistake we make. I'm sure I seem absurdly overcautious. But I don't mind making a fool of myself if there's the chance it may make a difference.

'With a top professional after him, I'm not sure how long we can keep Philip Kendall safe. But if despite all our efforts he ends up dead I don't want to think there was anything more I could have done to prevent it. If that means making a fool of myself, so be it. I don't want to make your job harder than it is already, so if you require that address I'll give it to you. But if it was your life on the line, I think you'd be hoping I wouldn't have to.'

He went on looking at her with the same speculative, ground-glass gaze until it took a real effort of will for her not to start shuffling. Finally he astounded her by nodding crisply and saying, 'All right, I'll give it some more thought. You move DI Colwyn in with you and show him where everything is. And, Inspector Graham?'

She paused in the door, expecting a late-firing rocket.

'If it *was* my life on the line, I'd be content to have it in your hands.'

Colwyn followed her dutifully and shifted his scant belongings from Donovan's office into hers. 'I'll try not to get in your way.' He had a light, ambivalent voice that sounded even younger than he looked.

Liz shook her head. 'I'm glad to have you here. I was trying to contact you yesterday. I need someone who can put some background to a list of rich foreigners. Round here their idea of a rich foreigner is a man from Peterborough with monogrammed socks.'

Colwyn laughed, apparently with relief. 'Let me have the list, I'll see what I can come up with. It's nice to have something useful to do. Mostly when we arrive somewhere I have to fight for the privilege.'

'I can't afford to stand on my dignity,' said Liz. 'Frank Shapiro leaves a big hole, I can't fill it on my own.'

'Will he be all right?'

She shrugged. 'He'll live. For all right we'll have to wait and see.'

DI Colwyn closed her door behind him. 'I'm sorry you and Hilton got off on the wrong foot. He's not an easy man to work for, but he is a good detective. Sometimes, people who get past the rather gritty exterior find themselves quite liking him.'

Liz stopped her eyebrows from soaring incredulously. 'You've worked with him before, then?'

'I've worked with him for the last eighteen months.'

'And this is what you do? Go round plugging holes in other people's dykes?'

'Pretty much. We're not very subtle, I'm afraid, but we don't have time to grow on people gradually. We're sent in because things have gone wrong and somebody needs to take control quickly. The Top People's Cop reckons you can make friends or get the job done but not both.'

Liz kept her face straight. 'The what?'

Colwyn grinned. 'Hilton—the Top People's Hotel? It's just a joke.'

'Does he know you make jokes about him?'

He shrugged. 'It wasn't me who came up with that one. I'm not sure, but I've always rather suspected it was him.'

FIVE

WHEN MADDIE COTTERICK saw the maroon Jaguar, refined and expensive and deeply conservative, she let out a hoot of laughter. 'I had you down for a GTi man. Something you could corner on two wheels.'

Donovan gave his saturnine smile. 'I always corner on two wheels. I'm a Kawasaki man: this is my Superintendent's.'

She was impressed. 'He must have a lot of faith in you.'

Honesty was always like a fox under Donovan's tunic. 'Actually,' he admitted, 'he had a lot of anaesthetic in him.'

He'd come in by the Cambridge road so he left by the Peterborough road. Not because he thought anyone would be waiting, just because if anyone was it would make his life that little bit harder. He didn't think anyone could have followed him. He wasn't convinced anyone would want to. But he'd been sent to collect a witness who was afraid to return to Castlemere alone, and it wasn't his job to decide if her fears were justified. Maybe they weren't, but the only way he'd know for sure was if he didn't take the proper precautions and it turned out they were.

There are police officers who specialize in close protection work, who develop keen instincts for who is in danger and where it will come from. Donovan wasn't one of them. He'd done the defensive driving course, and various counter-terrorism sessions—at which he always ended up playing the mad bomber—but all he knew of the work of a bodyguard was what any policeman needed to: keep moving, vary the route, avoid crowds, avoid wide open spaces. He would return by a different route because it was good practice to do so.

Maddie settled herself in the front passenger seat with an audible purr, cat-like in her pleasure. 'He's a man of taste, your Superintendent.'

For a moment Donovan felt indulgent, thinking such luxury was probably a rare treat for a girl like this. Then it struck him, deflatingly, that a girl like this would have sat in an awful lot more posh cars than he had, if only for ten minutes at a time. He said, 'Turn on the radio if you want. If you know how it works.' She did; and she did.

But not for long. She surfed through the stations but could find nothing to interest her; unless that was a guise and what she really wanted was to talk. As they left Lynn behind she said, 'Aren't you going to question me? You've come a long way, don't you want an explanation?'

Donovan shrugged. 'I'm just the babysitter. My Inspector will do the interview when we get back to Castlemere.'

She bridled at his lack of interest. At first, after she fled the hotel, she'd thought the police would be hunting for her and it was to escape them that she flung some things together and left town on Sunday night. News of the shooting at Kendall's house on Tuesday gave matters a whole new perspective, and by the time she'd worked out what it meant she knew that her best hope of safety lay in offering herself as a witness for the prosecution. She'd expected to have trouble persuading Queen's Street that she knew enough to need protection but thought that when they did turn up there'd be a barrage of questions to answer. The dark man's indifference stung her.

'You think I'm wasting your time. You think there's nothing I can tell you about Linda's death that you couldn't get from other, more reliable sources. You think I'm like those sad people who confess to crimes they didn't commit because it gets them a bit of attention!'

'I think,' said Donovan heavily, 'that my Superintendent's in hospital, there's a replacement due this morning and my Inspector wanted me out of the way for a few hours while she gets him broken in. I think if you hadn't called she'd have found some other fool's errand to send me on.'

Maddie nodded, a terse, jerky little movement. Watching the road, Donovan couldn't see the bitter disappointment on her face, but he heard it in her voice. 'At least we know where we stand. You think I'm a liar, I think you're a fool. The difference is, if you're right I still won't get you killed.'

That caught his attention. His eyes flicked sideways at her, surprised. If it was an act it was a good one. 'I didn't say I don't believe you. I don't know anything about you—well, nearly nothing. I don't know what you have to say. I'm not going to interview you in the car because that's not how it's done. For all I know you could be a suspect by now: I could banjax the entire investigation by chatting away to you just to pass the time. You're going to have to be patient, Maddie. DI Graham will hang on every word you have to say. Me, I'm just the chauffeur.'

She wasn't mollified, but she was damned if she was going to beg him to interrogate her. It wasn't even that she was desperate to tell the story. She just didn't appreciate being treated like a package. She didn't let clients treat her like an inanimate object, didn't see why she should put up with it from an officer of the law. She paid her taxes. Well, some of them.

The real reason she was angry with him was, of course, that she was afraid. Fear is disabling; anger empowers. It made her feel less helpless to be angry with someone and Donovan was handy.

A mile further on she said, 'Was it you went to my house?'

He saw no reason to lie but was obscurely uncomfortable about admitting it. 'Some of the girls thought you might be in trouble. After what happened to—Linda?'

'Linda Collins,' she nodded, 'we shared a flat when I lived in Cambridge.'

'She was'—he hesitated how to put this—'in the same line of business?'

Maddie nodded. 'It made sense to live together. It was a bit of mutual support and protection, and it meant we weren't annoying two other flatmates. I came to Castlemere when my grandmother died and left me her house.'

Donovan gave a grim chuckle. 'Must have gone down a bundle with the neighbours: swapping a little old lady for...' He ground to an embarrassed halt.

Maddie's laugh was brittle. 'I'm a prostitute, Sergeant. Don't let the word bother you, it doesn't bother me. It's an accurate description of what I do. Or a tom, or a hooker. Call-girl's rather nineteen-sixties, and I have to say I find whore a bit vulgar. Prostitute will do nicely.'

After a moment he said, 'You're not what I was expecting.'

She looked at the sprigged cotton dress and shrugged. 'This isn't my working gear. I *could* be what you were expecting. I can be just about anything.'

'Why do you do it?'

'Why are you a policeman?' she retorted instantly.

Donovan frowned, unsure if she meant it as an insult. 'I suppose, because it interests me and I'm some good at it.'

'That's why I'm a prostitute.'

'But—' It was: it was an insult. But it was a long drive back, he didn't want to spend it arguing with her. He fell silent.

She finished the thought for him. 'But...I let men I don't know inside me? That's not what sets me apart from other girls, Sergeant Donovan, it's the fact that I do it for money. How often have you taken a girl back to your place the night you met? Did you think it was love every time? Me and my clients don't even pretend. They don't take me to expensive restaurants, they give me the cash instead. I happen to think it's more honest that way.'

In fact she was talking to the wrong man. Donovan wasn't celibate either by nature or design, but the combination of a demanding job and a personality that did not encourage casual friendships meant that he had about as many one-night stands as the Singing Nun. But he took her point. 'It's still a hell of a risky job.'

'More than yours? Yes, I've been knocked about. I bet you have too. Since I learned the ropes there are certain individuals, and certain types of individual, I don't do business with any more. I bet that's a luxury *you* don't enjoy. Even when you're a superintendent with a flash car of your own you'll still be vulnerable to a bullet in the back because you haven't the right to say there are some jobs and some people it's just too dangerous to deal with.'

Again she'd misjudged him. Donovan would never be a superintendent. Barring a major change of policy at the top, Donovan would never be an inspector. Not because he wasn't up to it and not because he didn't deserve it, but because he wasn't The Right Type. Liz Graham was The Right Type. Oddly enough, Frank Shapiro wasn't, but at least he'd never been as aggressively The Wrong Type as Donovan. Superintendent Hilton wasn't the only member of the police hierarchy who remembered him as the surliest detective constable in the history of the force, and had never updated that image in light of subsequent successes.

He gave a dour sniff. 'That's how you see me? As a different kind of prostitute?'

Maddie nodded negligently. 'Pretty much. Look, if you don't like the word, call us hirelings. You're a body for hire, same as I am. Look what you're doing here. You're putting yourself at risk because I'm in danger. You're not doing it for love, or because you think I'm such a special human being I must be preserved at all cost. But if somebody comes after me with a knife, or a gun, you won't even ask yourself if I'm worth it. You'll do what your Superintendent did—protect me, even if it means getting hurt yourself. Because it's your job. Because you're paid to.'

His mouth opened and shut a couple of times before he was forced to concede that, in a particular narrow sense at least, she was right. He wouldn't go on doing this if they stopped paying him. It *was* a job: he took a pride in doing it well, but not always in *what* he had to do. That was the nature of the thing: you took the rough with the smooth, the boring with the hair-raising, the plainly right and important along with those things you only did because someone higher up had decided you should. He'd done a lot of things he'd taken no particular pleasure in, and a few he was ashamed of. He'd done them because it was his job. He consoled himself with the thought that handling whatever came along was the mark of a professional. He hadn't thought till now that such was also the prostitute's creed.

'Hireling,' he said finally. 'I've been called worse.'

EVEN AMONG THE NEW generation of computer-literate policemen Detective Inspector Colwyn was a class act. He was as familiar with the workings of the Police National Computer as Liz was with the contents of her own desk. He took Philip Kendall's list of delegates and started passing the names through successive databases, collecting information as he went.

By mid-morning he had reduced forty-odd men to a shortlist of five. Before he went any further he made a hard copy on the printer. He might be able to explain to DI Graham what the icons on the screen meant, but Superintendent Hilton would be a pieces-of-paper man to the end of his career.

'If we accept Maddie Cotterick's word that she can link the girl's death to the attempts on Kendall's life,' said Colwyn, 'then we can make certain inferences about the person responsible. He's a man who can call up first-class help at short notice, which means he has money or connections or both. He's from out of town, or he'd have taken more trouble disposing of the girl's body.'

'Which all points to one of the overseas delegates at the Bespoke Engineering conference,' said Hilton. 'He killed a prostitute then hired someone to tidy up the mess. This Maddie girl thinks he wants her dead because of what she knows. If he also wants Kendall dead, that suggests he knows something too.'

Liz refrained from saying that she'd reached that conclusion before he even arrived in Castlemere.

'With this in mind,' Colwyn went on hurriedly, 'I correlated information on everyone on the list, and discarded off the bottom those without that kind of influence or any kind of a track record. There's a mid-range of men who could cover up a murder in a foreign country but aren't likely to have committed one in the first place. And what rose to the top are five men who look like reasonable suspects.

'They have certain features in common. They're all foreign nationals. One of them was representing his government, the others are executive directors of private companies. All are wealthy men by any standards, and could additionally call on the resources of their state or company. Any of these five could afford the services of a top-flight assassin.'

He'd printed three copies of his research, one for each of them. He studied his own primarily, Liz thought, to give her and Hilton time to catch up.

Kim Il Muk managed a petroleum refinery in Pusan, South Korea. Four years earlier the underhousekeeper of a Paris hotel had accused him of attempted rape. The Paris police had it down as a misunderstanding due to lack of a common language. Mr Kim apologized through an interpreter and was released with a caution. He was a man of about forty-five.

Ian Selkirk's father owned a shrimping fleet, a cannery and most of a village in Yucatán. Selkirk, who was thirty-two, was known to be handy with his fists, and on one occasion with a baling hook. There were also suspicions that the shrimp-boats had been smuggling drugs into the United States, and that the death of a Federal investigator was linked to that. The FBI were still looking for proof.

Nicu Sibiu and his brothers ran the family munitions business in Romania. Twice during the civil unrest they used the finished product to defend the factory against angry mobs and Nicu, then in his late teens, was known to have shot a protestor dead. In view of the general chaos of the times, no action was taken to establish the legitimacy of this act.

Eduardo da Costa was in the arms procurement office of the Brazilian defence ministry. He was forty-three, a former soldier who reached the rank of colonel before taking his current position two years ago. His military career had been dogged by allegations of brutality.

Ibn al Siddiq was a minor member of the extensive Saudi royal family; he owned oil wells and racehorses. He'd had a distinguished career in the Saudi air force. The black mark against his name concerned the ill-treatment by one of the Siddiq wives of an African maid who travelled to London with the family. To avoid a diplomatic incident Siddiq paid the girl off and sent his wife home. Prince Ibn was in his early thirties and lived with his wives and children in a small palace outside Dhahran.

'As well as being able to deal with the consequences,' Colwyn continued, 'these five have some history of violence; except for the Saudi, who was covering up for his wife. I wasn't sure whether to include him or not.'

Hilton was running a jaundiced eye down his sheet. 'Are these names in any particular order?'

'Ye-es,' said Colwyn slowly. 'Likeliest first; but don't put too much weight on that. Is a man who may have tried to rape a girl, but just might have misunderstood the signals he was getting, more or less likely to have murdered a prostitute than someone with a reputation as a thug in his country's military? I don't know. Anyway, favourites don't win every race. These five men are more fanciable than the other forty-three at the conference, but it's still possible the killer is a rank outsider.'

'We have to start somewhere,' said Liz supportively. 'It

looks to me our best bet is to find these five and try to rule out four of them.'

Colwyn gave an eloquent shrug. 'Ideally, yes; in practice, I doubt if we can. Only two are still in the hotel; the others have already left the country and gone back to places where we can't count on the cooperation of the local police. The man who killed that girl believes he'll be safe once he's home: he was probably airborne before the body was even found.'

'You're saying the job's impossible,' Liz said baldly. She'd toyed with the notion herself, but she still didn't like the taste of it in her mouth.

'Not impossible, no. We may be able to identify the killer. But unless he returns to this country at some juncture, that's probably all we can do.'

'But if we can't arrest the principal, how do we stop the mechanic who's cleaning up after him?'

DI Colwyn had a round, open face on which deception sat uneasily. 'I'm not sure we can. I think the mechanic'll do what he's been paid to do.'

'Kill Philip Kendall. And possibly Maddie Cotterick.'

Hilton took a deep breath. 'All right, so it's going to be uphill work. But we can't just decide it's too difficult and not bother. Maybe the man who hired him can recall the assassin if it's in his interests to do so. We have to give him an incentive. Nobody's fireproof: the back-home interests who were happy to protect him while his identity was a mystery might be reluctant to go on helping someone who's been publicly named as a murder suspect.'

Liz elevated an eyebrow. 'Can we do that? With a foreign national who may be here representing his government? Won't the Foreign Office have something to say about it?'

'The Foreign Office,' said Hilton heavily, 'can only comment on what they hear about. You gave me a lesson on keeping secrets earlier today, Inspector Graham. Now let's see if the three of us can keep this one.'

For perhaps the first time, Liz saw clearly what Edwin

Hilton brought to the job that was worth a detective super-intendent's salary. It wasn't charm or an affable manner, it wasn't the sort of intuition that had got her out of some tight corners or the deep perceptive understanding of the human condition that was the secret of Frank Shapiro's success. It was moral courage. Her respect for him rocketed. He just might cost the three of them their careers, but it was the right thing to do and she saluted him for it.

'We still have to pin the tail on the donkey first,' said Hilton. 'One of these five men is probably a murderer. Finding out which one is still the name of the game.

'Inspector Graham, get on to the hotel, have those five rooms emptied and sealed. Get SOCO back there. He's looking for physical traces—fingerprints, a hair in the plug-hole, a tissue in the bin—that we can match to samples taken from Mrs Atwood's room. That'll tell us who we're dealing with even if we can't get at him. Meantime I'll call in some favours at Scotland Yard. They may be able to bring some pressure to bear. Have you had any experience of them, Mrs Graham?—they're a devious bunch of so-and-sos. They've a specialist in every imaginable discipline. I dare say they've got a whole desk devoted to Making Foreign Dignitaries Amenable.'

He turned again to DI Colwyn. 'James, you stay on the computer. Find out where those five men are now—what flights they took, if they went straight home. If we get a name, and it turns out he felt safe enough just getting out of Britain, instead of going straight home he thought he'd do a bit of shopping in Paris or Berlin first, he may not be beyond our grasp yet.'

SIX

IT WAS AFTER TEN and the roads were full of lorries: long distance, short haul, artics and rigids. For once Donovan was glad to see every one of them. Partly this was because, with a wheel at each corner himself, their immodest slipstream caused him no problems today; but mainly it was because, if Maddie Cotterick was right and still despite all their precautions someone had followed them, he'd have equipped himself with something more manoeuvrable than a 36-ton bulk carrier.

He felt safe ignoring anything that needed two minutes' notice to turn, confined himself to registering the cars around him. There weren't that many of them: most of the traffic was travelling the other way, heading for the coast. There was a white saloon ahead, a navy-blue hatchback a little way behind, a charcoal-grey Porsche bombing up the outside lane. He kept an eye on the Porsche until it passed, but it showed no interest in him, continued on its urgent, throaty, illegal way until it disappeared into the distance.

He found himself closing on the white saloon. He waited his moment, then accelerated past. He thought that, if he was allowed to, he could quite get used to driving a Jaguar. He watched the saloon in his mirror but it didn't speed up to keep pace with him. Soon enough it dropped out of sight.

Beside him Maddie had slumped in an inelegant collapse, arms folded tightly across her chest as if she was cold. A glance at her face showed her thoughts turned inwards, gnawing at her. While there had been things to do—setting up the meeting, vetting him, marking his card—she had been able to avoid dwelling too long on why she thought it was all necessary. Now they were on their way back she had nothing to do but think. From the tense little frown between her brows and the way she was chewing on the inside of her lip, her thoughts gave her no comfort.

Donovan was looking for something to say to cheer her up—and since he had never made cheering people his mission in life he had no ready stock of suitable remarks—when she broke the silence herself. He thought she was saying aloud what she'd been worrying about for some time.

'What I said before, about you risking your neck to protect me. Was I kidding myself?'

Taken aback, Donovan barked a little laugh. Then he shook his head. 'No. That's the job, it's what we do. But only when it comes to that, and thank Christ it doesn't very often. Mostly what policing is about is just being there. For every fight we have to break up, we prevent an awful lot just by being around. But if you're worried I'll run out on you if the going gets rough, forget it. I won't let anything happen to you.'

'That's easy to say when you're not facing a man with a gun!'

'I've faced men with guns before,' said Donovan, with a studied nonchalance that was more transparent than he probably supposed.

'Really? Were you scared?'

He thought a second, opted for the truth. 'Shitless. But I've never left anyone in the lurch yet, and I won't start with you.'

'Even if it means getting hurt?'

'If it comes to a direct choice, then yes. But...' He was about to add that it wouldn't come to that, it almost never did, the point of a police escort was not to stop the first bullet but to ensure that the target stayed away from people with guns. But Maddie forestalled him by bursting into tears.

'I know. I believe you. God damn it, I *know* you would—your Superintendent did it, damn near lost his life doing it, and for that little shit Kendall! That's what makes it so awful. I don't think I can bear it.' Clenched so tight the knuckles had turned white, her fists were hammering on her knees almost hard enough to do some damage.

Donovan had absolutely no idea what she was talking about. There was nowhere safe for him to stop, and anyway it was wiser to keep moving. But he snatched repeated glances at her, bent crying over her punitive fists. The sight disturbed him, more than he would have guessed. Perhaps because she wasn't the sort of girl to cry over nothing. 'Maddie, what is it?'

At first she only shook her head bitterly at him. But when the sobs abated and her hands lay exhausted in her lap she tried to explain. 'Linda was my best friend, had been since we were six years old. We'd lived together, looked out for one another. And I took her there—it wasn't her job, it was mine. But I let her die so I could escape.

'I'm nothing to you, but you'd risk your life for me. I loved Linda, but I let a mad bastard beat up on her, and then take her out and kill her, and all I could think about was getting away myself. Even when I was safe I hadn't the guts to call you people and tell you what had happened. Ironic, isn't it?—I wouldn't be in this mess if I had.'

Donovan could be a savage taskmaster, but his highest expectations were always of himself. It wasn't condescension, he genuinely saw no irony in the fact that she needed more from him than she had been able to offer her friend. It wasn't even that, as a man, he was stronger than her: it was what she said before, the money. For centuries Irish soldiers had toiled, suffered and died in the service of England's army for no better reason than that they had taken the King's Shilling. It was no criticism to say that their loyalty had been bought. They did the job they were paid to do or died in the attempt. In every sense, Cal Donovan was their heir. Another hireling.

Maddie Cotterick was a hireling too, but dying was no part of her contract. He didn't blame her for being so scared at the prospect that the only thing that mattered, the only thought her brain could encompass, was her own safety.

He didn't know what to say to her. He still knew precious little of what had happened; perhaps his sympathy for her pain was misplaced. But the pain was real enough, and you don't need to know what has made a child cry to want to hold it until it stops. He mumbled, 'You don't have to do this. Flay yourself like this. You didn't kill her. Probably you couldn't have saved her.'

'But I'll never know that, will I?' she wailed. 'Because I didn't even try.'

Donovan was fighting two urges, one less familiar than the other. He had no brief to question her, but procedure wouldn't have stopped him hearing her story if he thought she needed to tell it. He was used to ignoring procedure when it suited him.

He was less accustomed to feeling like this: as if he wanted to comfort her. Most of the people he dealt with were upset, but he didn't often feel moved to do anything about it beyond taking their statements and trying to nail the culprit. Conventional wisdom did not see him as a sympathetic man; though people who knew him well enough knew that when his compassion was stirred he felt more deeply and reacted more strongly than many a more obviously sensitive soul.

But there was something about Maddie Cotterick that troubled him, and he wasn't sure what it was or even which girl it was: the independent, unconventional straight-talker who made her living on her back because it pleased her to do so, or the girl in the sprigged dress and white loafers, her strong regular features pleasing rather than pretty, the sort of girl you could have known for years before it finally struck you what good company she was. Or maybe trying to separate them like that was itself an artifice, a way of being comfortable with who she actually was. Because actually she was both.

'Listen,' he said at last, 'if it'll help, tell me what happened. It isn't an interview, I won't ask you any questions, but if you need to get it off your chest we've got an hour's drive ahead of us, it'll feel a long way with you bottled up like a pressure cooker. If you talk about it, maybe you'll start to understand it better. Maybe you'd see there was nothing else you could have—'

His voice, low with an uncertain gentleness, stopped as if guillotined. He was looking in the mirror.

SHAPIRO HAD BEEN SLEEPING. Partly it was the drugs, partly the trauma, but he found he was likely to drift off any time he wasn't actually being prodded or poked or talked to reassuringly. He didn't fight it. It passed the time, and in his current state there was little else he could do to fill it. Except worry, and when the medical staff thought he was worrying they came and talked reassuringly to him some more.

It wasn't that he was ungrateful. But he'd got the message by now: they didn't know any more than he did. Only time would tell to what extent he would recover the use of his legs. That being so, passing time in the easiest way possible seemed sensible.

This time as he woke he was aware of someone beside his bed. He had the feeling whoever it was had been there for some time. He cranked round his gaze until he found the figure sitting in the utilitarian hospital chair, so familiar and so unexpected that for a moment it stole his breath away.

Angela had been watching him for half an hour, waiting for him to stir. She had seen his lax, heavy body, undignified in its awkward position, slowly firm and organize itself as his floating persona returned to animate it. Or at least, most of it. There was still no movement under the sheet that covered his legs; but there was something different from when she was here yesterday. Even the still bits looked as if they belonged to him now. When she first saw him, barely conscious, the bottom half of him had seemed dead; or not even that, more like a rough prosthesis. As if someone had stuffed a pair of pyjama trousers and bundled them under the sheet to approximate an appearance of normality.

'Hello, you,' she said softly.

For a moment he just breathed, taking her in. He hadn't seen her for two years. He had her address in Bedford but he'd never seen her house. She looked a little older. She looked tired. He was so glad to see her the tears sprang to his eyes and he had to sniff them away in an unconvincing simulacrum of a yawn.

'Have you been there long?'

'Not long. I didn't want to wake you—I thought the sleep would do you good.'

'Did I make the news, then?'

'You did, but I already knew. Mr Giles called me. I came straight over, but you were too groggy yesterday to notice. I stayed at your house last night. I hope you don't mind.'

They'd shared everything for over twenty years: how could he mind her being in his house? 'Do you like it?' He'd had no use for a family home after his family scattered, had moved into the stone cottage five years ago.

'It's charming. It's what you need.'

Shapiro snorted. 'It's what I used to need. Now I need a bungalow.'

But she knew him too well to tolerate his self-pity. 'You could always get a stair-lift put in.'

He stared at her, fully intending to feel hurt. But her magical blend of affection and pragmatism was exactly what he needed. He found himself smiling. 'I'm glad you're here. I've missed you.'

Her own smile had a dimple in it. 'I noticed. You never could see the point of vacuuming under things, could you?'

He considered that dirty pool. 'I have a woman—'

One fair, perfectly arched eyebrow climbed.

'I have a cleaner,' he elaborated sternly. 'She'll be offended if she finds you inspecting under the furniture.'

'That's the idea,' said Angela. 'She'll be offended; and then she'll get out the extension hose.'

'Can you stay?' he said. 'For a while.'

'As long as you need me.'

Shapiro tried to make a joke of that too, but before he could get it out his face started to crumple. 'Oh god, Angela. How am I going to *manage?*'

Her long hand grasped his and held it tight. 'The way you've managed all the other difficult things you've had to do,' she said fiercely. 'With courage. With strength. With intelligence and good humour, and the sort of personal reserves that get deeper the more you draw on them. You're a brave man, Frank Shapiro, and you'll get through this. Maybe in a wheelchair. Maybe on a stick. Maybe on your own two feet, with just an interesting limp to remind people what kind of a man you are. That isn't actually the important thing. If there is a permanent disability it may take you months, even longer, to get its measure and come to terms with it, but that still isn't the important part. The thing to remember is that you will.

'Whatever you're stuck with, however unfair, you will come to terms with it. You'll get past it to where the rest of your life is waiting. It may not be quite as you'd imagined it, but then, whose ever is? You're the same man you always were, you'll make a life worth having. Even in a wheelchair. I don't mean to minimize the enormity of that, I can imagine how it must seem to you. Like a mountain in your way. But don't underestimate yourself. You're an impressive bloody man, Frank, I don't think you always realize how much. How much people admire you. Well, now you're going to give them something new to admire. Either how quickly you get back on your feet again, or how well you cope without.'

His thick fingers inside her long ones were trembling. His voice broke up. 'I don't feel impressive,' he whispered. 'I feel frightened.'

'I know,' said Angela, holding him. 'But that's what courage is. It's not about not being afraid. It's about overcoming fear. And you will. I know you, Frank, I know you will.

'But you don't have to do it yet, and you don't have to do it in front of me. I don't need impressing. I know what you're made of.'

Inside the compass of her arms, his body shook with the relief of tears.

'IT'S PROBABLY NOTHING,' said Donovan. 'But there's a dark blue hatchback two cars back that's been there or there-abouts since we got on this road. I've passed stuff and stuff's passed me, but that hatchback is just about the same distance behind us it's been all along. Like I say, it probably doesn't mean a thing. But maybe we ought to make sure.'

There was nowhere to turn off. He indicated and pulled up on to the hard shoulder, taking out his mobile phone as a kind of explanation. The grey van that was immediately behind him sailed past without hesitation, and so did the navy hatchback. With the facility of long practice Donovan noted its number. There was nothing to note about its driver, except that he was alone. The car continued up the road and disappeared in the following traffic.

'False alarm,' said Donovan wryly. 'Sorry.'

'Don't be,' said Maddie Cotterick. 'I don't want reassuring, I want looking after.'

He put the phone away unused, waited for a gap in the traffic and got back on the road. He waited, too, for her to pick up where they'd left off. But the mood seemed to have been broken, and it wasn't for him to try to re-establish it. There was time and road enough ahead: if she wanted to talk she would. If not she could talk to DI Graham at Queen's Street.

He concentrated on his driving. But Fenland roads are flat and straight, the Jaguar might have gone on for miles if he'd fallen asleep at the wheel. It left a lot of mental capacity for other purposes. He found himself thinking about what had happened. More than thinking: reliving it. Standing flat-footed and uncomprehending in Philip Kendall's back garden while Shapiro flung himself in slow motion at the man on the steps. The rifle was far enough away for the sound of the shot to pass unnoticed; but Donovan saw it hit, and the way cloth and flesh dissolved and the blood fountained under the penetrating assault was more shocking, at a more fundamental level, than he could have imagined. It was like having your own mortality thrust in your face. Because your body worked pretty well most of the time, and so did everybody else's, you tended to forget how easily it could be made to come apart. Seeing someone shot at close quarters was the ultimate object lesson.

He found himself thinking about the mechanic. People hired this man to go round killing other people, and he was so serious about the job, so perfectionist, that after he set up his equipment he practised on live targets at the optimum range. Dedication to duty is always impressive; such dedication to such a duty was also deeply chilling. That one act told more about the man they were looking for than could have been crammed into a three-page biography. He was a professional. He was the ultimate professional. If he was sent to kill Kendall, for whatever reason, he wouldn't stop until he succeeded. Which meant, almost certainly, that Maddie Cotterick could have caught a bus back to Castlemere in perfect safety.

The Jaguar was slowing down. Puzzled, Maddie looked at her driver, about to ask why. The expression frozen on his dark face alarmed her. She jogged his elbow. 'Sergeant?'

Donovan blinked, and understanding rushed into his eyes like a cataract. His foot slammed down on the accelerator and the Jaguar took off like a greyhound leaving a trap. He steered one-handed, groping with the other inside his jacket.

When he had the mobile phone he pushed it into Maddie's hands and told her what to dial. His urgency frightened her. 'I don't understand. What's happened? What—?'

But like many people in receipt of a revelation he didn't make a very good job of explaining it. His eyes blazed. 'If the bastard's as good as all that,' he exclaimed, with an impatience that was more for his own stupidity than hers, 'how come he bloody missed?'

SEVEN

IF YOU LOOKED for two people with nothing in common but a job, you could hardly do better than Liz Graham and Cal Donovan. In every sense, they came from different places: different lands, different cultures, different backgrounds; different experiences leading to different ways of seeing the world. The odd thing was that, starting from diametrically different viewpoints, they had a knack of arriving at the same destination at pretty much the same time. They had been doing this since the earliest days of their association, a time when they could agree on almost nothing else. Donovan thought Liz an interloper, Liz thought Donovan a loose cannon, but they still had an uncanny ability to echo one another's thought processes.

So while, objectively, Donovan wasn't making a great deal of sense at his end of the line, at hers Liz was able somehow to reach past the hurried jumble of words and lift the notion he was trying to convey clean out of his mind. Her eyes saucered. 'You mean he *meant* to shoot Frank? Frank was his target all along? *Why?*'

'I don't know,' said Donovan. 'But boss, if a man like that wants him dead he's not safe in the public ward of a general hospital. You'd better get him out of there—or if he can't be moved, at least get him some protection.'

He was right, but that didn't make it any easier. 'Where from? There's nobody left!'

'Send Kendall home and let the chief have his minders. If Kendall wasn't the target he's never been in any danger.'

'Lord Almighty!' She was trying to follow it through, work out what it meant. But there wasn't time. It was more important to get the arrangements made: she could work out

the implications later. 'I can't do that. What if you're
wrong? But I'll sort something—get the chief out of sight
for starters. And we'll rake up someone to stay with him.
What about you? Have you got the girl?'

'Yeah, we're on our way back. We'll be back by noon.'

'Be careful,' said Liz. 'If we've read this wrong and he's
not looking for Kendall, it may be he's looking for Maddie
after all. Have you had any problems?'

'I don't think so. There was somebody keeping pace with
us a few minutes back, but I slowed up and he disappeared.
I haven't seen him since.'

'Did you get a number?'

He passed it on. 'But like I say, I don't think he'd any
interest in us. I'm just being a bit neurotic.'

'Stay neurotic,' said Liz severely. 'We obviously don't
know what the hell's going on, until we do we all need to
be neurotic. Get back here as quickly as you can.'

'Count on it,' said Donovan.

SUPERINTENDENT HILTON heard her out without interrup-
tion. As soon as she finished he called in DI Colwyn. 'Get
down to the hospital right away. Take a firearms officer.
Detective Superintendent Shapiro is to be put in a private
room as soon as it's safe to move him. Wherever he is, that
ward is closed to visitors and other than named staff unless
they've been personally vetted by DI Graham. Clear?'

'Sir.'

When he'd gone Hilton propped his elbows on the desk
and rested his chin on his folded hands. His eyes were troubled. 'What does it mean? If Superintendent Shapiro was
the intended victim?'

'That he knew something?' hazarded Liz. 'That he'd
worked out who killed the girl and had to be silenced.'

Hilton raised a sceptical eyebrow. 'He knew who committed a murder and failed to mention it to you? Oh no,
Inspector; oh dear me no. We don't keep secrets of that
kind. We've all seen too many midweek movies, we know

exactly what happens to detectives who say they've just one
more thing to check, they'll reveal all in the morning... No,
if Mr Shapiro had even suspected something important
enough to kill him for he'd have shared it with you.'

He heard the echo of that and gave a thin smile. 'You
know what I mean. After all, there was plenty of time. If
there was time to bring in a professional hit man, and for
him to carry out his meticulous preparations, whoever em-
ployed him must have known for at least twenty-four hours
that Mr Shapiro would need dealing with. It isn't credible
that he knew something vitally relevant to his case but ne-
glected to mention it for something over a day.'

She wasn't arguing. It wasn't an argument: they were
mulling it over, in the way that she usually did with Shapiro;
and if Hilton's methods and vocabulary were different, abrasive where Shapiro's were pensive, they were not neces-
sarily the worse for it. It was the feedback that was
important, tossing ideas between them until the patterns they
formed became less random and more significant.

Liz said, 'Maddie says they're connected—the girl's
death and Frank getting shot. How?'

'Philip Kendall is the connection.'

'Kendall's house is where the shooting took place. But
perhaps the mechanic merely followed Frank there. He
needed him out in the open, this was his chance. Maybe he
took the pot-shot at Kendall's back door just to bring him
out.'

'So Kendall was never more than a red herring?'

Liz shrugged. 'I don't know. We'll have to ask Maddie
that too.'

'You could have asked when you were talking to her,'
Hilton said pointedly.

Liz gave a rueful shrug. 'I did try. I think she was afraid
that when we knew as much as she did we'd leave her to
cope alone.'

'Is her life really in danger?'

'I don't know that either,' admitted Liz. 'I didn't feel it

was safe to dismiss the idea. And I wanted to hear what she had to say.'

Hilton nodded. 'So it wasn't just a matter of getting Detective Sergeant Donovan out of my way for a few hours.'

Liz cast him a startled look; but immediately she realized it was a shrewd little joke. She was beginning to see how DI Colwyn could enjoy working with the man. She fought to keep her face straight. 'Of course not, sir. He's looking forward to seeing you again.'

'Of course he is,' agreed Detective Superintendent Hilton with a thin smile. 'True as I'm strangling this ferret.'

THERE WERE THIRTY-FIVE miles of good road between King's Lynn and Peterborough; Donovan expected to cover them in fifty minutes. (In a car: on his bike he'd have aimed at half an hour.) Another twenty-five miles, say forty minutes, would see him coming into Castlemere. They'd been on their way for half an hour when he saw something he hadn't expected to see again. The navy-blue hatchback.

Only the fact that he was looking out for trouble made it seem at all sinister. It had passed him before when he pulled on to the hard shoulder. Since then he'd been told to get a move on: probably he'd increased his speed just enough to catch it. These weren't local roads, they were long-distance routes: every second car would be going to Peterborough or beyond. If he slowed down he'd probably meet the white saloon again; if he accelerated enough he might even catch the Porsche. It was the nature of good roads in open country.

And yet...and yet. The woman beside him believed her life was in danger: that someone was hunting her and would try to kill her. Even if it turned out she was wrong, Donovan thought the belief was absolutely genuine. He hadn't worried much till now because he thought the man who shot Shapiro was still in Castlemere, trying to find out where Philip Kendall had got to. But if Kendall was never the target he wouldn't be wasting time looking for him. He might be intending to finish his business with Shapiro; or he might have Maddie in his sights.

He could no longer afford the luxury of strict adherence to protocol. Their lives just might depend on things only Maddie knew.

He kept his eyes on the traffic ahead, watching the hatchback for any change in its speed, but he spoke to Maddie. 'Tell me what happened.'

THE CONFERENCE TRADE was something of a speciality and Maddie had never got involved before. She wasn't planning on working at all that weekend. She had a friend to stay, intended to spend the time with her, catching up on one another's news.

But it's the same in all businesses: it's hard to refuse a favour to a regular customer.

She covered the phone with a hand. 'I'll tell him no. Damn it, I expect more notice than this even when I haven't got other plans. I'll tell him I'm already booked.'

Linda shook her golden head and grinned. She was Maddie's age but she'd cornered a slightly different market. At twenty-six she still looked about twenty. In the right gear she looked an incredibly promiscuous fourteen. 'Say we'll both go. It'll be fun.'

Maddie frowned. They'd been going to go to a film, she'd been looking forward to it. But Jane Austen was more her sort of thing than Linda's, she suspected her friend was glad of an excuse to get out of it. Linda wasn't a natural spectator. She was keener on participation. 'Are you sure?'

'Of course. Bit of fun, bit of grass, bit of cash—my idea of the perfect night.'

It was Maddie's experience that, while a lot of prostitutes talked like this in company, not many really and honestly felt that way. They looked on it more like a job in an abattoir: a messy old business but somebody has to do it. They were often uneducated women with limited options for making serious money. But Linda loved the game. She'd have gone on doing it if she'd won the lottery. She enjoyed the excitement, the risk, the rush it gave her; the sensation of power. Maddie recognized that it was an illusion of power and acted accordingly; but Linda was too swept up in her own myth of woman rampant to see that the weaker can only exploit the stronger as long as the stronger consent. Somehow, in the seven years she'd been doing this, she'd never had to deal with a genuine sadist: a man who obtained sexual release from physically abusing his partner.

In all the commotion of a big conference winding up they had no difficulty passing the desk of The Barbican Hotel unnoticed. The man met them at the lifts. It wasn't Maddie's regular but his friend, the visitor for whom he wanted to lay on a treat. She wasn't worried when the man who'd phoned her didn't join them. He was a civilized punter who always paid up without demur; any friend of his was acceptable to her.

She weighted the client up covertly as the lift rose. He was a few years older than her but still a young man, strongly made, with the elegant, tensile power of a cat. A man of expensive tastes and extravagant good manners. He was a foreigner, but Maddie had no problems with that. The only drawback might be if he tried to pay by American Express.

Thus far Donovan had seen no need to interrupt her. He concentrated on his driving, and on the car up ahead, and let the story she was telling pour into his mind unfiltered by much in the way of analysis. But there was something he wanted to know now. 'Did he give you his name?'

Maddie shook her head. 'He said to call him Sir.'

Donovan had a bizarre picture flit through his head then; but no. Even if he could fake a foreign accent, nobody'd have described Superintendent Hilton as having extravagant good manners. 'Go on.'

It came as no great surprise to Maddie when the man produced some cocaine. Crack, for smoking. He passed it round, along with the means of taking it, and started dragging it in. Linda followed suit enthusiastically, Maddie with circumspection. It was a basic precaution in her business always to be in full command of one's senses. But Linda didn't believe in taking precautions. She thought the free availability of mind-altering substances was a bonus.

'How much detail do you want?' asked Maddie.

Donovan shrugged. 'Whatever it takes. Don't worry, you won't shock me.' But she did, a little.

Perhaps because she seemed younger, perhaps because she was keener, the client concentrated his attention on the bubbly blonde, excited by the combination of a cheeky schoolgirl face, a pneumatic woman's body, and the total lack of inhibition of an enthusiastic whore. The crack drove both of them to mounting excesses: Maddie found herself propped in a corner with a half-smoked spoon, watching with bored tolerance that grew slowly to unease.

She realized sooner than Linda, who'd been freer with the crack, that the girl was beginning to take some punishment. Not just a little rough and tumble, that was par for the course. But this man was starting to use force on her. Cocaine is an anaesthetic: if she hadn't been high she'd have known she was getting hurt. When the drugs slowed her reactions he shoved and shook her into compliance. He slapped her face, and Linda was spaced out enough that when he laughed at her objections she laughed too.

'I knew it was getting out of hand,' said Maddie in a small voice. 'I knew he was getting vicious, and he was going to hurt her. He was pulling her about like a rag doll, and she was so high she'd no idea she was in danger.'

'But you weren't?—high?'

She shook her head. 'A drag or two, to get in the mood. He kept pushing more at me. I pretended to use it to keep him happy.' She forced a smile. 'If there's one thing a prostitute's good at it's faking.'

A knot of lorries slowed the traffic in front. Donovan pulled the Jaguar into the outside lane and powered past. The road ahead was clear.

It might have been, Maddie admitted, that she too had taken more crack than she thought. But her recollection was that the tone of events really did change between one breath and the next. One moment she was sitting in the corner, in a litter of discarded clothes, pretending to smoke and watching two consenting adults play a game of rough love that at least one of them would regret when she came to her senses; and the next the game had changed to a deadly reality. The man was hitting the cheeky schoolgirl face as he might have hit another man: with his fists, with his weight behind them. He split her lip and she mewed a kittenish protest. Maddie thought the blood on his hands excited him. He hit her in the face again, this time under the eye. The skin over her cheekbone parted. The man laughed again. This time he laughed alone.

Maddie Cotterick was haunted by her failure: not just that she couldn't save her friend, but that she made almost no effort to. By the time she realized how critical matters had become she was paralysed with fear. So it was important to her that the man beside her knew she had tried. Only once, and without success, but she had at least tried.

'I got up then. Linda didn't: I think it was more the crack than what he'd done to her. If she'd been able to stand up for herself, maybe… But she couldn't, and he knew he could knock either of us alone into the middle of next week. I said I was leaving, I was going to get help. But he'd locked the door. I yelled but no one heard—everyone was at the party downstairs, and they were making too much noise to hear anything.

'I thought for a second I'd brought him to his senses. He left Linda and stood up. He gave a little smile—almost like an apology. He said, "I get carried away sometimes." He came over to the door. I thought he had the key: I stood back for him to unlock it.'

She remembered then, with the prospect of escape so close, that she'd hardly a stitch on. She looked round to see where her clothes had got to.

He hit her so hard, with the back of his fist across her ear, that she literally flew, crashing into the wall, her limbs sprawling among the legs of the furniture, her wits fluttering around the cornice like a flock of startled birds. The violence of it, abrupt and extreme, left her stunned. Her eyes remained open, she saw everything that happened thereafter, but dizziness, shock and terror prevented her from making any further intervention.

He returned his attentions to Linda. Kneeling on the bed now, she'd found a tissue and was dabbing ineffectually at her face. 'You shit,' she mumbled plaintively through broken lips. 'You shit.'

He hit her. He hit her and hit her and hit her. In the face. In the belly. About the ribs. She fell off the bed, curled foetally around the hurt, and he picked her up and hit her some more. Before he finished her face was raw meat. Blood from her nose and mouth sprayed the walls as he pounded her head from side to side.

Surreally, it all happened in near silence. After it started the girl never had enough air in her lungs to fuel a cry. Even when she fell off the bed her body was already too limp with abuse to make much of a thud. She spilled bonelessly along the rug. Maddie heard a little broken moan as the man picked her up, and that was all.

She couldn't be sure if Linda was still conscious when it ended or not. In any event her involvement was not required. At a certain point the man was ready. He stopped hitting her, pulled her roughly spread-eagle on the bed, inserted himself and hunched to a rapid climax. It was over in seconds. All that build-up to so little satisfaction. It wasn't about sex. Sex was the excuse. It was about pain.

Slowly then he seemed to come to his senses. He looked around and saw what he'd done, the mess he'd have to clear up. Maddie closed her eyes before his gaze reached her, let him think she was unconscious. Even better, let him think she was dead. Anything that would keep him from turning his attentions on her.

She stayed where she was, motionless, half under the furniture, listening to him move around the room. Once he lifted her chin with his foot, and she was surprised to discover that he'd put his shoes back on. She made no visible reaction, didn't open her eyes, and he moved away.

The next thing she heard was the door opening and when she dared a look they were both gone, Linda and the man. So was the bloody sheet off the bed. But there was still a jumble of clothes littering the floor, so she grabbed anything that looked familiar, got into just enough of them to pass a casual glance, and ran. She met no one in the corridor. She found the back stairs and left that way.

'I didn't know until later that he'd killed her,' she whispered. 'But I did really. After I got home I called the hospital but she wasn't there. All the damage he'd done to her, I knew that if she wasn't in hospital she was dead.

'I thought he'd come after me then. I didn't know his name but I'd seen his face, I knew what he'd done. If he'd killed her he had to kill me too. The other one knew where to find me, I couldn't think of anything but getting away. I should have come to you but I was too scared. I thought he'd buy his way out of trouble somehow. I thought it would be my word against his, until he stopped me from talking altogether. I thought if I just got out, went where nobody could find me... I suppose that sounds stupid.'

'It sounds like you were scared out of your mind and probably concussed as well,' said Donovan. 'Nobody's responsible for what they do in circumstances like that.'

'But I left her!' cried Maddie. 'I left her to die. I let him kill her.'

'He bounced your head off the wall,' said Donovan tartly. 'He thought he'd knocked you out or he wouldn't have left you in the room alone. The wonder is not that you couldn't help your friend but that you managed to save yourself.'

'You think so?' Her voice was a tiny plea; she was desperately looking for some kind of redemption.

'Maddie, you're talking to a policeman! I've been beaten

up too. I know what it's like to have the strength and the wits knocked out of you. All the faculties you have left concentrate on one thing: survival. Any way, at any cost. You just don't have enough reserves left to worry about anyone else.'

'She was my friend…'

'It wouldn't have made a difference if she'd been your mother.'

She was crying again. But it was different; softer. Telling her story had robbed it of much of the pain, the self-recrimination. She was crying with relief.

But she hadn't finished the story. She hadn't reached the part Donovan was waiting for. He left a decent interval before prompting her. 'What happened at Kendall's house? Who shot the chief? And did he mean to, or were we right the first time and he was aiming at Kendall?'

Maddie wiped away her tears and blew her nose. Her voice was calmer, the edge gone out of it. 'I'm not sure. When it happened, when I saw it on the news, I thought Kendall was the target. That's what scared me. I thought, if he was on the hit list, damn sure I was. I don't know who did the shooting. A pro, I suppose: someone else he hired to do a messy little job for him.' The little wan smiled flickered again. 'Another hireling. The man who killed Linda sent him, to silence me and to silence Kendall.

'Or maybe to stop Mr Shapiro, because he was getting too close. There are places in the world where it doesn't matter what you do as long as you can afford a cover-up. That's the kind of place he's from. Back home he'd have used his influence and the local chief of detectives would have looked the other way. Here he needed to stop him with a bullet.'

Donovan didn't understand. 'What do you mean, getting too close? We hadn't a single idea who was responsible. Our list of suspects was the same as Kendall's guest-list, and we weren't even sure he was on that. He'd nothing to gain by shooting either of them, Kendall or the chief. Neither of them could put the finger...'

His voice died away. Like an echo, something she'd said before came back to him. His brows knit. 'You said there were two men. You said it was the other one who called you. He was a regular. So—he's a local man?'

Maddie rubbed her eyes with the heels of her hands. 'I'm sorry, I'm really not telling this very well. Yes, of course. I don't think he meant us to get hurt, but afterwards he helped his friend get away, and he must have warned him that the police had his name. Maybe you had forty others as well, but as a local man he knew that if anyone could whittle that list down to one it was Mr Shapiro. I was wrong, wasn't I?—the little shit was never in any danger. He wasn't the target, he was the bait. The bullets were for me and Mr Shapiro.'

Another echo; another little bell ringing in the background. She'd called somebody that before, though she wasn't a woman from whom expletives flowed naturally. That little shit—

'*Kendall?*' exclaimed Donovan, ripping his eyes off the road to stare at her. 'Kendall set him up?'

'Philip Kendall. Yes.'

SUPERINTENDENT HILTON cleared his throat. 'So the mechanic took a shot at Kendall in order to bring Mr Shapiro out to the house. Did he mean to kill Kendall as well?'

'No,' decided Liz. 'Donovan's right—a man as careful as this one hits what he's aiming at. If he'd been aiming at Kendall the man would be dead. Frank would still have gone to his house. If anything it would have been easier to hit him bent over a body on the back steps than moving around.'

Hilton sniffed; it looked as if his moustache was shrugging. 'So Kendall's part of it?'

'If he's not the target—if in fact the mechanic went to some trouble to avoid shooting him—I think maybe he's in it up to his neck.' Liz was thinking on her feet: until the words came out she hadn't much more idea than Hilton what she was going to say. 'He set up the conference, and when one of his clients asked for a tom he fixed it up. He called a girl he used himself. Then he fixed somewhere for them to meet that wasn't the man's own room. Maybe he suspected this could get nasty, maybe it was just a matter of discretion. Either way, he invited Mrs Atwood out for supper so they could use her room.

'He wasn't there when the girl was killed, and maybe he had no reason to expect that. The man must have cleaned up by then or Mrs Atwood would have screamed blue murder when she went up to bed. So maybe the first Kendall knew of what had happened was when Frank talked to him on Monday morning.

'To protect himself he gave Frank everything he asked for, including the list of delegates. But as soon as he could he called his friend to warn him we were on his case. Kendall knows Frank, at least by reputation—he may have overestimated how far we'd got with the investigation. Or maybe he recognized that Frank was their biggest danger: that as long as he was in command discovery was a real and imminent possibility. The rest of us didn't worry them too much, but Frank Shapiro's brain is like the mills of God: it grinds exceeding small. To be safe they had to get him out of the picture.'

'You mean, Kendall suggested killing him?'

'Maybe, maybe not. Maybe they just wanted him in hospital for a couple of weeks until they had the thing tidied up. And maybe even that wasn't Kendall's suggestion but what his friend—his client—whoever we're talking about— thought would be best. He made some calls of his own, and within a few hours a first-class mechanic was on his way to Castlemere. To get Frank Shapiro off the case, and to dispose of the only witness who hadn't every reason to keep quiet.'

'You're making a pretty persuasive case against him.'

Liz had rather surprised herself with how strongly it had come out. She rocked a hand. 'It's easier to believe he was involved than that he was an innocent dupe. It could just about have happened without his cooperation but it would be an awful lot harder. Oh, I know, none of this amounts to proof. In fact it's going to be very hard to prove. But it is suggestive.'

A shock wave lurched through her expression. Her eyes saucered and her lips blanched and parted. 'Oh my God!'

Hilton stared at her. 'What? Inspector?'

'Kendall,' she managed. 'I talked to him last night. At that point I had no reason to suspect him of complicity. I was just keeping him up to date, reassuring him...'

'What did you tell him?'

'I told him about the girl. I told him I was sending Donovan to collect her first thing this morning. Sir, if he is involved—'

The superintendent finished the thought for her. 'It would be the easiest thing in the world for the mechanic to follow Donovan as he left. Yes.'

Liz felt someone had kicked a ladder out from under her. Her mind windmilled as she fought for balance. 'He thought there was a car following him. He gave me the number. Then it disappeared and he thought he'd been wrong. But maybe he wasn't at all.' She clutched for a passing straw. 'Kendall's in hiding—he'd not supposed to use the phone.'

Hilton shrugged. 'That was for his protection. I don't suppose DC Morgan sat all night watching to make sure the man didn't cut his own throat.'

'So he knows.' Liz's voice was low, stunned. 'He knows about Maddie, and that she's coming here and who's fetching her. They'll never make it!'

Detective Superintendent Hilton was not widely known as a kindly man. But he had no interest in rubbing salt into a self-inflicted wound. He stood up abruptly. 'All right, this is what we do. I'll go and see Kendall. You call Donovan, warn him he may have a tail. Find out where he is, then organize him some support, from whatever station's closest. If he can keep out of trouble for another ten minutes they'll be all right.' He reached for his coat and headed for the stairs.

But before he got there he stopped and turned back. 'Ah—Inspector Graham?'

'Sir?'

'That address in Northampton? I think this constitutes a need to know.'

EIGHT

DONOVAN HAD HIS HAND on his phone when he saw the navy-blue hatchback again. Behind him, this time. He remembered the knot of lorries that he'd passed. The car must have been on the inside, shielded from view. That wasn't the sort of thing that happened accidentally. To make it happen the driver had manipulated the speeds and positions of three other vehicles, a task comparable with juggling petrol bombs. No undertaking for an amateur.

First things first. He left the phone in his pocket. 'We have to get off this road,' he said tersely, 'I think we've got a tail. No'—he grabbed Maddie's shoulder as she went to screw round—'*don't* turn round: I don't want him to know we've spotted him. We need the element of surprise if we're going to lose him.'

'Him?' she echoed breathlessly; as if there could be two answers.

Donovan shrugged. 'I guess you were right all along.'

'You were supposed to protect me!' she wailed, clutching her seat as if it might try to throw her.

'I *am* protecting you,' said Donovan indignantly. 'We're halfway home'—this was an exaggeration—'and the worst that's happened so far is that we're sharing a road with the ungodly. And I'm going to do something about that.'

His narrow face screwed up with thinking. He was trying to picture exactly where they were, as on a map. The road had divided a mile back; he'd headed south towards Castlemere. But there was another road, coming up on his right, and off that were a whole series of minor roads wandering round the fen. There were those, probably, who knew the little back-ways through the fen even better than Donovan, but most of them were waterfowl. He could take the secondary road as if he was still heading for Peterborough, then double back out of sight and rejoin this road a few miles further on.

The junction loomed. He slowed the Jaguar, indicating in good time and then making the turn as if he had no idea there was a paid killer behind him.

For perhaps twenty seconds, which was long enough for him to start wondering if he'd misunderstood, nothing followed. He eased back on the accelerator, watching his mirror. Finally it was there: the navy-blue hatchback. 'All right,' he said with a kind of leaden calm. 'So now we know what we're dealing with.'

Maddie had known for three days. She'd known her life was in danger before she fled The Barbican Hotel. She'd known it was still in danger as she hid in King's Lynn, and after she saw on the news what happened at Kendall's house she knew that the danger was closing in.

And still it came as a shock that what she had feared, what she had been so sure would happen, was actually happening now. A man who had been paid to silence her was in a car quarter of a mile back up the road, and her life depended on an unarmed detective who'd be reluctant to put his foot down for fear of damaging his superintendent's suspension.

Donovan watched for the first road off on his left, but then cruised on past it apparently oblivious. A mile further on was another, and a third half a mile beyond that. They all came together, along with a fourth that rapidly divided into a fifth, in the middle of the Bedford Levels. Maybe he didn't know them as well as he knew the Castlemere Levels a little further south, but if he couldn't lose a stranger there it was time he took up a less demanding profession.

Between the second and third turnings he pulled his seatbelt tight and advised Maddie to do the same. 'It'll get hectic for a minute or two, but hang on, there are half a dozen chances to lose him in the next couple of miles. If you're going to scream, do it quietly; if you're going to throw up, *not* on the chief's upholstery.'

'In your dreams,' gritted Maddie Cotterick.

With the moment when he had to make his move coming up at a steady forty-five miles an hour, what Donovan needed most in the world was a distraction. Experience had taught him, however, that Fate tended to save her surprises for when a man desperately needed a smooth run. So when a tractor began emerging from an adjacent gateway, for a split second Donovan wasn't sure if he was actually seeing it or if it was just wishful thinking.

After that, though, instinct took over. He wanted that tractor between him and the hatchback when he turned off the road. He eased up on the accelerator enough that a gap appeared ahead of him and the tractor moved into it. Donovan slowed some more, and saw the hatchback reduce speed behind him. Then he went to pass the tractor.

But as soon as he had the road in front of it he braked sharply. The tractor braked too, blaring a horn like a coaster in dense fog; behind it the hatchback, which had begun to overtake, was forced to brake as well. Donovan yanked hard at the wheel and the big car answered with well-bred tolerance, cornering snugly into the minor road. A glance in his mirror showed the tractor stalled across the junction and the hatchback flashing its lights in frustration. Castlemere had its share of farmers: Donovan knew that the only thing capable of making them hurry was the promise of an EEC food subsidy. He vented an evil chuckle and floored the accelerator, and the next bend, and the next junction, appeared fast enough for him to lose sight of the pursuit.

If he hadn't known about the crossroads further on he'd have taken that first available turning. But he did; and he hoped that the man behind him, who probably didn't, would assume that was what he'd done. He drove on, as fast as he could steer, and took the second turning, and immediately turned left again. Already he was pointing back towards the Castlemere road.

The only drawback was that now he had three miles of minor road ahead of him. That hardly mattered if he'd already lost his tail, and he thought there was a good chance that he had. He'd had a choice of five routes since he last saw the navy hatchback; the logic of the one he'd taken was only evident to someone familiar with the area.

They were through the long straight stretch and into the next bend, and still there was nothing in the mirror. Donovan allowed himself the luxury of a breath that went deeper than his Adam's apple. Maddie, still clutching her seat as if only death would part them, said in a small tight voice, 'Are you going to tell your Inspector what's happening?'

Until then there hadn't been time for Donovan to deal with anything but his driving. In truth, though, he'd forgotten the phone inside his jacket. He was just old enough to have learned this job in the pre-Cellnet era, when a policeman's best chance of summoning urgent assistance was a lapel radio that only worked if he was in the right place at the right time and there wasn't an R in the month. Even that made him a child of the technological age in Shapiro's eyes. When he was a beat copper they depended on whistles.

'Er—yeah. You dial.' He passed her the instrument, repeated the number. 'When you get DI Graham, I'll talk to her.'

She got Queen's Street. She got Sergeant Bolsover, who performed his function with a weighty deliberation that made the Bedford farmers look like gadflies. She explained that she had DS Donovan for DI Graham, and Sergeant Bolsover said he'd enquire as to whether DI Graham was currently on the premises. Maddie waited. And waited.

The waiting came to an abrupt end when the Jaguar creamed round a slight left-hand bend and found the road blocked by a navy-blue hatchback and a man holding what appeared at first sight—which is all they had time for—to be a bazooka.

DC MORGAN WAS A naturally cautious man. He came from the same Fenland stock as Sergeant Bolsover and believed

in looking before he leapt. All the same, he didn't keep
Detective Superintendent Hilton waiting on the doorstep
while he checked his credentials all the way back to Division, which is what he should probably have done. He might
never have seen the man before but he knew him by repute;
and those cautious Fenland genes told him that the greatest
danger he faced right now was incurring Superintendent Hilton's displeasure.

'They're in the back room, sir. WPC Wilson's with them.'

Kendall was working at the table, the contents of his
briefcase spread across its surface. His wife was trying to
watch television, but distractedly: she hadn't noticed that in
flicking between the channels she'd managed to turn the
sound off.

Hilton introduced himself, helped himself to a chair and
looked around. The furniture was more old-fashioned than
worn. Most of the time nobody lived here at all; and when
they did it was usually only for a few days at a time. The
only up-to-date item in the room was the TV, because it got
enough usage when there was someone in residence to wear
out. Sometimes, Hilton supposed, if someone was worried
and frustrated enough, it wore out very quickly from the
sudden introduction of an ash-tray through the screen.

'Well, Mr and Mrs Kendall, I have some good news.' He
smiled. It was like the smile of a newly-boiled gin-trap.
'You may be able to go home sooner than we were hoping.
It seems Mr Kendall wasn't the assassin's target after all.'

Still with that steely smile in place, he watched their faces
minutely. He saw the information hit them and the implications sink in. And what he saw were two quite different
reactions. Mrs Kendall's heart rose, pushing surprise and
hope up through her eyes and rounding her lips on an unspoken question.

Philip Kendall's heart sank.

Well now, thought the Top People's Cop. Either you were
looking forward to a few days off work, in which case why

did you bring so much of it here with you? Or you know that us making progress with this investigation isn't good news but bad news from your point of view. If we know you weren't the target, we know Shapiro was; and if we're sure of that we probably know why; and if we know why we probably know the rest.

And sometime soon, he thought, before you commit yourself to saying almost anything else, you're going to want to make sure just what we do know, what we have reason to suspect and what we're running up the flagpole to see if anyone salutes. He held his peace, and his smile, continued to watch Kendall, waiting for the tension to become unbearable.

Mrs Kendall didn't understand what was passing between them. She looked at her husband, and at the policeman, with mounting confusion, growing impatient with them. 'That *is* good news. Isn't it? Philip?'

For a second he looked as she had looked watching a television with the sound off. 'What? Oh—yes. Yes, of course. Um—have you made an arrest, Superintendent?'

Which was fairly sophisticated thinking for a man unexpectedly delivered from the sword of Damocles. 'No, sir, not yet. But we know now who we're looking for, we know who *he's* looking for, and we know where he is. Good heavens, we even have the number of his car! We'll have this sorted out in a jiffy, you mark my words.'

Looking at Philip Kendall then was like confronting one of the Easter Island statues. His face had the same resolute lack of expression, and pretty much the same colour. But behind the frozen face his brain was racing. Hilton could almost hear the wheels clicking and whirring like a clock.

He knew—from Hilton's presence here he knew—that the next thing he should say was 'I want my solicitor'. Almost certainly. Unless he was jumping the gun. If Hilton was merely kite-flying, or even just bringing him up to date and it was the man's weird manner that was investing the exchange with sinister overtones, demanding to see his solicitor would be the same as blurting a confession. But anything else he said would dig him deeper in the mire if he had become a suspect.

His wife's eyes on his face, puzzled and increasingly uneasy, did nothing to aid his decision. What he needed most of all was some thinking space, and it didn't look like he was going to get it. He didn't know much about police procedure, but enough to suspect that detective superintendents don't habitually drive thirty miles just to tell someone he mightn't be in much danger after all.

But a man doesn't get to be sales director of a respected company in a difficult and competitive international field if he can't keep a cool head and take a calculated risk when the need arises. Philip Kendall wasn't ready to admit defeat while any chance remained that he could get out of this scot-free. There was no evidence against him. There couldn't be: he hadn't actually *done* anything—nothing that left fingerprints, or hairs on the carpet. There was only one person who could connect him to any of this, and if she'd talked they'd be conducting this interview at Queen's Street. The police didn't *know* anything. They were guessing, and Hilton needed him to incriminate himself. That was why he was here.

Kendall pushed out a slow smile, just smug enough to offend the policeman without giving him cause for complaint. He got up from the table, and stretched, and put an arm around his wife's shoulders. 'Well, that's splendid, Superintendent—isn't it, dear? I appreciate you coming to tell us.'

Instincts honed by a quarter of a century in this job told Superintendent Hilton that Philip Kendall had come within a hair's breadth of making a full and frank confession, hoping that by assisting in the detention of the major criminals his own contribution could be made to look as minor as possible. And he'd decided against.

He was right. Hilton couldn't fault his decision—he was bluffing. He'd come here with a fair idea that the man was

involved, had been convinced totally by his reactions, but
the actual evidence against him could be written in large
letters on the back of a postage stamp. It would have been
a mistake to break down at that point; but it's what most
people would have done, and the fact that Kendall declined
to told Hilton, in case he hadn't already realized, that he
was dealing with a tough and intelligent adversary. He had
to get this right. If he got it wrong, Kendall would wriggle
free.

His expression didn't flicker. 'Well, there was something
else I needed to ask you. Did you make any phonecalls last
night?'

Again the pregnant pause while Kendall worked out the
implications. Oh yes, thought Hilton, this man is guilty as
hell. But he's clever as the devil. 'Iris phoned her mother
this morning.'

'No one else?'

Kendall shook his head. 'No.'

Hilton didn't believe him, but when he glanced at DC
Morgan and WPC Wilson for confirmation, neither was able
to assist him. He went to the phone and pressed the last-
number-redial. He got Kendall's mother-in-law. Rather than
talk he hung up.

'So what happens now?' asked Kendall, emboldened by
his success. 'Can we go home right away?'

'I think so, sir, yes.' He paused just long enough for Kendall to suppose he'd finished, then added, 'Then it won't be
such a long haul next time I want to talk to you.'

DONOVAN'S PHONE was switched off. To save the battery,
thought Liz bitterly. What about your goddamned neck? Until she talked to him, found out where he was, she couldn't
send help. She put a message out to neighbouring forces to
stop Shapiro's car if it was spotted; that was all she could
do until Donovan called in.

By eleven-fifteen it was beginning to feel a long time
since she'd heard from him. Probably it meant only that

things were proceeding smoothly and he had nothing to report, but she was uneasy. The fact that Kendall could have sent someone after him didn't mean he had. Probably she'd overreacted. Because it had been her mistake to talk that freely to him, she'd assumed the worst. It was only ever a possibility, and not a strong one.

And the fact that Donovan was maintaining radio silence didn't mean he had a problem. Among her sergeant's many failings, a tendency to engage in inconsequential chit-chat was marked by its absence. If he had nothing to say he wouldn't call. She kept dialling his number; he kept being unavailable.

She called down to the switchboard. 'You haven't heard anything from DS Donovan, I suppose?'

Sergeant Bolsover gave the set a slow, puzzled blink. 'You mean, in the last twenty minutes?'

Liz favoured him with an unseen scowl. 'Twenty minutes? What are you talking about?'

Patiently, Sergeant Bolsover explained. 'He called in. Twenty minutes ago. Asked for you. I put him through—well, her, it was the woman. At least, I thought I put her through. You didn't get her?'

'No. We must have lost the connection.' But Liz was reassured. As recently as twenty minutes ago they called in. Donovan was driving so Maddie used the phone. Maybe she hit the wrong button; or maybe the signal was lost. He'd try again in a little while. 'That's OK, Sergeant. At least we've heard from them.'

She looked at her watch. They were still forty minutes away, and Hilton wouldn't be back until after that. Nothing on her desk needed her immediate attention.

'I'm nipping down to the hospital,' she told Colwyn, 'see how the chief's getting on. If Donovan calls in, bring him up to date and tell him to stand by. Then call me. If I don't hear from you I'll be back in half an hour.'

Colwyn made a note of her mobile number. 'I'll hold the fort.'

Constable Dimmock, the Authorized Firearms Officer, was stood down when Shapiro was moved to a private room. WPC Flynn sat outside the door, reading a magazine. Liz suspected that if she'd been a professional killer, and had therefore not made a point of saying, 'Good morning, Cathy,' as she went inside, Flynn might never have noticed her. Liz made a mental note to send DC Scobie to relieve her. He was no brighter than Cathy Flynn, but if errors were going to be made it was better to have the ward orderly in an armlock than an assassin let in merely because he'd picked up a white coat somewhere.

Shapiro looked a great deal more comfortable than last time Liz saw him, lying on his back with a couple of pillows behind his head. At first glance she thought he was asleep. Then she realized that he wasn't: instead he was staring at his feet through lowered lids and concentrating really hard.

'Frank—what are you *doing?*'

He looked up and beckoned her over urgently. 'Come here. Sit there.' He pulled the chair up beside the locker. 'Now, watch.'

She wasn't at all sure what she was supposed to be watching for. And then she was. She felt an idiot smile spread over her face. She didn't know whether to laugh or cry. 'Frank, that's terrific. How long—?'

'Just this last half hour. I was asleep, and I dreamt I was running. Me!—never mind this, I haven't run anywhere for years. And when I woke up I saw—that.'

They looked together at the foot of the bed. Under the white sheet Frank Shapiro was wiggling his toes.

He wanted to know how the investigation was progressing. Liz hardly knew how to answer. She told him about Maddie Cotterick, who might have something useful to contribute when Donovan brought her back but then again might not. And she told him about Donovan's flash of inspiration.

He heard her out in a silence so profound it was like

another person in the room with them. Until he broke it she
couldn't tell what he was thinking.

'You mean, my brave and noble self-sacrifice was nothing
of the kind?'

Liz beamed sympathetically. 'It *was*, Frank. You had no
way of knowing the sod was shooting at you all along.'

'All the same...' He sounded hurt. This last half hour,
since he'd woken up to find the first signs of life returning
to his legs, he'd begun to feel just a little smug about what
had happened. Not that getting shot in the back had much
to recommend it. But for the thirty-odd years he'd been
doing this job, he'd known and so had everyone around him
that he did better work in his head than on his feet. It was
nice to be seen as a man of action for a change. Who'd have
thought it of the old desk-jockey? (they'd have said up at
Division)—hurling himself in front of an assassin's gun like
that? Good old Frank Shapiro (they'd have said), slower
than a speeding bullet. But it was different if the gunman
was shooting at him anyway. 'So what's happening about
Kendall?'

'Mr Hilton's gone to see him now. I don't know if he'll
arrest him or not. The trouble is, there's no evidence. It
makes sense, and Maddie Cotterick may be able to confirm
it, but if he insists he knows nothing about it I don't know
how we set about proving it.'

'And Donovan's fetching this girl now, is he?' Shapiro's
eyes narrowed. Behind them he was thinking. Specifically,
he was counting—the vehicles available, and the jobs that
had to be done with them. And he came up one short.

Liz had decided against worrying him with her remarks
to Kendall. It was easier to tell him about his car. 'Everything else was tied up, and it was just sitting in the yard so
I told him to take the Jaguar. I hope that's all right.'

Shapiro sniffed; but it was too late and anyway a shade
graceless to complain. He wouldn't have thanked them for
leaving it at Kendall's house, and it would have been un-

reasonable to expect Donovan to drive it back to Queen's Street and then take the bus to King's Lynn. All the same…

All the time his children had been small he'd driven a lumbering great estate big enough to take half a hockey team. And when they grew up there was the divorce to get through, and he'd limited himself to a mid-range saloon until he knew how big an impact the settlement was going to have on his finances. Only last year, with his promotion, had he decided the time had come to treat himself, and he'd spent months agonizing between the pros and even-more-pros of three or four seriously classy cars before opting for the Jaguar. He hadn't been disappointed. Every time his backside settled into the upholstery he got a small thrill of pleasure.

And now Donovan was driving it. Well, what if he was? He was a good enough driver; he didn't race amber lights or tailgate people who overtook him. He had the mildly disconcerting habit of leaning into sharp corners, but perhaps that was something all bikers did.

Shapiro sniffed. 'As long as he doesn't scratch it.'

NINE

IT WASN'T A BAZOOKA, it was an RPG launcher. When the rocket-propelled grenade hit the front of Shapiro's Jaguar, instantly the question of scratches to the paintwork became academic. It blew the bonnet off. It blew the windscreen in and all the other windows out. It blew up the engine and then, just as the debris was beginning to rain down, it blew up the rest of the car. A gout of fire surged through the passenger compartment, filling it like molten steel filling a mould. Flames roared in the empty windows. When the heat reached the petrol tank, the explosion lifted what was left of the vehicle clean off the road and dropped it upside down in the ditch.

Ditches in the fens aren't primarily to provide hedgehogs with a hiding place until they see an approaching car. They're to drain the surrounding land, and they're usually full of water. Most of them are deep enough to drown in; some of them are wide enough to sail on. This one was almost big enough to swallow the blazing wreckage of Shapiro's Jaguar: the water quenched the fire as far back as the front seats in a noisy chorus of hissing steam. Smoke and bits of charred debris continued roiling out of the back half where it lay inverted on the steep bank.

The man in the middle of the road put his RPG down and drew a handgun. He wasn't expecting to need it, but a man didn't succeed in his profession by taking any chances at all. He didn't see how anything could come out of that car except more steam and an oddly sweet smell like roast pork. But it wasn't a decision he needed to take. If they were dead, they wouldn't stop being dead because he had a gun in his hand; and if by any chance one of them had survived he was ready to rectify the situation. He waited a moment for the breeze to shred the pall of smoke and steam, then advanced towards the burning wreckage.

But he knew before he got there, before he could see how much of the car was left, that his job wasn't finished. He knew the smell of burning flesh, he'd encountered it before, and he missed it from the rich and acrid cocktail—burning petrol and burning electrics and hot metal and singed leather and melted rubber—rising from the ditch.

'Damn,' he said mildly. Then he stepped away from the car, crossed the road in a couple of deceptively swift strides and peered down the opposite ditch. 'Ah—'

HE'D PROMISED to protect her. He was *paid* to protect her. But in the face of an RPG there was nothing Donovan could do for Maddie Cotterick except scream, 'Get out!', and hope that while he was bowling out of the driver's door she was doing the same on the other side. The Jaguar had come almost to a standstill but not quite. When he saw what was being aimed at them Donovan needed his brake foot back because he couldn't leave without it.

Nor did he jump a moment too soon. He acted on pure instinct, getting out of a situation that was plainly untenable. If he'd paused just a second to weigh up the alternatives, to wonder if he could get past the hatchback or shunt into reverse (and never mind his Superintendent's gearbox) and roar back the way he'd come, he'd still have been in the car when it exploded. As it was he was somewhere between the seat and the open door, and his own impetus and the sudden expansion of the air behind him shot him out like the cork from an inexpertly opened bottle of champagne. The sound and force of the blast, and the searing flame riding upon it, swept over him before he hit the ground, shrouding him in choking chemical smog.

He thought, insofar as he had the time or the mental capacity to think, that he was dying. He didn't see how anyone could survive an explosion like that, and the reason it didn't hurt more was that he was already past that stage. He'd seen people who'd been burned too badly to recover. They seemed to suffer less pain than someone with lesser burns. If there was enough tissue damage, the pain-sensitive nerves were largely destroyed.

And Donovan thought that was probably the state he was in now: his clothes, his hair and his skin turned to ash, his raw flesh still too shocked to react. He thought, Any second now...any second now.

Then the squall of air generated by the petrol tank detonating behind him tore a rent through the smoke, and for a moment he saw his hands. They were splayed out on the road, one either side of his face, and he could see them clearly. They looked fine. Not dissolved to ash. Not blackened and cracked. Not, so far as he could see, burned at all.

Which raised the possibility that the rest of him was all right too; and that if he wanted to stay that way he'd better do something about getting out of here.

The smoke disorientated him. He wasn't sure where the gunman was, or even where the remains of the car were. But when he stretched out his right hand he felt the tarmac surface give way to dust and then to grass, and he rolled over his shoulder on to the bank and down into the drain. He had just enough time to think, quite calmly, If I'm wrong about this and I *am* burned, the shock of this'll kill me; and then the water closed over him with a faint weedy slurp that no one any nearer the fire would have heard.

MADDIE COTTERICK saw what Donovan saw at the moment Donovan saw it, and though she couldn't identify it she certainly knew what it meant. She was evacuating the car even before Donovan yelled.

She hit the ground hard because the Jaguar still had some forward momentum. All the breath left her in a rush, and she curled round her collapsed lungs gasping for air. For a couple of seconds none came; she thought she was going to die flapping on the tarmac like a landed fish. Then the car blew up.

It might have been the shock wave hitting her that finally got her breathing again. Certainly she got the smell, and a wave of heat rolled over her like a breaker on a beach. But she was further away than Donovan and the flames missed her, and so did the great cushion of smoke that spread out, filling the lane from side to side. More by luck than design, it made a perfect smokescreen between her and the man hunting her.

She got her knees under her, still bent low to the road, whooping the stinking air into her lungs, desperately watching the smoke and waiting for it to part around a striding figure. But it didn't. Nor could she see Donovan. For all she knew he'd never got out of the car. She thought she was on her own. She knew she couldn't outrun a bullet; in her current state she couldn't have outrun the man either. Whatever chance she had, and she knew it wasn't much of one, depended on finding cover. There was nothing back the way they'd come for much further than she could hope to escape pursuit. That left the ditches on either side of the road.

She'd gone out the nearside door and landed closer to the nearside ditch. But even as she crouched there, gasping for breath, the Jaguar slewed into that left-hand ditch, adding white steam to the oily smoke pouring into the air. She had no idea if any more explosions were likely, but the possibility was enough to decide her. Hidden by the roiling cloud, she crawled on her hands and knees to the opposite verge and rolled down the bank out of sight.

PC WILLIAM WARREN was on his way back to Peterborough when he saw the smoke. If he'd seen it on his way out of Peterborough he'd have thought that the Flixton family domestic that he was on his way to deal with had gone a bit further than usual and it was the demise of Flixton Farm he was seeing. But he'd left the parties fuming over their unresolved grievances at opposite ends of the eighteenth-

century farmhouse, Mrs Flixton nursing a black eye and Mr
Flixton treating his scratches with udder cream, and the sudden belch of smoke was ahead of him and a little way off
the main road. At the first junction Warren turned towards
it, and within a couple of hundred yards he came on the
accident.

At least, he supposed it was an accident. There was one
car blazing merrily in the ditch, another parked across the
road. A man was standing on the grass. He looked up at the
sound of the police car and waved.

His eyes wide, Warren hurried over to the burning car.
'Is there anyone in there?'

It was the right question, but actually the answer was
immaterial. If there was it was already too late to help, for
which PC Warren was heartily grateful. If he'd got here a
minute earlier he might have had to try.

The man shook his head and pointed north across The
Levels. 'They went that way. A couple of young lads; I
think they may have been joyriders.'

'What happened?'

The man gave a minimal shrug. He was a tall man of
around fifty, well dressed and well groomed: a businessman,
thought Warren, or perhaps a solicitor. 'They came round
the corner up there'—he pointed—'at about seventy. I
braked hard, which is why I ended up slewed across the
road like this, but they couldn't stop. The driver pulled on
to the bank—I think he thought he could squeeze past me—
but it was steeper than he was expecting. The car rolled, the
boys got out, then it caught fire. They high-tailed it across
the fields. The way they were laughing, it wasn't their car.'

The constable was looking at the wreckage. 'I shouldn't
imagine it was. That was a Jaguar, that was.'

'Pity,' said the man.

'I'm going to need some details from you,' said Warren.

'Of course. But can I come into the police station and see
you later? I'm a surgeon, I work at a private hospital near
Godmanchester, I'm needed there in half an hour to scrub

up for a hip replacement. I could come by on my way home this afternoon, after I finish.'

PC Warren had no reason to quarrel with that. He took the witness's name and address, and noted the number of his car, then he thanked Mr Dodgson for his cooperation. He wished him well with the hip replacement, and when the navy hatchback drove off he stayed with the smouldering wreckage and waited for the assistance he'd summoned to arrive.

BY NOON LIZ WAS seriously worried. Donovan should have been back at Queen's Street by now. Of course, anything could have happened to delay him, including a flat tyre, but if he'd been held up he'd have called in a revised ETA. He should have called in anyway, particularly after his earlier attempt failed, if only to say he was all right. Liz tried three more times to raise him, with the same results as before. Every word of her exchange with Kendall hammered in her head like a drum.

When Superintendent Hilton returned from Northampton and there was still no news it was time to take action. She phoned the police stations in Peterborough, Cambridge and Ely warning them what was happening and asking if they had any information on a maroon Jaguar.

After a few minutes Peterborough rang back.

She sprinted the short distance to Shapiro's office, flinging open the door without even a cursory knock. 'They're in trouble.'

The name and the address given to PC Warren had been checked and found to be false. But the registration number he'd taken was real enough: Donovan had called it in when he noticed the navy hatchback travelling his way. He'd thought it was probably a coincidence but reported it anyway. Its presence by the roadside while Shapiro's Jaguar burned in the ditch said it was no coincidence. Further enquiries revealed it to be a hire car. The man who rented it had given the same false name to the hire company.

'It was definitely Mr Shapiro's car in the ditch?' asked Hilton.

'No question about it.'

'But there was no one inside.'

'No, thank God.'

'And we don't believe in joyriders running away across the fields giggling.'

'No, sir.'

Superintendent Hilton took a measured breath and let it out again. 'It was him, wasn't it? This man calling himself Charles L. Dodgson—it was the mechanic. He ran them off the road, they got out of the car before it caught fire, he was about to finish the job but Constable Warren came along and distracted him. I think Detective Sergeant Donovan and Miss Cotterick may owe their lives to Constable Warren.'

'And what does Constable Warren owe his life to?' asked Liz. 'I mean, this is a professional killer, he's been paid to silence Maddie Cotterick, and the only thing stopping him was an unarmed PC. Why didn't he gun him down and finish what he was there to do? He could have been on his way home by now.'

Hilton didn't know. 'Not ethical considerations, anyway. So it was a matter of practicality or of pride. He didn't have to kill him—he could talk his way out, and it could be hours before anyone realized who he was. Whereas if he shot Warren it wouldn't be long before someone reported the fire, the body would be found and the area would be crawling with policemen. It was a sound decision. It got him away from the scene with nobody chasing him, and ensured that Peterborough would treat it as taking-and-driving-away instead of launching a murder hunt. Yes, it was a good decision. He's a calm and clever man, our Mr Dodgson.'

Liz frowned. 'I know that name from somewhere.'

Hilton did the gin-trap smile again. 'Of course you do, Inspector. You've read *Alice in Wonderland*. Charles Lutwidge Dodgson—Lewis Carroll?'

That was it. Liz nodded, her lips pressed into a thin line. 'Nice. A hired killer with a sense of humour.'

'I'm sure he'll have the judge in stitches,' said Hilton coldly. 'If we find him; if we catch him.'

'Right now I'd settle for finding Donovan and the girl. They got out of the car before it caught fire or Warren would have seen the bodies. But they couldn't have got far: the crash had only just happened, and if they'd run off Dodgson'—she had nothing else to call him—'would have gone after them. They had to be in the immediate area when Warren turned up. So why didn't they show themselves?'

'Donovan's not some probationer wet behind the ears who thinks that putting a suspect under arrest is the same as clapping him in irons. If he'd revealed himself and told Warren what was happening, Dodgson would have killed the three of them. That constable's life hung in the balance until Dodgson got back in his car and drove away. Donovan knew that asking for his help would be the same as signing his death warrant.'

'But Dodgson *did* drive away. He persuaded Warren to let him go about his business, and he left the scene. Why didn't they wait until he'd gone and then clamber out of the ditch?'

As soon as she'd asked the question, the answer seemed obvious. Her head rocked back and her lips parted. 'Maybe we're wrong. Maybe they didn't get away. Maybe he killed them, and he'd just pushed them out of sight when Warren arrived. Maybe what we need to do next is drag those damned ditches.'

Hilton regarded her for a moment before replying. He was still adjusting to the novelty of working with a woman officer above the rank of sergeant, and it *was* different even if the differences were subtle ones. This was a case in point. A time came in every policeman's career where he had to face the possibility of a colleague's death. Some react with bitter fury and some seek sanctuary in a kind of black humour. The simple honesty of Liz Graham's reaction, her ability to show her feelings without any sense of being diminished by them, was new to Hilton. Most of the men he'd worked with would have felt compromised by admitting either to fear or to grief. The interesting thing was that caring enough about a colleague to feel pain at the prospect of losing him didn't make Inspector Graham appear weak, it made her seem strong.

'We will,' he said, 'but I don't think we'll find anything. Dodgson wouldn't have driven away and left a policeman—who'd seen him well enough to identify him, who'd got the number of his car—in charge of a scene where he'd concealed two bodies. He'd have killed him, and been twenty miles away before anyone came to see why Warren wasn't answering his radio. No, he left because he'd lost one chance but he thought there'd be another as long as he was free to take it.'

It made sense. So perhaps they weren't in immediate danger. She felt the tension in her body ease a little. 'But Donovan has a mobile phone. Why hasn't he called for help?'

Superintendent Hilton cocked a sceptical eyebrow. '*My* mobile phone doesn't work if it spends any length of time upside down in my pocket. *His* has been in a car crash, may have been dropped on the ground, may have been swimming in a ditch. My guess is, the next we hear from Sergeant Donovan he'll be in a telephone kiosk. They can tell us about their adventures over a late lunch.' He paused then, noticing her silence. 'You don't look convinced.'

'Sorry, sir. It's just—' There was a big map on the wall of Shapiro's office. It showed the country around Castlemere for thirty miles in every direction. It showed the Castlemere Levels to the east, and the Bedford Levels up to the north. And though it was a large-scale map, a lot of what it showed was nothing at all. 'The fens are strange country. You can get lost out there. All that flatness, all that sky, it all looks the same. And every few fields you have to turn aside because you've hit another watercourse with no way over it. You need a compass to find your way across. Otherwise you can go round in circles.'

'The same applies to Dodgson.'

'No. He only has to look at his map and identify the nearest phone, whether that's a public phone or a house. He can go straight there, and if they're not there he can go to the next. They're on foot, trying to find their way back to civilization. It's country that favours the hunter, not the quarry.'

'What if I ask division for the helicopter?'

That sounded better. Liz nodded. 'Yes, that'll find them. I'm sorry to seem paranoid. But so much has gone wrong already. Now they're out there in a green desert with a killer on their trail, and it seems to me that a man as serious about his job as this one won't be put off by losing their scent for a while. But the helicopter will find them before he does. Can you spare me? I'd like to be on the scene.'

The more angular of Hilton's eyebrows shot up his forehead. 'Can you fly a helicopter, Inspector?'

'Of course not. But—'

'Then I think we can safely leave the search to those who can. There's still plenty of work to be done here. Kendall: I'm going to have him, and it isn't going to be easy because he knows that we know, and he knows that we can't prove it. Go and see Mr Shapiro again, get a statement from him—everything he can remember about his visit to Kendall's house. Maybe there's something we can use.'

'All right.' It was better than having nothing to do but wait. 'How much should I tell him? Do I treat him as a witness or part of the investigating team?'

'I think I can leave that to your discretion, Inspector Graham. There's no point concealing from him that Kendall is under suspicion, simply because if it becomes an issue in court nobody'll believe that we did. So yes, tell him anything he wants to know. He's too experienced an officer to let it influence him. Just bear in mind that the man's in hospital because he's been shot. He's still weak, he doesn't need all the problems of this department dropping in his lap.'

Liz knew what Hilton was saying, and she couldn't altogether blame him. He had a difficult enough job without his officers constantly turning for a second opinion to the man whose desk he'd taken. She nodded. 'I'll be careful not to tire him, sir. If he's got anything useful I'll call. I could meet you at Kendall's house.'

'No, come back here. Once I've got the search organized I'm going to bring Kendall in. Whether or not Mr Shapiro can help, I think it's time to take the gloves off.'

PART THREE

ONE

MADDIE COTTERICK rolled into the water without knowing how deep it was, aware she might only have swapped one death, fast and hot, for another cold and slow. But her feet touched the bottom, and as she straightened carefully she became aware of someone else, wet and weedy as herself, only a metre away. She whispered, 'Donovan?'

He mouthed back, 'Don't talk. Turn round, head that way. Keep low. If he starts shooting, get under the water.'

But the man with the gun was still waiting for a gap in the smoke, still of the belief that his job was done. The few seconds that he kept believing that were all the head start they were going to get. Wading breast-high, silent in the scummy water, they put distance between them and him, every metre another small triumph.

There was a junction twenty metres back where a smaller ditch run into this one. Donovan pushed Maddie round the corner and out of sight. A second later the man with the gun looked into the drain and saw the peaty hole in the surface algae where something solid had gone through. Donovan was still close enough to hear his murmur of satisfaction. He ducked back out of sight, but he knew that they'd left a trail as clear as footprints in the water. The man had only to walk twenty metres up the bank to have a clear view, and a clear shot, into the channel where they were hiding.

Donovan squeezed his eyes shut, trying desperately to think, but there was no solution to find. If they stayed where they were, in half a minute they'd be dead. If they climbed out of the channel and tried to run, they'd be dead rather sooner. This was a man who practised on targets quarter of a mile away. Donovan considered himself fit, but across rough pastureland and weighed down by wet clothing he doubted if he could cover quarter of a mile inside three minutes. Maddie, even if she'd managed to hold on to her shoes, would take five. She wouldn't have got a hundred metres before this man had strolled back to his car, got out his sniper's rifle, assembled it if need be, adjusted the sight, loaded it, strolled back to the dyke and drilled a hole clean through her head.

He didn't know what to do. He pushed her behind him because there was no other cover and waited.

They heard the car, and the voices. Maddie looked up at him, sudden burgeoning hope in her eyes. Donovan had to restrain her physically to keep her from giving them away. He mouthed, 'Stay here. I'll look. *Don't move.*'

A little time from now Superintendent Hilton would credit him with a rather clearer grasp of the situation than was in fact warranted. When he saw the police car and PC Warren standing beside it, Donovan's first thought was the same as Maddie's—that their problems were over. He filled his lungs to call out. Reality interceded just in time. Two unarmed police officers, one of them in a ditch, were no match for a professional killer. If he opened his mouth the man would kill both of them, and Maddie at his leisure.

She didn't see that. Her muddy face was astonished and horrified. 'But—he's a policeman! He can help us.'

'*I'm* a policeman,' Donovan shot back very quietly, 'and a lot of good that did us! Take my word for it, the only chance we have is getting out of here while the sod's busy explaining about this terrible accident he stumbled on. If a moment comes where he thinks his story isn't being believed, he'll shoot the woodentop and get on with searching these drains. We need to be gone by then. We'll find a farm and phone from there.'

Donovan backed away from the overflow—hearing as he did the name the man gave and thinking, as Liz would later, that Charles Dodgson sounded vaguely familiar—and pushed Maddie ahead of him. He knew she wasn't convinced. Almost, she resisted him. But she'd asked for help and he was what she'd got, and he'd kept her alive this far so maybe he had a better idea what he was doing than it sometimes appeared.

Actually he hadn't. Except that he knew they had to vacate this area, and there would never be a better moment than now.

There was a sluggish flow as the seep-water dropped towards the main drain. They forged their way against it, taking every turn that offered. Maddie was close to exhaustion, but Donovan pushed her on until they came to a tangle of willow scrub overhanging the ditch. He clambered to the lip of the bank, his clothes shedding the thick water only reluctantly, and looked back. He could still see the mounting plume of smoke, but neither the cars nor the men in attendance. Presumably that meant they couldn't see him either.

He reached down into the dyke. 'Come on. It gets easier from here.' She had almost no strength left: pulling her out of the water was like lifting a dead weight. They collapsed on the bank in a sprawl of limbs, too tired to go any further, letting the stinking wetness run off them into the dry grass.

But a few minutes' respite was all they could afford. When Donovan felt his limbs growing light enough he pushed himself on to his knees, then stood up. 'Get up. We have to go.'

Maddie didn't move. It was as if she thought he might go on alone if she pretended to be dead. Actually, the element of pretence wasn't that great. She had never in her entire life been so close to collapse.

'Maddie! Get up. We have to keep moving. I can't carry you, but I'll drag you if I must.' When she opened one jaundiced eye he pointed. 'There are some buildings over there. Maybe a mile away. Twenty, twenty-five minutes. Just like walking the dog.'

'I don't have a dog,' she growled feebly.

'Me neither,' Donovan chuckled damply. 'I've got the

reincarnation of Attila the Hun.' He offered his hand and, after a moment, she took it and let him draw her to her feet.

'Twenty-five minutes,' she said sternly. 'After that I lie down and die.'

'It's a deal.'

LIZ DIDN'T HAVE TO volunteer the information. As soon as he saw her face Shapiro knew things were not going well. 'Tell me what's happened.'

She forced a smile she didn't much feel like. 'Do you want the bad news or the very bad news?'

'I want it all,' he said firmly. One of the very few causes for optimism, she thought, was that every time she came here Frank Shapiro looked and sounded more like his old self.

She took a deep breath and got it out in one action-packed sentence. 'Your car's upside down in a ditch in the Bedford Levels, and Donovan and Maddie Cotterick are missing with a hired assassin on their trail.' Then she filled in some details.

He heard her out in silence. He was sitting up quite normally now; every so often the sheet over his feet moved as he practised unconsciously his rediscovered talent. When she'd finished he said, 'I presume somebody's looking for them.'

'Peterborough are organizing a search. Hilton's trying to get the helicopter. But Frank, you know what The Levels are like—you could lose an army in there. Hilton thinks they'll turn up in half an hour. I'm afraid they'll still be scrambling in and out of drains when it goes dark; unless Dodgson's caught up with them by then.'

'He may not still be after them. He got away from the crash without blowing his cover, he may have decided to call it a day. You're right, it's a maze—once they disappeared in there he wouldn't know how to begin finding them. He'll go away, change his car, and think of something else.

'Queen's Street, for instance. Wherever they are now, however long they wander round before emerging from The Levels, sooner or later they're going to end up back in Castlemere, driving down Queen's Street. It's a good place for an ambush. You could check the houses overlooking the street—better still, check those overlooking the backyard. Shooting a woman in a car's going to be difficult, even for him. But once in the yard she has to get out of the car and go up the back steps.' He twitched a sombre little smile. 'He's good at steps.'

Listening to his calm assessment, Liz felt more at ease than she had for the last hour. It made sense; it was what a man like this would do; and it meant Donovan and Maddie Cotterick weren't gong to die in the middle of The Levels because of her error of judgement. She had to believe it. 'I'll get on to it. If that's what he's going to do, there's only a tiny window of opportunity where we have to protect her. They're safe until they're almost home.' She smiled, relaxing. 'Damn it, Frank, even in a hospital bed you think clearer than the rest of us!'

Shapiro shrugged. 'In a hospital bed there isn't much else to do but think.' But secretly he was pleased.

Liz got up to go. 'And Superintendent Hilton wants to know if you're ready to give a statement.'

'A statement?'

'About what happened at Kendall's house. Assuming you remember what happened. The man's in this up to his eyeballs—of course, if you *are* going to make a statement I didn't just say that. If we can prove it he'll tell us which of his customers killed the girl because that's all he'll have to bargain with.'

Shapiro was nodding slowly. 'So we get a name. But the man himself is long gone. No point being a foreigner if you're not going to skip the country after committing murder.'

'I don't expect we will get him,' agreed Liz. 'But if we know who he is he might as well call off the assassin he's paying to protect his identity. We don't have to arrest him for Maddie to be safe. We just have to mark his card.'

There was a pause while Shapiro thought. 'Leave it with me, I'll draw something up. Liz—call me if there are any developments.'

She nodded. 'I expect Hilton's right and we'll find them soon enough. I'll get back to Queen's Street and make sure nothing happens there.'

'Be careful,' said Shapiro. 'Remember what this man's done already. He's clever, resourceful and quite amoral. He'll kill anyone to get to his target.'

'He can't shoot her if he can't see her. I'll put screens up in the yard so he never gets a look at her.'

A slow grin spread across Shapiro's rumpled face. 'That's my girl.'

AFTER FIFTY MINUTES of walking, wading and clambering Maddie was too tired to look up. So she didn't see, as Donovan did, that the farm buildings that had been inching closer were near enough now for the broken empty windows to be clearly seen. He bit his lip and said nothing. At least it would be somewhere for her to rest. He could leave her there and go on alone. There had to be a phone somewhere in this frigging fen.

He too was tired, right down to the bone. It didn't have to matter. It was twelve-thirty, Queen's Street would know by now that something had gone wrong, might even know where it happened. But they wouldn't know where to send help until he called in. The upside of that was that Dodgson too would have no idea where to find them. They had broken their trail so often. Sometimes deliberately, sometimes for lack of choice, that a team of bloodhounds would have been foxed. Colour-washed by the contents of half a dozen drains, mud in their hair and on their faces and thick on their clothes, they could have evaded discovery anywhere in this fen merely by lying on a bit of bare earth. He hated to think what they'd find when they finally got the chance to take their clothes off and clean up. He'd seen *The African Queen*.

Between the last drain and the derelict farm there was a tumbled fence. Donovan didn't so much help Maddie over it as lift her over. 'Nearly there,' he said. 'But Maddie—'

Finally she looked up. They'd made it. More than an hour ago someone had tried to kill her; since then she'd been trudging through a nightmare landscape of empty fields turned into islands by their drainage system. Logic insisted there must be a way to pass dry-shod between them, for tractors and the like; but perhaps it was never necessary for tractors to pass directly from *these* fields to *this* farm. Once they'd found a proper bridge; twice they'd found a plank serving as a footbridge; otherwise it had been a matter of sliding into the drain, wading across and—suddenly twice the weight—labouring up the far side.

But they'd made it. The farm buildings stretched across her sight like a hamlet. Even today, even allowing for mechanization, such an enterprise must employ ten, fifteen men. Too many for even a professional killer to confront. Of course, some of them would be out in the fields. Not the fields they'd come through: others, behind the house…

Even after her gaze had taken in the reality, her mind was still trying to supply a less upsetting alternative. With a range of buildings this extensive there'd always be broken windows. Indeed, some of these outhouses would benefit more from ventilation than protection: probably they'd never bothered to replace the glass. It would be different at the house. There would be curtains at the windows, and maybe roses round the door, and when they knocked a fat little farmer's wife would exclaim in horror at their appearance and then usher them inside…

'There's nobody here,' she said in a tiny voice. 'Is there? It's abandoned. Even the farmers couldn't live out here.' Slowly as a tree falling she sank on to her knees, and buried her face in her hands, and cried as if the world had come to an end.

'It's not as bad as that,' insisted Donovan, though there was a secret bit of him that would quite have liked to cry as well. 'It's shelter. They'll have left things behind—maybe some blankets, maybe we can get dry. Maybe there'll be a stove I can get going. And there'll be a road. Even if it's overgrown now, it'll be a damn sight easier than the way we came. Come on, Maddie, let's get inside. You'll feel better once you're out of the wind.'

But her spirit was entirely broken; she couldn't go another step. She'd lost her shoes in one of the drains—for all he knew, in the first of them. She'd been walking barefoot for over an hour through stony cornfields and tussocky pasture, and under the all-concealing mud her feet were bruised and bloody. She waved a limp hand vaguely. 'Go on,' she gulped. 'I'll stay here. Get help. I'll be here.'

But he couldn't leave her in the open for maybe another hour. 'It's all right,' he said softly. 'I'll look after you.' Bending, he put her arm around his neck; then he put one hand behind her back and the other under her knees, and somehow straightened his weary back, lifting her off the ground like an exhausted child. She buried her face in his shoulder, and he carried her through the empty yards and under the gaze of the broken windows until he found the back door into the farmhouse. Without dropping his burden he kicked it open and carried her inside.

TWO

MORE BAD NEWS waited at Queen's Street. Philip Kendall had come armed with his solicitor—and as a wealthy man he had an expensive solicitor. And the helicopter Superintendent Hilton had asked Division for was grounded with technical problems.

'Damn and blast!' swore Liz. 'What kind of technical problems?'

Hilton stared at her. 'Does it matter? It won't fly. That means that as a search tool it's rather less use than a bicycle.'

'And there's still no word of them?'

'No. But nobody's seen a man in a navy hatchback carving notches in his pistol either.' It wasn't that he thought it a suitable subject for levity, more that he'd learned there was nothing more pointless than tearing his hair out over things he couldn't alter. A bit of bleak humour was sometimes the only sane response to things going wrong. 'What did Mr Shapiro have to say?'

'He's writing his statement. One thing he said which I hadn't thought of: if Dodgson has lost them in The Levels he may come back here to wait for them. I'll rig some screens in the yard when we know they're on the way in—not before, or he'll find some other place for an ambush.'

Hilton's small, hard eyes widened. 'He thinks Dodgson could be here—now—at a window overlooking this police station?' He thought about it, vented a silent whistle. 'He's right, isn't he? Why didn't you think of that, Inspector?'

Liz was beginning to read this man and knew it wasn't a genuine criticism. 'Deferring to rank, sir. I knew you'd want to think of it first.'

The superintendent swallowed a smile. 'Have a discreet word with the neighbours, see if anybody's seen anything. Be very careful: the last thing you want to do is walk in on this man oiling his rifle. I'll get back to Kendall. I hoped you might bring me something to use against him. Never mind, perhaps a bit of all-purpose harassment will do instead.' He headed downstairs to Interview Room 1.

If he'd been a local man he'd have recognized the significance of Kendall calling Mr Browne of the solicitors Carfax & Browne. Mr Carfax didn't do police work any more, though he would stretch a point for a business client who found himself temporarily embarrassed by a breathalyser. Ms Holloway was fast building a reputation for defending the indefensible, but she wasn't yet perceived as a heavyweight. Shapiro would have recognized instantly that Donald Browne was the solicitor of choice for the man who had everything except a criminal record and meant to keep it that way.

He began by trying to take control of the interview: not aggressively, just laying out some ground rules that subtly suggested the ground was his. 'Mr Kendall is happy to answer any questions which might help you get to the bottom of this unfortunate affair. But he wants to make clear that he was not part of any conspiracy, either before or after the fact. If the young woman was indeed killed by someone at the sales conference, then plainly he was there at Mr Kendall's invitation. But that is the extent of his involvement and responsibility. He doesn't know which of his clients might be the man you're looking for. If he had any suspicions he'd tell you.

'It appears that someone used him in this matter, and if you have any questions that might help to identify that person Mr Kendall will be pleased to answer them. He considered these people friends: he'd like to know which of them thought he'd make a good scapegoat.' Mr Browne sat back with the smug air of a man who's covered all the angles, lacing thick fingers across an impressive expanse of waist-coat.

Despite his lack of equivalent girth, in his own circles Superintendent Hilton was considered a heavyweight too. He nodded, his thin face expressionless. 'We'll be glad of all the help we can get, and at the moment Mr Kendall seems likely to have more information than anyone else we can talk to. Though that may change in the near future.' Not exactly a threat; perhaps a little more than a warning.

'The attack on the girl,' he went on, 'took place in the room registered to Mrs Atwood at a time when Mrs Atwood was having supper with you, Mr Kendall. Do you recall whose idea that was?'

Kendall had already told them. It was an invitation to lie which he respectfully declined. 'Mine. We're old friends, we hadn't seen one another for a while; we'd spent all week-end trying to get five minutes together and I thought it would be nice to have a quiet meal before she went home.'

'So you asked her out to supper.'

'Yes.'

'There's something wrong with the Barbican's catering?'

'Of course not. But it wouldn't have been a quiet meal with the rest of the delegates tucking in all around us.'

'Where did you take her?'

'The Hereward Inn, on the Cambridge Road.'

'A long way out on the Cambridge Road,' said Hilton, who'd done his homework. 'Actually, closer to Cambridge. Was there a reason for that?'

Kendall didn't quite have the composure to shrug. 'I like the place. They do a nice meal.'

'And going that far meant you'd have her company for an extra hour or more.'

'I suppose so. That wasn't why I chose it.'

'No? You wanted to see her quietly, but not for too long?'

The faintest dew of a sweat broke on Philip Kendall's upper lip. 'I mean, I wanted to have supper with her. I wasn't watching the clock.'

'Really? So if Mrs Atwood got the impression that you were, she was mistaken?' It was a question, not an allegation: Grace Atwood had said no such thing.

'Yes. She was.'

'What time did you leave The Barbican, and what time did you get back?'

Kendall made a show of thinking. 'We left about a quarter to nine, I think. And got back maybe about half eleven.'

'And you were unaware that by keeping her away from the hotel for nearly three hours you were making it possible for a man to entertain two prostitutes in her room, kill one of them and clean up afterwards.'

'Yes. Of course.' No further elaboration. He thought he had to keep to the point to avoid trapping himself.

'Who else knew you were going out for supper?'

'I don't know.' Kendall relaxed visibly; this was safer ground. 'I suppose almost anyone in the bar could have overheard us.'

'And would anyone in the bar have known where you were going, and therefore how long you were likely to be?'

'I don't remember. I may have told Mrs Atwood about The Hereward at that point, I may not.' So he hadn't, he just didn't want to have to say so.

'But only someone who knew you were going more than halfway to Cambridge could have been sure of having Mrs Atwood's room for long enough for a party. The hotel bar is probably the only place he could have heard it.'

'Then I suppose I must have done. I honestly don't remember.' It was one of Shapiro's Laws of Successful Detecting always to suspect someone who uses the word Honest, but Superintendent Hilton had noticed the paradox too.

'Neither does Mrs Atwood.'

Mr Browne knew that if he did nothing else useful today he could earn his fee by filling that gap in the conversation before his client felt obliged to. 'Mr Kendall has said quite clearly that he doesn't remember if he referred to the restaurant or not. If Mrs Atwood doesn't remember either, it seems likely that he did do and that's where he was over-heard.'

Hilton nodded slowly. No one could have looked less convinced. He changed tack abruptly. 'Your delegates were largely from overseas.'

Again the fractional relaxation as the ground under Kendall seemed to firm. 'Most of them.'

'So, on the balance of probabilities, we should be looking for a foreigner?'

Mr Browne again. 'You're asking Mr Kendall to speculate on something he cannot possibly know. It may be reasonable for you to make a working assumption to that effect, but you can't expect him to confirm it. He's still having difficulty believing that *any* of his clients are capable of all this.'

'Yet it seems one of them was; and it seems likeliest it was one of the foreign delegates. We've compiled a shortlist of those men who were in the hotel on Sunday who have a history of violence. Of course, Mr Kendall would not have had access to this information when he was issuing his invitations.'

'That's right,' said Kendall, marginally too quickly.

'What puzzles me,' said Hilton thoughtfully, 'is how someone who only arrived in Castlemere on Friday, probably from abroad, who spent most of the weekend discussing your products in The Barbican Hotel, could know enough about the surrounding area to recognize from a chance remark overheard in a bar that The Hereward Inn was far enough away for him to use Mrs Atwood's room for his activities.'

He didn't dwell on that, just left it to fester. 'Tell me,' he went on, 'do you remember who was in the general neighbourhood when you asked Mrs Atwood to supper? Close enough to overhear, I mean.'

This gave Philip Kendall a problem. If he said he didn't remember, the policeman would raise one of those narrow eyebrows in disbelief that he had been so wrapped up in

Grace Atwood's company that he didn't notice anything that was happening around them. These were his clients, men he was hoping to make money out of, it was inconceivable that he would ignore them at the final get-together. They must have been talking together, however inconsequentially. So he had to remember.

But if he failed to name the man they were looking for, and subsequently they identified him—even if they couldn't catch him—they would take that as proof that Kendall was involved in a cover-up. On the other hand, if he named the killer and the killer learned of it, the man who was currently hunting down the escaped hooker could very quickly be diverted to another task.

All this passed through Kendall's mind in just a few seconds. The solution came as quickly. 'There was a lot of circulating, I couldn't vouch for who was standing where at what point. But I do remember exchanging a word or two with…' He reeled off all the names he could remember of men who were definitely still in the hotel on Sunday evening. In a list of maybe thirty the one they sought could be of no significance.

Hilton wrote them down, slowing Kendall as he got ahead. When he'd finished he made no immediate response but turned back the pages of his pocket-book to where Kendall could glimpse another, shorter list. The superintendent gave a little hum that, to the nervous ear, sounded distinctly satisfied.

He went through Kendall's list, underlining five names. Five is a much smaller number than thirty; much more personal. 'What can you tell me about Eduardo da Costa?'

It was too late for Kendall to start picking and choosing who he'd talk about. 'He's in arms procurement at the Brazilian defence ministry. His wife's an artist.'

'He was a soldier?'

'Made colonel, I believe. Before I knew him.'

Hilton breathed heavily. 'Talk to me, Mr Kendall. What

kind of a man is he? The sort who might enjoy hurting people?'

After a moment Kendall nodded. 'Maybe. He's supposed to have been a bastard to his own men, and worse than that to dissident civilians.' He smiled. 'Though he may have started the rumour himself. Being known as a ruthless bastard is what got him where he is today.'

Hilton didn't comment. 'Kim Il Muk?'

'Runs a petroleum refinery in Pusan. I don't know anything about his home life.'

'What about this business in Paris?'

Kendall grinned. 'Yes, I know about that. Look, the man made a fool of himself over a woman in a foreign city. It happens.'

'You don't think he was trying to rape her?'

'I doubt he's the type. Mind you, they're inscrutable, these Orientals.'

'Nicu Sibiu?'

'Youngest of four brothers running the family munitions business. You know how things were in Romania: imagine you were responsible for defending an arsenal. I know he talks tough, I imagine he *is* tough, that he had to be.'

'He killed someone.'

'You find that surprising? If rioters had taken over the factory the death toll would have rocketed. Was he prosecuted?'

Hilton shook his head. 'Either the authorities called it justifiable homicide, or they weren't willing to take on the wealth of the Sibiu clan when the boy had at least an arguable defence. Do you know if he's married?'

'He's single. I believe he's considered a great catch in Bucharest.'

'What about Ian Selkirk?'

'His father emigrated from Scotland soon after the war. He was a fisherman, so that's what he did in Mexico—ended up with a small fleet and a cannery in Yucatán. Ian was here shopping for a new automated plant for the cannery.'

'And the drugs connection?'

For a moment Kendall considered denying all knowledge. Then he shrugged. 'I've heard the stories, I don't know if they're true.'

'The FBI think they are. They think the Selkirk fleet runs drugs into the United States. An undercover agent was murdered.'

'By Ian?'

'They consider that a distinct possibility.'

Kendall shook his head in wonder. 'I'd no idea.'

'How about the Saudi? Ibn al Siddiq.' He had to read that from his list. 'Is he a real prince?'

'Yes; though there are a lot of real princes in Saudi Arabia, he's only a distant relative of the present king.'

'What does he do for a living? Does he do anything for a living?'

'He owns oil wells.'

'Wasn't he in the services during the Gulf War?'

'He was a pilot in the Saudi air force. Did he kill people?—I expect he did, I think that was the whole idea. If you'd had Iraqi tanks heading for your borders you might have done too.'

'There was an incident in London two years ago. Are you aware of that?'

Kendall frowned. 'The business with the African maid. It was most unfortunate; Prince Ibn was deeply embarrassed. Though in fact it was his wife who was responsible.'

'Tell me what you understand of the episode.'

'The girl was travelling with the family as a lady's maid. She was admitted to hospital with burns on her back caused by an electric iron. The younger of Siddiq's wives had found creases in her best frock.'

'So she burned the girl with an iron?' Incredulity was like a bad taste in Superintendent Hilton's mouth.

'She was sent home in disgrace,' Kendall said. 'Siddiq was as horrified as you and me. He tried to make amends: looked after the girl's expenses in this country and provided generous compensation to see her back safely to her own. He did all he could to remedy the situation.'

'I see.' Hilton made a note. 'Is there anything more you can tell me about any of them?'

'I can tell you,' said Kendall, measuring his words, 'that they're all good customers. That those in the market for armaments are acceptable to our government as end-users. They pay their bills, and don't expect backhanders. What else should I know? They're not personal friends, I can't vouch for what they do on their nights off. If you tell me one of them committed this crime I'll be shocked but I won't argue, I don't know them that well. The only genuine friend I had at the conference was Mrs Atwood, and she and I were having supper when the murder was committed. I can tell you she wasn't involved. Beyond that I can't tell you anything for sure.'

'And the fact that Detective Superintendent Shapiro was shot while responding to a call from you is—what, coincidence?'

'I shouldn't imagine it was anything of the kind,' said Kendall tersely. 'I imagine it happened exactly as planned. The man terrorized me in my own house in the confident expectation that I'd call the police, that the town's senior detective would want to see where the shots were fired, and that as he came up those steps he'd be a sitting duck. That may make me stupid—it's certainly how I feel right now. But it doesn't make me involved, Superintendent. He used me, I didn't help him.'

'Him? Who?'

Kendall spread a hand. 'Whoever we're talking about. The Mexican, the Korean, the Arab—whoever the others were.'

'Oh no, Mr Kendall, you misunderstand.' Hilton did that cold smile of his. 'I don't think the man who killed the girl shot Mr Shapiro. He was perfectly capable of beating a young girl and throwing her off a roof, but he wouldn't take on a senior police officer. I think when he realized Mr Shapiro was on his trail he hired a professional to stop him. The miracle of modern communications, eh, Mr Kendall?— pick up the phone, transfer money to a Swiss bank account, and within a few hours someone who was threatening your peace of mind isn't any longer. No exchanging of bulging envelopes on park benches—nothing to photograph, no one to follow. All pretty untraceable. You can imagine how hard that makes our job.'

He paused just long enough for Kendall to think he'd finished and begin to relax. Then abruptly he went on. 'Fortunately, we have technology on our side too. Pretty soon I'll be able to tell you which of your guests is a murderer. Samples taken from Mrs Atwood's room are being compared with those from rooms occupied by those five men. I think we'll find a match, and then we'll have him.

'Well, we may not have him exactly. If he's any sense he'll have skipped the country by now.' Hilton's tone hardened. 'After all, that's why you bought him that bit of time—that, and to cover your own involvement. You got Mrs Atwood out of the way so he could use her room, and when you learned what he'd used it for you may have been appalled but you didn't pick up the phone and tell us. You helped him to make his escape.'

He leaned back in his chair, regarding Kendall speculatively. 'Did you try to find the other girl too?—to buy her silence or ensure it some other way? But she was already gone. She hadn't told the police either or we'd have been swarming all over the hotel when you got back from your supper, so maybe she just panicked and fled. Maybe she'd keep her head down and never be heard of again. Every hour that passed left you a little more confident.

'But not for long. Fourteen hours after the murder Mr Shapiro had established where it occurred, and you were having to answer questions that put you perilously close to naming the man you'd gone out on a limb to protect. So you warned him, and he sent a mechanic—a professional, Mr Kendall, a hit man, an assassin—to deal with it. Maybe you weren't expecting that. Maybe you hadn't thought he'd want your help to shoot Mr Shapiro. But it was already too late to refuse.

'After that you were committed. You'd do anything he asked, because your safety depended on it. When Detective Inspector Graham, in a worthy if unwise attempt to set your mind at rest, told you the missing girl had been in touch and how, when and by whom she was being brought back to Castlemere, you passed the information on.

'But you see, technology's going to help us there too. Every call made on that phone is logged. When we find a number on the list that is suddenly, unaccountably unobtainable, and the call was made at a time only you, your wife and my officers were in the house, you're going to find yourself in severe difficulties.

'For a cannery contract, was it?—or some oil industry equipment? By God, Mr Kendall, I hope you're on commission. It wouldn't be worth it otherwise.'

Mr Browne fielded that too. His jowly face was ideally suited to convey outraged disapproval. 'Superintendent, you really mustn't throw blanket accusations at Mr Kendall without any evidence to support them. I realize this is a difficult time for you, which is why my client's trying to help. But he won't *keep* trying to help if you're going to accuse him of everything that's happened in this town in the last week.

'If you want to treat him as a suspect, that's your prerogative. But I'll then have to advise him that he's already given all the information that can reasonably be expected of him and he should say nothing more unless at some point you have some evidence against him. I'd be reluctant to do that, Superintendent, but if there is now a possibility, however remote, of Mr Kendall facing charges it's my duty to protect his interests rather than assist with yours. Perhaps you'd like to consider that before we go much further.'

Hilton looked at him for a long moment before replying. 'No need, Mr Browne. I believe we've achieved all we can, for the moment. I'm ending this interview at'—he glanced at his watch—'one twenty-two p.m. Mr Kendall is free to go.' He turned off the tape.

Kendall went on sitting, eyes flicking between the man at his side and the man across the table as if he wasn't sure who'd won. 'That's it?'

Hilton shook his head. 'No, Mr Kendall, that's not it. I have a dead girl in the morgue, an injured colleague in the hospital, and a scared girl and another police officer missing in the fens somewhere. It won't be, as you say, *it* until someone is made amenable for these crimes. But don't worry, it doesn't have to be today. I'm not going anywhere. Neither are you.'

THREE

THE FARMHOUSE had been abandoned for a decade. Fewer people working more land with bigger machines made it economic to combine into larger units farms which had once supported several families, with the consequence that some of the dwellings became surplus to requirements. This was an old one, and it had been vacated in favour of something smaller, newer and less remote. But whoever built it, two hundred years earlier, had known it would have to withstand savage Fenland gales with a minimum of cosseting, and ten years of them had hardly been enough to dislodge a slate or penetrate the rendering on a wall. The broken windows were more vandalism than wear: essentially the house was still weather-proof. There was no warmth inside, but there was shelter.

Abandoned houses are never entirely emptied. There are always bits and pieces that nobody wants enough to come back for. The kitchen range had been removed, because it was worth serious money, but a little pot-bellied stove in the scullery had been left. There were a couple of wooden chairs in the kitchen; and scavenging upstairs Donovan found two pairs of enormous red plush curtains, musty but not mildewed, neatly folded into a cupboard.

He hauled them into the scullery and, using anything dry that came to hand, got the stove burning. He wrapped one of the curtains round Maddie and sat her in a chair where the warmth would reach her. 'When you feel up to it,' he said, 'get out of those clothes and give them a chance to dry.'

Outside in the yard he found a trough served by a big rainwater butt. The water wasn't exactly clean, but it was cleaner than what had been in the drains. He stripped off and rinsed his body and his clothes. He was going to have to find help, his best chance was stopping a car on the road, but *he* wouldn't have picked up someone looking like he looked when they got here. If he was reasonably clean, hopefully no one would notice he was wet until after they stopped.

When he'd struggled back into his damp clothes he returned to the scullery. It was a small room, already the little stove had made inroads into the chill.

Maddie was huddled up in her curtain, but she'd done as he suggested and draped her clothes around the stove. If anything, the smell of the mud drying was worse than when it was wet.

Donovan stood as close to the stove as he could without stealing her heat, felt the glow begin to percolate through to his flesh. Given half an excuse he'd have spent an hour here, thawing out and resting. But time mattered. Even if Donovan couldn't see how Dodgson could have followed them here, given enough time he would find them again. It was impossible to say how long they'd got, only that the longer they waited the likelier it was they'd regret it.

'Maddie,' he said quietly, 'I have to leave here now. We need help, and no one knows where we are. I have to get to a phone.'

Maddie's voice was an exhausted little plaint. 'You have a phone. Ah—' She remembered. It had been in her hand when they drove round the corner into the sights of an RPG. She had no idea what happened to it after that, but she hadn't hung on to it and she didn't know when Donovan could have gone back for it. Either it was in the burnt-out car or at the bottom of the ditch. 'I can't...'

Donovan shook his head, spraying droplets of water like a labrador. 'I know. You stay here. I'll get back as soon as I can, but it could be another hour or so. Will you be all right?'

She thought, hunched herself deeper into her curtain. 'Don't go.'

'I have to. I have to let my boss know what's happened. Then she'll send us some transport. Maddie, if we wait to be found it could be days, and it may not be my people who find us.'

She was terrified of being left alone. 'What if he comes before you do?'

'He won't,' said Donovan, with all the confidence he could muster. 'There hasn't been time for him to track us down. The Levels is all like this, isolated farms at the end of long tracks. He doesn't know which way we went—Jesus, *I* don't know which way we went!—so he has to go up every one. There's time enough if I go now. I may not be that long. I might meet a car, or somebody ploughing a field, in the first mile. I could be back here in half an hour. You'll be all right for half an hour, won't you?'

She didn't think she would. For some reason, and it couldn't be his success in keeping her out of trouble, she had confidence in this long streak of black Irishness. He'd said he'd stick by her, whatever the cost, and though Maddie had heard the words before she'd never heard them from someone who obviously, genuinely meant them. She knew that all his earnest commitment—all right, to his job, but this time that meant to her too—wasn't enough to guarantee her safety. But she'd spent a lot of her life at the lower end of people's priorities and it felt good to be on top for a change.

She didn't deceive herself that it was personal regard that put her there. He was taking care of her to the best of his ability because he'd taken the shilling and was too proud to say that any of the ways of earning it were too difficult. That didn't lower him in her estimation. Anybody could be great in bed with someone they fancied the socks off: the mark of a professional was to do their level best for someone when it was just a job. It *was* something to be proud of. The labourer was worthy of his hire.

Of course, the same thing applied to the man hunting them. Hunting her, rather—Donovan was incidental, only at risk as long as he was with her. Another professional, another hireling. He'd taken the money and he'd finish the job if there was any way at all. He didn't hate her, any more than Donovan cared for her or she loved the men she bedded. But it was a contract, you had to give value for money. You didn't just go through the motions. You did your best, even when you wished heartily to be anywhere but here. She wouldn't put her clothes back on and run because the man turned out to be more Proteus than Adonis. Donovan couldn't cut and run because circumstances had turned him from a taxi-driver into an unarmed bodyguard. And the man out there couldn't call it a day simply because it had got messy and taken too much time and on reflection it seemed a pretty sordid way to make a crust, hunting a woman to exhaustion and then snuffing her out.

Donovan was right: he would keep coming. If they waited he would find them. She didn't look up, didn't want him to see how afraid she was. 'Yes,' she mumbled. 'Yes, of course I will. I'll just stay here by the stove.'

He didn't need to see her eyes. He knew she was terrified. She had every reason to be. When he left here he'd be reasonably safe, but she wouldn't be safe until she was at Queen's Street. If then. A top mechanic had been paid to end her life. He'd already tried; only luck had saved her. If Donovan was wrong and Dodgson had already picked up the trail, he'd get back here to find her dead. It really didn't alter anything. If he didn't go, Dodgson would find them for sure.

Donovan didn't kid himself that his presence in the house at that moment would make more than a fleeting difference. Armed, he would have been no match for a professional gunman; unarmed, all he could do was offer an additional target. He'd have done that if need be, but not with any hope that his death would do more than delay the inevitable by a few moments. It was almost the hardest thing about what he had to do next: that he would be leaving the worst of the danger behind.

He crouched down so that his face was level with hers and he smiled. Donovan's smile could surprise people who had known him for quite some time, partly because he didn't do it often and partly because it was a gentler, more tender thing than anyone who knew his fierce, feral grin ever expected. His grin made those of a nervous disposition hide behind the furniture, but his smile was like a secret gateway to an altogether sweeter place in his soul. What surprised people was that such a place existed.

'You're doing great,' he said. 'And I'll be back before you miss me.' Then he left.

Realistically, he didn't expect to see another living soul for half an hour. Even then he could still be some way from the nearest phone. At least he didn't have to decide which way to go. Unless he was prepared to return to the fen, there was only one way. He set off at a walk, his long stride lending speed to the apparently easy pace. He did a lot of walking at home, it took nothing out of him. Even after the morning he'd had, after a few minutes he had energy to spare for an economical jog.

Drainage for cultivation had shrunk the fields on either side so that the track stood two metres above the rest of the landscape. Donovan felt desperately conspicuous, had to keep reminding himself that was probably a good thing. Of all the people who might spot him from a mile away and wonder who the hell he was and what he was doing there, only one was bad news. An irate farmer loaded for bear was just what he needed right now.

But if anyone saw him they did nothing about it. He walked and jogged for ten minutes, and then the track joined a metalled laneway. There were no signs: he might as well have flipped a coin as try to work out which way would serve him best. He turned right simply because walking into the spring sunshine was pleasanter than walking away from it.

Finally a hard-of-hearing God responded to his not-very-practised prayers and sent a car.

Over the flat landscape he saw it even before he heard it. He could make out no detail except the one he absolutely had to be sure of: that it wasn't navy blue. In fact it was cream, a big load-carrying estate capable of accommodating a large family, several sacks of grain and a sick sheep. Donovan breathed a sigh of relief. If they were all out together, the sheep could take its chances while he got Maddie to safety.

As the car drew closer he stepped into the middle of the road, flagging it down. He had just time to wonder what sort of a figure he cut, and whether an elderly man or a woman driving alone would not have every excuse to speed past him, or indeed over him, and then it started to brake.

The driver was a middle-aged man in a cloth cap and shirt sleeves. He wound down the window as he stopped. 'Got a problem?'

Donovan nodded wearily, resting his arm on the roof. 'You could say that. Listen, I'm a police officer. Do you have a phone?'

'Hang on.' The man reached under the dashboard.

But it wasn't a phone he came up with, it was a gun. Donovan never even saw it. The noise and the impact hit him simultaneously, at point-blank range, flinging him off the car. He hit the road, rolled once and came to rest face-down in the dirt with his long arms flung out as if his last conscious thought had been the fear of falling.

FOUR

AT ONE O'CLOCK there was still no word of the helicopter. Peterborough had started a foot-search of Bedford Levels, radiating out from where the car was found, and Division had contributed a pair of tracker dogs.

'Dogs?' exclaimed Liz. 'What use are dogs going to be? The one thing everyone knows about tracker dogs is that you can lose them by crossing water. The one thing we know about where Donovan and Maddie Cotterick have gone is they must have crossed water, several times.'

Hilton understood her frustration, but he could offer her no more than Division had offered him.

Frank Shapiro phoned from the hospital and asked Liz to collect his statement. She'd meant to send a PC, but in fact there was nothing to keep her at Queen's Street. She felt rushed off her feet with all that was happening, but it was that particular kind of rushed-off-her-feet that involved a lot of staring at the wall, hollow-eyed, imagining the worst. She had the screens ready for use; she'd visited the surrounding houses and none of the residents reckoned to have an assassin in the attic. There wasn't much more she could do for now. Getting out of the office for twenty minutes would help pass the time.

He was waiting for her, waiting for news. 'Have they turned up yet?'

Liz shook her head. 'It may not mean much. It's only this last half hour they've had people out there looking. If it'd been our end of The Levels, Giles would have had everyone including his arthritic mother tramping the fen within twenty minutes of the car being found.'

'Mm,' said Shapiro thoughtfully. 'Next time Donovan

wrecks my car he'll have to be more careful where he does it.'

Liz smiled dutifully, but actually neither of them felt much like joking. They weren't used to being sidelined. Quite possibly the outcome would have been the same if they'd been running the search, but at least they'd have known they were doing all that could be done.

'So. You got your statement written up?'

'Yes.' There was a portable typewriter sitting on his bed-side cabinet with an envelope beside it. But he didn't immediately offer it to her. 'You reckon Kendall's the key to this?'

Liz nodded. 'I think so; and Hilton's sure. But he can't pin him down. Which wouldn't matter if we had the time to play games with him.'

'And if he could pin him down?'

'If we can prove Kendall was part of it, I think he'll give it up. Make a full-and-frank. He didn't kill anyone; if he never anticipated that anyone could get killed he'll want to get out from under that. I think he'll tell us everything.'

'And if he doesn't?'

'In time we'll get at the truth. We'll match DNA from Mrs Atwood's room with a sample from one of the men's rooms, and we'll know. But it'll be too late to catch him. It's probably too late now.'

'And the witness? Donovan?'

Liz frowned. She wasn't sure quite what this conversation was about. 'Surely to God they'll have found a phone by then!'

'What if he's still out there? What if I was wrong and he never thought of coming back here to wait for them? Liz, what if he's still out there looking?'

'Then we have to find them first. He's on his own, re-member; and hell, we've got dogs!' But Shapiro was in no mood to respond to irony; she wasn't even sure he'd no-ticed. 'Frank, what is this? What's bothering you? I mean, apart from the obvious.'

He looked white and strained, somehow more than when he had been more ill. He looked troubled. He reached for the waste-paper basket. It was full of crumpled balls of half-typed paper.

She didn't understand. 'Couldn't you remember what happened?'

That wasn't it. 'I remember perfectly. I remember that Philip Kendall did and said nothing we can use against him.' He lifted hunted eyes from the bin to her face. 'I wanted to lie. All these scraps—they're different versions. Different lies.' He forced a shaky little laugh. 'Pretty convincing, some of them. You'd have believed them. Hilton would have charged him on the strength of them. Liz, I've been doing this job for more than thirty years, and I've never put my name to a lie before this.'

He'd quite knocked the wind out of her. She sat down on the edge of the bed. Her lips formed a question mark. 'Then—why?'

He answered carefully, one word at a time. 'Because I thought they needed me to. Because I thought of them out there, lost in that green desert, with a hired killer on their heels, and I thought their lives were worth more than my integrity.

'I didn't mean for Kendall to go to jail because of it,' he added quickly. It mattered to him that she know that. 'Once they were safe, or past help, I'd have admitted what I'd done. I'd have had to resign, which isn't the way I'd have chosen to end my career, but I was ready to do it. I thought the prize was worth the cost. I thought I could improve their chances, and I thought it was worth it.'

Liz looked at the envelope on the cabinet. She didn't know how to put this. She was—not shocked but taken aback—and at the same time her heart was swelling with compassion and sheer regard for the man. Whatever she said, she didn't want it to sound like criticism. 'And this one. Is the best version of all?'

Shapiro flicked her a brief smile for that. 'Yes, and no.

It's the truth. The honest, unadulterated, totally useless truth.
I couldn't do it.' He ran a distracted hand through his hair,
already tousled from the pillow. 'Liz, I had the chance to
help them. Maybe. Maybe not, but maybe I could have got
Dodgson called off. Maybe I could have saved their lives.
And I couldn't do it. God in heaven, Liz, when it came to
a choice between my word and the safety of two people, I
couldn't do it! If they die, it'll be my fault.'

She couldn't let him think that. He'd startled her, she'd
need a little time to know how she felt about what he'd
confided, but whether he'd been right to consider it or right
to dismiss it she knew he was wrong to feel responsible for
the consequences of his honesty. She leaned forward, her
eyes sparking with indignation.

'Don't you dare say that! It isn't true, not even slightly.
In the first place, we're going to find them before they come
to any harm. And in the second place, if by any chance
things go badly, it still won't be your fault for not lying. If
it's anybody's fault it's mine, for telling Kendall about Maddie. I'm hoping and praying that maybe it didn't make that
much difference, that even if I'd kept my mouth shut Dodgson would have found them somehow. I don't know if it's
true but I have to believe it. And you have to believe that
even if you'd sacrificed your career, it might have made no
difference except that Castlemere would have lost a Detective Superintendent it desperately needs.

'But even if it could have helped—even if we could get
past Kendall to whoever he's protecting and there was still
time to call off the mechanic—nobody who knows you, and
that includes Donovan, would expect you to do it. It's not
who you are, Frank. And those of us—like Donovan, like
me—who have most to be grateful to you for would be
sorriest to see you turn into a man for whom ends justify
means.'

'But Liz.' He was looking at her as if she might somehow
have missed the point. 'This is his *life* we're talking about.
The lives of both of them. I know, it's better that ten guilty

men go free than that one innocent man go to jail. But what about a guilty man who's willing to protect himself by killing other people? You really think it's still that clear-cut?'

Liz took a long breath to steady her voice, aware that what she said next was vitally important to both of them. 'In a general philosophical way?—no, I don't. I think it's open to debate. But it's not our job to debate it. We're paid to uphold the law, we're not entitled to hold that view. We have to do the best we can within the framework of the law, and recognize that sometimes it's not enough but that's not our fault. If we start to think we can step outside the law sometimes, when it really matters the whole business of law enforcement will fall apart. We won't be police officers any more, we'll be vigilantes.

'We don't have a choice, Frank. We can think about it, we can wish we had—there's nothing wrong with agonizing over the paradox, that basket of crumpled dreams is a testament to your humanity—but in the end we have to hold the line. Because if the time comes that even we think we can cross it with a good enough excuse, there'll be no line left.'

Shapiro's eyes were shut. His restless hand had fallen still across his mouth, except for the little caressing movements of the fingers. It was a racial thing. His father, his grandfather and all his forefathers had grown serious beards and stroked them like pets when they were thinking. Frank Shapiro didn't have a beard, but sometimes he stroked where it ought to be, like a man scratching an amputated foot. Finally he gave a tiny nod. 'You're right,' he said through his hand. 'Of course.'

Liz nodded at the bin. 'Frank, you don't need anyone to tell you what's right. You have the best instincts of anyone I've ever known. But you're like the rest of us: sometimes it's good to hear someone say it. One of the privileges of rank, I'm afraid, is that all the hardest decisions you have to take alone. OK, nobody ever tells you you're wrong, but they don't tell you you're right either, and everybody needs that sometimes.'

Shapiro vented a shaky sigh. 'You're a good friend, Liz. You've always been a good officer, but I've had more from you than that. I hope you know I'm grateful.'

She shrugged, pleased and embarrassed, her cheeks warm.

Shapiro gave his old businesslike sniff. 'Right. This isn't buttering any babies.' When it came to metaphors, he could mix them like a Kenwood Chef. He passed her the envelope. 'Hand this to Mr Hilton, with my apologies. Then I suggest you get on to Division again, and if they still can't get their helicopter in the air ask Mr Giles to hire you a spotter plan from the airfield here.'

Her eyes widened. She simply hadn't thought of that. She nodded crisply. 'We'll find them, Frank. We'll bring them back safely.'

'Of course you will.'

THE MAN WHO CALLED himself Dodgson made very few mistakes. He planned his work in meticulous detail and performed it with consummate skill. He was one of the top men in his field, and it was a source of pride to him that he'd never seen the inside of a police station.

He'd left the navy hatchback in the farmyard where he found the cream estate. When the owner returned from livestock sales in Northampton sometime this evening to find a strange vehicle in his yard and his wife locked in the dairy he would of course alert the police. By then, though, this job would be finished and Dodgson would be out of the country.

He'd recognized the policeman flagging him down in plenty of time to decide what to do about it. He toyed with the idea of picking him up—he didn't think DS Donovan had seen him clearly enough to recognize him in a different car and the hat that came with it—and letting him lead him to the girl. But it was a bit complicated, and simple plans work best. He knew the direction Donovan had come from, had passed only one lane he could have come down. The girl had to be up that lane. It would be quicker to go and look than to spend time trying to get the information out of the detective; and much safer to leave him in the ditch than to have him, desperate and plotting, in the seat beside him.

Donovan's death hadn't been bought in the way that Maddie Cotterick's had but Dodgson was a professional, had no compunction about removing obstacles. He owed it to his principles to get the job done quickly.

He'd shot a lot of men in his time. Sometimes they took longer to go down than you'd expect, but mostly once they were down they stayed that way. Even so Dodgson approached the body in the road with caution. He didn't think there was any fight left in it, but you couldn't be sure. He didn't think it had ever been armed, but you couldn't be sure of that either. He kept his handgun trained on Donovan's spine, the bones knobbly through the damp shirt, and prodded him with his foot. When there was no reaction he aimed a solider kick.

It was one of those rare mistakes. It left him momentarily off-balance, his attention on the moving foot rather than the steady hand; when the long shape he had thought little better than a corpse rolled abruptly under him he found himself unable to fire without shooting his own knee. By then Donovan had hold of his foot and, surging upwards with all the strength he could muster, threw the older man backwards on to the road. He landed with enough force to knock the air out of his lungs and the gun out of his hand. It skittered across the cracked tarmac.

Both men dived for it. Both believed that everything depended on getting there first. But Donovan was coming up while Dodgson was still falling, and his long-fingered hand clapped over the weapon with seconds to spare. He reared back, pointing the gun like an accusing finger in the other man's face.

They hadn't been this close before. Donovan had got only

an impression of a middle-aged man in a suit—he'd taken
off the jacket since they last met—tall, lean, athletically
built for a man who was no longer young. Now he had a
face to put with that. Quite narrow and chiselled, with high
cheekbones and deep-set, light grey eyes. Thin lips; grey
hair cut ruthlessly short. There were no handles on him,
Donovan realized: nothing to grab hold of, either actually
or descriptively. A man who could pass through a customs
hall lined with his portrait and never be stopped. Even
sprawling in the road he managed to look as respectable and
indignant as any businessman tricked by a ruffian. If the
area car from Peterborough had come back this way, the
driver would have tried to arrest Donovan rather than the
hired killer.

He ground breathlessly, 'You're nicked.'

The man in the road regarded him with calm, faintly
mocking disdain. 'Don't be absurd.' Donovan was no good
at English accents, except that he knew an expensive one
when he heard it. It always made his hackles rise, even when
the speaker wasn't trying to kill him.

If he hadn't been so tired he'd have snapped back with a
smart retort of his own. So it might have taken him longer
to appreciate his dilemma, which Dodgson had already identified. They couldn't sit here all day, face to face with the
gun between them, waiting to be discovered. But the moment they moved the potential existed for Dodgson to turn
the tables. Donovan had no illusions about his own abilities:
against a professional mechanic he was way out of his
depth, merest luck had preserved him long enough to see
the ghost of a chance and take it. But alone and far from
home, how long could he hope to keep a man like this under
control? He didn't even have a set of handcuffs.

Just the gun. He could shoot the man dead. Nobody'd
blame him, even if he admitted that at the moment it happened he was in command of the situation. That could
change in the blink of an eye. He'd seen what Dodgson was
capable of. And it wasn't just his own life at stake, it was

Maddie's, a girl he'd been sent to protect, a girl who had witnessed a murder. Her safety was still his first priority, but she couldn't be considered safe while Dodgson could regain the upper hand at any moment.

'Listen to me,' said the man in the road, the well modulated voice quiet and persuasive. 'I don't need you. You can walk away from this. I only need the woman.'

Donovan stared, astonished by the sheer effrontery of the man. As if this thing in his hand was a lump of inert metal, a piece of pig-iron or a length of lead pipe. It was a gun. It was supposed to be the deciding factor.

But only if he used it.

There were alternatives, there had to be. Donovan gave them some thought. He could shoot to disable. If he broke a major weight-bearing bone, say a femur, all the professionalism in the world wouldn't enable Dodgson either to pursue him further or to escape. But if he left the man by the roadside with a gunshot wound and a broken leg, the next person who came along would stop to help. He'd kill them with his bare hands, take their car and somehow find the sort of help that people with enough money and nothing to lose can find anywhere.

'She's a hooker,' said Dodgson softly. 'She isn't worth dying for. You did your best. Walk away while you can.'

Or he could use the gun as a truncheon. A passerby would still stop to tend an unconscious man, but was less likely to find him snapping their hyoid bone in the process of manual strangulation immediately afterwards. Hit a man over the head hard enough to lay him out for hours and you run the risk that he'll never wake up. But that troubled Donovan hardly at all. He couldn't justify the risk either of taking him along or of leaving him here with his wits intact, and though there was much to be said for a permanent solution, ultimately he ran up against what had stood between Shapiro and his helpful lie. It wasn't right. It was pragmatic, it was sensible, but it wasn't easy for a law-abiding man to end a life, even this life, in cold blood.

But he was tired, and scared, and angry: angry enough, with the day he'd had and the pain in his side, to hold the weapon rock-steady on Dodgson's left eye. He grated, 'Turn round. Slowly.'

Dodgson didn't move, stayed where he was on his knees with his hands spread wide. His voice was calm. 'You're not going to shoot me, Sergeant.'

Donovan blinked. But of course the man knew who he was: he'd followed him to Maddie. He still didn't know how, but that was the only way he could be here. 'Wanna bet?'

Dodgson smiled, but then he did what he was told. 'A small bet, perhaps; but not my life.' Still on his knees, he shuffled round to face the car.

Donovan knew things they didn't teach at police training college. He knew that a rising shot through the back of the skull was as sure an execution as the guillotine. He knew where to find the brachial plexus, and that severing the spinal chord above that point would paralyse the man from the neck down while severing it below would leave him the use of his hands. And he knew that he'd never have to justify what happened next.

He swung the gun in his hand with all the force of his fear and anger, and the man who called himself Dodgson cannoned sideways off the blow, spilled along the roadway and lay still. A slow trickle of blood wormed from his ear.

FIVE

DETECTIVE SUPERINTENDENT Hilton was reading Shapiro's statement for the third time, resigned to the fact that there was nothing in it that would help and never suspecting how different things could have been, when DI Colwyn burst into his office with the most cursory knock imaginable and a positive sunburst of expression on his round young face. 'We've got him, sir!'

Hilton's eyes widened, then narrowed. He didn't intend to be disappointed. 'Who, exactly? And got how?'

Colwyn nodded and got a grip on himself. 'The man who killed the girl. And no, we haven't got him, but if we can get hold of him we have enough to convict.'

The superintendent breathed lightly. 'You can put one of them in Mrs Atwood's room?'

Colwyn nodded. 'We have matching DNA samples from Mrs Atwood's room and one of the men's. Better than that: they both match semen taken from the girl's body. We can put the occupant of room 606 not only at the scene of the attack but actually having sex with the victim.'

He wanted to be asked. Impatiently, Hilton obliged. 'Well?'

'The Saudi,' said Colwyn, his eyes aglow with satisfaction. 'It was the oil prince from Dhahran. Ibn al Siddiq.'

Even without the witness of Maddie Cotterick, the forensic evidence now formed a physical chain tying Siddiq to the murdered girl that would put the matter beyond reasonable doubt with any jury in the land. In the unlikely event of it getting to court. The murderer was undoubtedly safe in his own country. But the man who facilitated both his crime and his escape was still in Castlemere, and a jury could be asked to judge his guilt.

'Get Kendall back in here. Then call Mrs Graham's mobile number. She'll want to know this.'

Colwyn reached for the phone. 'Where is she?'

Hilton scowled. 'On her way to the airfield. She seems to fancy herself as Amelia Earhart.'

ANOTHER SUMMONS to Queen's Street following so quickly on the first could only be bad news. Kendall and his solicitor both entered the building with trepidation. Kendall thought the days of his liberty might be numbered. Mr Browne saw his chances of making his 3.30 tee-off time on the wane.

So both were mentally prepared for the fencing to stop and for events to move forward. One look at Detective Superintendent Hilton's face as he came in and started the interview tape confirmed surer than words that something fundamental had changed.

His very first words put it beyond doubt. 'You contacted Prince Ibn al Siddiq on Monday to update him on our inquiry. He responded by sending a professional assassin to remove the senior investigating officer. Now I want you to contact him again and tell him we have proof of his guilt, and to call off his hit man since it can only make things worse for him and for you if anyone else dies.'

In all his years as a solicitor Mr Browne had never heard anything like it. Partly, of course, because he'd spent his career in Castlemere which got its fair share of crime but didn't see a lot of either princes or professional killers. But partly because police officers investigating major crimes didn't often commit themselves that comprehensively. There were always alternative scenarios, the possibility of error.

For a detective superintendent to say what this one just had, on the record, it had to be true.

He said smoothly, 'Superintendent, I wonder if I might have a word with—?'

Kendall didn't let him finish. From the mere fact that he'd begun that sentence he knew what his solicitor wanted to say. There was no point in delaying further; indeed, further delay could only do him harm. 'It's all right, Mr Browne; thank you, but I understand the position.'

He filled his lungs. 'You're right, I've been less than frank with you. I can cast some light on events at The Barbican at the weekend. I should have spoken up sooner. I was reluctant because Siddiq's been a good client of mine, even a friend, for ten years and I believed him when he said it was an accident. He said they were smoking crack, he got a bit overenthusiastic, and the girl panicked and fell. I thought we were talking misadventure, just maybe manslaughter; if I'd thought it was murder I wouldn't have helped him. Now you're telling me he had Mr Shapiro shot, and he wants Maddie dead too, and that alters everything—'

Hilton put a mobile phone on the table in front of him. 'Save the excuses for a more appropriate time. All I want right now is for you to call him.'

Kendall did. But when he got a reply the conversation did not go the way Hilton was expecting. In the first place it didn't seem to be Ibn al Siddiq he was speaking to. Then Kendall rang off before passing on his message.

Hilton frowned. 'Mr Kendall, now is not the time to get coy.'

Kendall shook his head urgently. 'You don't understand, Superintendent. I didn't think you'd want me to say anything. He isn't at home; he isn't on his way home. He's at a Thoroughbred stud about twenty minutes' drive from here. If you want to arrest him you can.'

THE CREAM ESTATE was too damn big and too damn heavy for manoeuvring in narrow lanes. Donovan nearly lost it a couple of times, expecting to turn it with a spin of the wheel and finding himself still heading for a gate-post. But he didn't dare slow down. He wanted Maddie safe in the seat beside him and the still prone body of the man who called himself Dodgson falling behind at a rate of a mile a minute. Then he could afford to relax. He knew he was tired. He needed to get her to safety before exhaustion set in.

He didn't stop the engine, just abandoned the vehicle in the middle of the yard. He heeled his hand down on the horn as he got out. 'Maddie! It's me—Donovan. I've got us some transport. Let's get the hell out of here.' He leaned against the car for a moment, hoping she'd appear and he wouldn't have to go and fetch her.

The farmhouse door creaked open and she stood there, uncertain, barefoot and swathed in red plush. She looked at the car, then at Donovan. Her pale lips parted. 'You're bleeding.'

He shook his head. 'It's nothing. A flesh wound. Looks worse than it is.'

But she was staring at him with unreassured horror. 'Donovan, you're bleeding a river!'

Finally he looked down.

The round had punched through his side, glancing off his bottom rib and carving a bloody trench you could have laid your finger on before hurtling on to oblivion in the fen. It was a fiery stitch in his side, it hurt when he moved, but there were no vital organs there and apart from the shock he thought he'd got off lightly enough. But she was right, he was bleeding like a stuck pig. The estate wasn't that big, the steering wasn't that heavy and the space wasn't that tight. All his strength was ebbing out along with his blood.

His knees buckled and he lurched against the vehicle,

sliding down the door until he was sitting in the dirt, his eyes stretched with shock.

Maddie gathered up her cloak and ran to him, shutting out the gritty stones under her raw feet. She knelt beside him, exploring his injury with shaky hands. 'Dear God, you met him, didn't you? He shot you!' She looked around in terror. 'Where is he?'

Donovan shook his head, in which strange gravity-defying forces were at work. 'I knocked him out. I may have killed him, I don't know. We have to get away from here.' His voice was frail and breathy.

'You can't drive like that!'

'You drive.'

'All right. Let me get some clothes on.'

'There's no time…'

'I can't drive wrapped up in a curtain!'

Toasting on the stove, her clothes were dry enough to pull on without difficulty; except for the white cotton slip and the remains of her tights, for which she had another purpose. She hurried back and bent over Donovan again. She eased his shirt carefully out of his belt to reveal the wound gouged in his side.

'We have to stop the bleeding or you're going to die.'

She wadded the bundled cotton hard into the wound, ignoring the hiss of breath in his teeth. She put his hand against it. 'Hold it there. Harder!' She pressed down on his slack fingers, making him do as she said. 'Now, lean on me.' She pulled him forward until his head was on her shoulder, then reached round him with the micromesh bandage. 'It may not be St John's standard,' she said with terse humour, 'but if it's tight enough it'll control the bleeding. Does it feel tight?'

'Oh yeah,' groaned Donovan, laid over her shoulder like an extremely large baby in need of burping.

'OK. Let's get you up.' She'd managed perhaps half an hour's rest since they got here. Five minutes ago she'd have said it wasn't enough, that they'd have to carry her out on a stretcher. But bodies are more resilient than their owners ever think and minds even more so. He needed her help, so somewhere she had to find the reserves to give it. The alternative was watching him bleed his life away; or worse, driving away and leaving him to do it alone. This had happened to him because of her, because of the lifestyle she'd chosen. Donovan may not have been the best bodyguard anyone ever had but he'd certainly tried hard. He'd fought for her, he'd bled for her. Maddie wasn't turning her back on another desperate human being as long as she lived.

She took his arm over her shoulder and straightened. Donovan's head swam, but he fought it and once he was on his feet, as long as she steadied him he could walk. She steered him round the car and reached past him to open the passenger door. He slumped on to the seat. Maddie lifted his long legs in as if he were an elderly arthritic aunt she was taking for a drive. Then she hurried round the bonnet and got in behind the wheel.

The roughness of the track hadn't bothered Donovan much when he jogged out this way. He hadn't been particularly aware of it driving back, had been fully occupied with what he'd then believed was the dreadful handling of the vehicle. Now every pothole sent pain thudding through his side. He gritted his teeth and told himself it would be better when they reached the better road; then abruptly the car turned and they were on the better road already. Somewhere he'd lost a couple of minutes.

He tugged weakly at Maddie's sleeve. 'Other way.'

She braked and looked anxiously at him. He was drifting in and out of the fog, she wasn't sure she should pay any heed to what he said now. 'Why?'

'I came this way,' he explained, as clearly as he could manage. 'I met Dodgson a quarter-mile further on. If he's feeling better by now, I don't want to meet him again.'

Maddie wasn't going to argue with that. She backed just far enough into the lane to turn the other way.

At least the pain in his side was easier now. But the light-headedness was growing worse. He wasn't unconscious in the sense of being unaware of his surroundings, he just couldn't keep his mind on them. It kept wandering off, without aim or purpose, sifting through what had already happened and was past repair with the idle curiosity of a window-shopper browsing along an arcade.

He tried to concentrate on what was happening now, on their immediate needs and the quickest way of meeting them. But he had no sense of direction left. If Maddie couldn't find her way out of the fen alone, then they would drive round it until either the car's tank or his veins ran dry, whichever came first. Lacking the strength to hold it, he let his mind ramble off again, to think whatever thoughts it chose and remember what it cared to.

He'd wrecked Shapiro's car. Well, that was bound to rankle: no wonder he kept going back over it. He'd thought he could lose his pursuer in The Levels, that he knew and the man behind him couldn't possibly, but still he was outman-ouevred in the end and it cost Shapiro his car. He mustn't have followed them into the fen at all. He must have sped back the way they'd come, back on to the main road and off again at the next junction. He'd guessed Donovan would come that way. He didn't need to know the precise layout of all the lanes, where they joined and where they led. He only needed to know where Donovan was heading, and to get there first.

Donovan's jaw dropped. He reached for Maddie's sleeve again. 'No, wait...'

If Dodgson was still lying unconscious in the road they could pass him without danger. If he was back in business he wouldn't still be sitting there, nursing his head in his hands. He'd have worked out what Donovan would do next and moved to intercept him. He only needed to know where they were heading and get there first...

Maddie glanced at him but didn't brake again. 'It's all right. We're going to be all right.'

She drove round a bend and found the lane full of sheep. 'What the—?' She braked then; of course she did, no one with a spark of decency in them accelerates into a press of living animals.

'Don't stop,' gasped Donovan. 'Drive on. Drive, damn you!'

She stared at him as if he was mad. 'I can't. I'll flatten them.' Perhaps then, in the split second that was left, she realized that he wasn't as far gone as that, that there was good reason for his insistence; she may even have caught a glimpse of it. But by then the cream estate car was stationary and surrounded by a flock of sheep escaped through the open gate on their right, and the man who called himself Dodgson was standing on the left-hand verge pointing a small silver gun through the near-side window.

He'd made another of those rare mistakes. Or perhaps that wasn't fair, because although he knew he'd shot Donovan the events that followed suggested that he hadn't inflicted much damage. He expected the policeman to be driving and the woman to be in the passenger seat. After loosing the sheep he'd positioned himself accordingly.

Almost more than the fear, Maddie was overwhelmed by disbelief. She hissed at Donovan, 'You left him the *gun?*'

Donovan shook his head the least amount necessary. 'No. It's in here somewhere...' His hand moved towards the back of the car, almost immediately stopped. If it had been in the glove compartment it would have done him no good. There wasn't time to use it, let alone find it. 'He had a spare.' His voice was flat, all out of hope.

Dodgson stepped forward carefully. Caution was, of course, his stock in trade, but this time he also had a ringing in his head to contend with. If Donovan had been in better shape it might have made him vulnerable, but then again it might not. It might have meant he'd shoot at the first sign of trouble because he wouldn't trust himself to see the second. 'Get out.'

With the gun a handspan from his ear Donovan didn't argue. It wasn't a very big gun, but it was big enough to punch a hole through the glass and into his head. Besides, there was nothing he could do in here. Out there he might come up with something, if it was only fainting at a judicious moment. He reached for the door catch.

Weakness, and yes, fear, made him clumsy. He fumbled it. Dodgson lost patience and snatched the door open with his left hand. Then he grabbed Donovan's collar and trailed him out on to the verge. He barked a little laugh when he saw the blood. 'I thought I was losing my touch!'

Donovan licked his lips. But he still couldn't think of a smart retort. 'Drive,' he murmured, not to Dodgson. 'Go. Now.'

It was a very small gun. It had to be, to be capable of concealment. Even in the hands of an expert it wouldn't be reliable over more than a few metres. If Maddie stamped on the accelerator, batting sheep out of her way as she went, and if Donovan could keep him occupied for just a second or two, Dodgson would certainly shoot at her, he might even hit her, but his chances of stopping her with that gun at increasing range would sink rapidly from poor to nil. And this was his last chance. If she had the courage to act now she could save herself.

But Donovan, and Dodgson himself, knew she wasn't going to do it when she let the moment go and looked at them instead.

Dodgson with a smooth motion took the gun off her and pushed its muzzle up under Donovan's jaw. 'You're right,' he said softly, answering the unspoken question, 'it isn't much of a gun. I could miss you. But I sure as hell can't miss him.'

'Go,' whispered Donovan. 'Maddie, *go*.'

'Hush,' said the gunman mildly, grinding the weapon into Donovan's throat. 'Miss Cotterick, listen to me. I won't kill you—I won't hurt either of you—if you give me back the car. Get out of the car. Then I'll go away and leave you alone.'

It didn't work like that. Donovan knew it didn't work like that. If he'd just needed transport he'd have helped himself to the first car that came along, he didn't need to go to these lengths to recover this one. He was still doing what he'd been doing all along, what he'd been paid to do.

'Don't listen to him—'

Dodgson took the gun away from Donovan's throat just long enough to thump him in the side with the butt end. An agony like fire exploded outwards from the wound, ripping a thin cry from him; he'd have gone down except that Dodgson held him on his feet. His vision dimmed, his body went heavy as lead. His head rocked.

'No, don't!' Maddie was out of the car and backing away from it, one hand held up, the palm spread. 'Don't hurt him. I'll do as you say. You can have the car. Just—don't hurt us.'

Donovan had served his purpose. Dodgson let him go and he folded bonelessly on the grass, too weak to move. Blind and disorientated, hearing was the only sense remaining to him.

Dodgson stepped over him. His voice was calm, reassuring. 'It's all right, Maddie. Everything will be all right now.' Then a shot rang out. Then, a few seconds later, another one.

LIZ KNEW EVERY STABLE YARD, every cross-country course, every saddlery and every stud within twenty miles of Castlemere. She knew this one. She led the way, and drove like Jehu.

There's always something happening around horses. Farriers coming, vets coming, owners coming, horses getting loose, dogs getting kicked. All that goes double for studs, where there are also mares arriving, foals arriving, stallions getting excited, mares getting bored, stallions getting kicked, owners getting cross and stud managers getting drunk.

Even so, no one working at the Collington Stud could remember a day quite like this one. First an Arab princeling looking for a promising yearling or eight; then four cars, two of them in police livery, squealing to a halt in the yard; then a dozen police officers, some of them armed, fanning out in all directions. It was so interesting that even Collington Silver Superman, who was on top of Luckworth Lili Marlene at the time, stopped what he was doing to watch.

Like many police officers, Liz had a sneaking fondness for cop-shows on television. Not because the realism was particularly impressive but because they made it look so good. Like a well-oiled machine. In actuality there were no rehearsals, so that there was less of the well-oiled machine about it and more of the blue-arsed fly. It was as much as you could do to ensure that everyone knew who the target was, what sort of back-up he was likely to have, if they would be armed, and how to put on body-armour.

This one took place with more than the usual sense of urgency, not only because of what might be happening on the Bedford Levels but because Liz had gambled that the situation would not deteriorate significantly in the half-hour it took to muster a posse and get it here from Castlemere. There hadn't even been time to talk it through except in shorthand. But nor had there been any need for detailed discussions: both she and Hilton understood the nature of the gamble. If Kendall phoned a warning to Siddiq, he might call off his mechanic but whether he did or not he would certainly make his escape. If the first thing Siddiq knew was that he was under arrest, the executive jet waiting at the nearby airstrip would do him no good at all. So he'd make the call, because if he didn't he'd have to answer for two more lives—but that extra half-hour just might have made the whole thing academic.

Hilton made sure Liz appreciated the implications of the decision, but he left the making of it to her. She knew things he didn't: how quickly they could reach the stud if they really had to, and whether Donovan knew these fens well enough to still be ahead of the game. Of course, even she could only guess, and if she guessed wrong she would blame herself. But it was probably better than guessing right and having to watch a superior officer do it all wrong anyway.

'We'll go for the arrest,' she decided. 'If we don't, he may think his best interests would still be served by silencing the witness.' Eight minutes after that they were on the road, leaving DI Colwyn to locate a Saudi interpreter. She didn't want anything she didn't understand passing between the accused man and his entourage.

She had no idea how much trouble they would have making this arrest. For all she knew, the personal bodyguard of a Saudi princeling might carry sub-machine-guns and use them at the first sign of trouble. But in the event there was no such drama. Ibn al Siddiq was taking tea with the stud manager and his wife when the cars arrived, and his bodyguard was in the bathroom. By such vagaries of fate are great events decided. If Castro's poisoned milk shake hadn't been left too long in the fridge... If the gallant six hundred had charged down the right valley... And if Ibn al Siddiq had been aware that there are parts of the world where even the potent combination of sex, rank and bank balance don't guarantee immunity to a murder charge, he'd have been out of the country before the dead girl was found and never mind if it cost him the Dubai Cup.

But he was used to having it all: to giving orders and making funds available, and leaving the rest to people whose life's work consisted of smoothing his passage. He wanted a Derby prospect?—they'd find him a choice of three. He wanted pretty blonde girls to entertain him on business trips?—the question was not how but how many. He needed someone to tidy up after him?—that too was only a matter of paying the bill. It wasn't bravado, it genuinely hadn't occurred to him that the people he paid to protect him couldn't protect him from this too.

As far as Siddiq was concerned it was already history— an indiscretion that could have caused some embarrassment at home if he hadn't taken steps to deal with it. But it was done. He'd put the girl he killed, and the one he was having killed, so far out of his mind that when police officers with guns burst into the living-room, his first thought was that they were here to save him from some unforeseen danger.

Superintendent Hilton quickly disabused him. 'Ibn al Siddiq, I'm arresting you for the murder of a woman, identity as yet unknown, in The Barbican Hotel, Castlemere, on Sunday evening. You do not have to say anything, but I must caution you that...'

Siddiq heard him out in stunned silence. It wasn't that he

didn't understand: his English was perfect. It was that he didn't *understand*. 'Superintendent—you do know who I *am?*'

'Indeed I do,' said Hilton crisply. 'You're a man who hurts people weaker than himself for pleasure, who kills people when they become a nuisance, and who's going to find Wormwood Scrubs something of a culture shock.'

Carefully Siddiq put down his cup. 'There must be some mistake,' he said distantly. 'I have killed no one. I was at the hotel. It was a business conference.'

'It was business for the girl too,' said Hilton. 'But beating her up and pushing her off the roof weren't part of the deal.'

Siddiq still thought there might be some mileage in an outright denial. 'I don't know what you are talking about, Superintendent.' But the beginnings of a shake in his voice suggested that he was seeing, for the first time, the possible consequences of his night on the tiles.

Liz leaned over the table in front of him and slapped down her mobile phone. 'Call him off.'

Siddiq's voice was reedy with mounting panic. If they knew that... 'Him—who?'

'You *know* who,' she spat. 'Call him off, now, and it's worth about ten years to you. So far you've killed a prostitute—a good brief can argue that was consensual sex that went too far. You've also had someone shoot a detective superintendent; but we won't get the mechanic so that'll be hard to prove, plus Mr Shapiro's on the mend so even if we do manage a charge it won't be murder. But now your Mr Dodgson is after another of my colleagues and the girl he's protecting, and if he kills either of them your defence goes down the tubes. Nobody—not your ambassador, not your second cousin the king—will lift a hand to help you then. Call him off, and you might get home before the oil well runs dry.'

A lot of what Ibn al Siddiq had was because of who he was, but even without the silver spoon he'd have done well for himself. He wasn't a stupid man. He was intelligent and astute, and no one knew better than he that a distant cousin who caused the king embarrassment abroad was unlikely to prosper further. He thought about it for perhaps half a minute. Then he picked up the phone.

It rang; then it funnelled through some kind of electronic filter; then it rang some more. Then someone answered.

Siddiq didn't use a name or give his own. In a terse, clipped voice he said, 'This is my cousin's cousin. Come home; all is well.'

There was a pause at the other end. Liz waited, her ear close to the handset, not daring to breathe. When there was no response she looked questioningly at Siddiq and he gave a perplexed shrug.

Finally the phone crackled to life again. It might have been interference, or the bleak chuckle of a craftsman constantly having to compromise his professional integrity to accommodate the vacillations of amateurs. The man who called himself Dodgson said, 'It's too late.'

HALF AN HOUR'S HEAD START was all he needed to be safe. In that time he could change the car a couple of times, change his clothes, take on a whole new persona. He knew from long experience that he could walk through a police checkpoint and never be spotted as long as his clothes were different and he didn't look guilty. He never looked guilty, because guilt was something that he didn't feel.

The sheep had tired of being a roadblock and set about cropping an adjacent hayfield. He ignored them: whoever found them would swear a lot and then return them to their pasture. He might blame walkers or picnickers; he wouldn't be looking for evidence of anything more sinister than that.

Dodgson dragged the body of Maddie Cotterick into the field and bundled it into the ditch under the hedge. Then he went back and looked down at Donovan. 'Can you walk?'

Donovan didn't reply. His heart raged within him that if he'd been able to walk, if he'd been able to do anything, he wouldn't have sat by and let someone put two bullets into the girl's brain. He knew, in his head and in his heart, that he'd done everything in his power to keep her safe, that she'd died in spite of his best efforts not because he hadn't tried hard enough. Soon that would be a consolation, as would the fact that the man who defeated him was an expert who was being paid more for this day's work than Donovan would earn in three years.

But now all he felt was a sense of loss. He hadn't known Maddie Cotterick very long, he hadn't known her very well, but he'd liked her, admired her resilience, her determination to make a good job of the lonely furrow she'd chosen to plough. And now she was gone, her life judged an embarrassment and erased as a careless typist might erase a slip of the finger. It wasn't good enough. It was an offence against natural justice and human worth, and the impotent fury he felt was not just because he hadn't the strength left to do anything about it. He'd have been helpless to avenge her if he'd come this far without a scratch on him. He was outclassed. He'd been outclassed all along. Dodgson would get away with her murder, as he'd got away with all the others, because it was his job and he'd take whatever steps were necessary to get it done.

'No, of course you can't,' said Dodgson, weighing him up. When he wasn't actually killing anyone he came across as a serious, thoughtful, intellectual man. It wasn't concern in his eyes as he took in the blood that had already soaked the dressing Maddie had fabricated from her underwear—her last, or rather her last but one act of kindness in this world—but it was understanding. He knew Donovan wasn't going to jump him and wrestle his weapon away again. The policeman was a threat whose bolt was shot.

'All right. Bottom line? The bottom line is, I need half an hour's head start. After that I don't care who knows what happened, or how good a description you give them. It won't make any difference. Every police computer in the civilized world has a description of me, but I go where I like.

'Now, I can make absolutely sure you don't talk to anyone, in the next half hour or indeed ever. Or I can take the small risk of leaving you here. The chances are it'll be all of half an hour before you're found: it could be a lot longer. The way you're bleeding it could be too long.

'Or I can take you with me and leave you at the first service station. They'll call you an ambulance. But I'll need your word that for at least half an hour you won't give any information that'll help catch me.'

'My word?' Donovan's voice was sunk to a whisper. It was only the surprise that wrung any response out of him at all.

Dodgson gave a little smile, ruefully lopsided. 'Oh yes, Sergeant Donovan, I'll take your word. Look what you did to keep your promise to Miss Cotterick.'

'Go to hell,' whispered Donovan.

Dodgson breathed heavily at him, impatience tempered by respect. 'Donovan, you don't need to die over this. There's nothing more you can do for the girl: all that's at stake now is your pride, and it's not a good enough reason to watch your life seep away. Nobody—*nobody*—would want you to do that. But we have to reach an understanding, and soon. I have a plane to meet. God damn it, man, give me your word and then break it if that's what it takes!'

There are times, as a Hollywood film-maker once observed, when nothing is a real cool hand. Donovan shook his head. Then his eyes slid shut and he keeled over slowly on the grassy bank, denying the professional killer scowling down at him even the satisfaction of bawling him out.

THE CREAM ESTATE CAR didn't seem to want petrol. It pulled up at the far side of the forecourt, where the air pump and jet-wash machines were. The attendant looked up from his paper but there was nothing for him to do so he stayed where he was in the garage shop.

There was a pause while the driver made or answered a call on his mobile phone. Then he got out of the vehicle, walked round to the back and opened the tailgate. Reaching inside he dragged something heavy out on to the tarmac. Then he got back into the car and drove away.

For several seconds the garage attendant went on staring at the abandoned object. He was a man of the world. You see a lot of things dumped on garage forecourts: unwanted hitch-hikers, unwanted dogs, he'd even had a baby left in his washroom once. But he still didn't believe that someone had left the main road for just long enough to dump a body here.

It took a moment for what he'd seen to filter through into some action. Then he put the paper aside—carefully, he might still be able to sell it—and, moving like a sleep-walker, went outside. Maybe it was just a bundle of rubbish—grass-cuttings, something like that... But he knew it wasn't.

But it wasn't a corpse either, at least not yet. When he was close enough the attendant extended a tentative foot and nudged it, and it responded with a moan and a lax, uncoordinated movement of one hand that revealed a slash of dark blood all the way down its right side.

SEVEN

LIZ DELAYED TELLING Shapiro until there was confirmation. It would be bad enough when they knew it was true; the uncertainty was a burden a sick man could do without.

Hilton was dealing with Siddiq. He offered her the chance to be involved, but though she appreciated the gesture she doubted she could do it justice. Besides, if it was anybody's triumph it was James Colwyn's. She was happy for him to take the second seat while she sat by the phone in her office, thinking of all the times Donovan had driven her to distraction and wondering how on earth she'd replace him.

When the call came saying she wouldn't have to, that DS Donovan had been found unconscious on a garage forecourt and was currently on a drip in Peterborough District Hospital, she was hit by a maelstrom of conflicting emotions. Donovan was safe: he'd lost a lot of blood, but he'd be back on his feet in a day or two. He'd returned from the dead, Liz thought with relief, more times than Dracula.

But there would be no resurrection for Maddie Cotterick. Even when he was able to talk Donovan wasn't able to give a clear picture of where Dodgson had finally caught up with them, and Peterborough police were still searching for the body. But he had no doubt that she was dead; and what Dodgson told Siddiq on the phone confirmed it. Liz had thought he'd killed them both. A fresh cause for guilt was the way her heart lifted when she knew that, though the girl was dead, Donovan was safe. It was only natural—she told herself anyone would have felt the same—but it was no cause for celebration that the disaster had been a little less than total.

Maddie had known she was in danger. She'd turned to Queen's Street for help, and they'd failed her. Liz couldn't see what she should have done differently, and clearly Donovan had done his level best, but the unavoidable fact was that a witness in a murder case had been eliminated after she'd put herself into the hands of the investigating officers. An inquiry was inevitable. Even that didn't bother Liz as much as wondering if they should, or even could, have done better.

Shapiro. Time to tell him how things stood. Like her, his first reaction would be relief; and his second, like hers, a pang of remorse that he was more concerned about his sergeant than the woman he'd been sent to protect.

There was more good news than bad. Donovan safe; Ibn al Siddiq in custody; Philip Kendall in custody. But the bad news weighed heavier. A second girl had died. Even knowing all they did by then, they hadn't been able to prevent another murder.

Perhaps because he'd been on the periphery during later events, Shapiro managed to be philosophical. 'We can't change the world, Liz. We do our best. We all did our best: me, you, and Donovan who if he'd tried any harder would have ended up on a slab. Sometimes it isn't enough. Sometimes the odds are just too great. We were up against a man with a bottomless pocket and no conscience, and I can't imagine a more lethal cocktail. You got to the bottom of it. It has to be enough.'

It didn't feel enough. Maybe if they'd got the mechanic as well, but although every airport and ferry terminal was being watched, Liz wasn't optimistic. If he could be picked out of a crowd he'd never have stayed in business long enough to reach the top. The man who called himself Dodgson had disappeared back through the looking-glass.

She tried to look on the bright side. 'We've evidence enough for the first murder charge to stick. What about conspiracy to murder Maddie—will the CPS have any trouble with that?' She meant, would their nerve fail them. The Crown Prosecution Service was notorious for backing off any case that didn't more or less make itself, as if the cost of losing one would be deducted from the Directors' pension fund.

Shapiro didn't answer right away, and when Liz looked at him, puzzled, his face was screwed up as if he was wondering how to break bad news. 'Frank? What is it?'

He was doing the thing with his toes again, watching them so he didn't have to look at her. 'Liz, don't set your heart on seeing this man in court.'

She stared at him, a blaze kindling in her eyes. 'What do you mean? We know what he did. We have forensics connecting him to the girl in the hotel. We have Kendall's testimony. We even have his own actions—if it's all a case of mistaken identity, how the hell did he know how to contact the mechanic? Of course we've got him!'

There were times, he thought wryly, when it seemed Liz Graham had managed to claw her way up to the exalted rank—for a woman—of detective inspector without ever learning what a corrupt place the world was. Not the criminal substrata, you expected them to behave like that, but the place where the so-called decent people lived. As soon as people had a bit of money they began to think they could behave as they liked; as if middle-class values only applied when you couldn't afford to pay for your vices. Coming as he did from a great bastion of middle-class values, Frank Shapiro didn't have a lot of time for the seriously rich. He could understand people who stole because they were too

stupid to earn what they wanted—not excuse, but understand. He honestly couldn't understand people who had all
the advantages and still couldn't conduct themselves de-
cently.

'I know it shouldn't matter who he is, but we may find
that it does. He's a high-ranking foreign national—he's the
second cousin of an absolute monarch, for God's sake! This
whole business is going to be a massive embarrassment for
both governments. If the Saudis say they want him back,
they'll deal with him at home, I think the Home Office may
go along with that.'

When they were as wide as this Liz's eyes were more
green than hazel. 'They can't! What the hell kind of a message does that send to the world?—Come to Britain, see the
Palace and Shakespeare's birthplace, commit a murder or
two and if you're important enough we'll brush it under the
carpet in the interests of the next trade agreement! Frank,
are you serious?'

Shapiro shrugged. 'Maybe I'm wrong. We all know I
have a nasty suspicious mind, maybe it's working overtime.
I just—wanted to warn you, I suppose. There are things that
officially don't happen but in fact do happen and are just
kept quiet. This may be one of them.'

She still didn't believe. Until she got back to Queen's
Street and found her parking space occupied by a black
limousine with a uniformed chauffeur.

Inside the police station she found a lot of people carefully not looking at her.

'What's going on? Whose is the hearse?'

Sergeant Bolsover was on the desk. 'Home Office,' he
said morosely. Of course, he could sound morose ordering
a chocolate digestive for his elevenses, it was just his way,
but he didn't usually look like he wanted to spit and then

wipe his mouth on his sleeve. 'Detective Superintendent Hilton said—'

'I know,' she said shortly. 'To see him when I got in. I'm on my way.' She started resolutely up the stairs.

You can tell a genuine Fenlander not only by his glum expression but by the slow deliberation of his speech. Liz had disappeared round the angle of the stairs before Bolsover rumbled, 'No. He said to keep out of the way.'

So Shapiro was right. They were going to Reach an Understanding. To protect Siddiq's family and the British government from public embarrassment, they were going to circumvent the process of law and send the transgressor home for a slap on the wrist. As if the lives of Maddie Cotterick and her friend were of no consequence. As if three murders mattered less than the risk of offending a major export customer. Mounting outrage and a savage determination to get justice for the dead girls, and for the homeless man called Wicksy, powered her up the stairs two at a time.

Hilton either heard or anticipated her arrival. He met her in the corridor. More than ever his expression was internalized, tight and wary. He was expecting fireworks. He thought he'd slammed the blast-proof door just in time, was alarmed to hear a fizzing sound on this side of it.

'Inspector Graham. Didn't you get my message?'

Her eyes were hot on his face. 'No, I don't think I did. You've got the Home Office in there.' She jerked her head at his door.

'Yes. And the Assistant Chief Constable, and a gentleman from the Saudi embassy. It's not a big office,' he added pointedly, 'when I go back in there it'll be full.'

'You're going to let him go.'

Hilton elevated one thin eyebrow. 'Really? You've got a crystal ball, have you?—you know what the outcome of this meeting's going to be? Excellent; you can save us all a lot of time.'

But she was too angry to wilt under his sarcasm. 'God damn it, sir! He killed two women and a man: one with his hands, the others with his chequebook. He had Frank Shapiro shot in the back to stop him investigating, and Donovan almost bled to death. And you're going to let him go. Because he has friends in high places, and after all, we do some valuable business with his cousin! And they were only a couple of working girls; oh, and your colleagues.'

If she'd been a man it's just possible he might have decked her for that. Detective Superintendent Edwin Hilton was not blessed with unlimited personal charm, but he was an honourable man with twenty-five years' service under his belt and he found both her tone and her words deeply offensive. The more so because, though they hadn't worked together very long, it had been enough for each to gain an appreciation of the other's worth. He had come to respect Liz Graham's opinion, was hurt by her judgement of him.

Another man might have tried to explain, to justify himself. But Hilton had a pride as brittle and impervious as porcelain, fired long and hot for maximum lustre and minimum flexibility. His lips just tightened and his eyes grew hard and cold. 'What you think of me, Mrs Graham, is of very little moment; but if you imagine I don't care what happened to Mr Shapiro, and indeed to Sergeant Donovan, you're mistaken. I also care about the murder victims. But I'm a police officer: I have superiors, I have orders, and ultimately I have to defer to them. I may not like it any more than you do, but I don't actually have a choice.

'When we're done here I shall go back into my office and try to persuade my visitors that they've got it wrong, that upholding the rule of law is worth putting some pressure on even a profitable friendship. But if I don't succeed, and I'll tell you frankly that I don't expect to—if they start talking about the public interest and diplomatic immunity—then I shall do what I'm told by those with the authority to tell me. And so, Mrs Graham, will you.'

With that he turned on his heel, crisply as a storm trooper, and returned to his office, shutting the door with an audible snap behind him.

Liz remained where she was in the corridor, frozen like Mrs Lot, for perhaps a minute. She could hear the murmur of voices through the door without being able to pick out the words. After a few exchanges the voices began to rise, becoming querulous.

Liz was already growing aware, even through her fury, that she'd been unfair. Hilton was only a link in the chain, like herself—a bit further up the chain maybe, but a long way from where decisions like this one were made. He was wasting his time even pressing for a rethink. The decision had already been made, not by the people in that room, and was not open to negotiation. They were here to inform him, not to engage him in discussion.

As soon as Ibn al Siddiq had telephoned his embassy, which as a foreign national in police custody he was entitled to do, the great wheels and little wheels stirred into motion and soon the machines of state were clanking along at maximum revs. If Hilton or any of them got in the way they'd be mown down, and the machines wouldn't even notice. They were concerned with world events, not the ant-like activities of a few people in a town whose existence history would hardly acknowledge. There was nothing more he could do. There was nothing she could have done, had it been her call, or Shapiro had it been his. Ultimately, as Hilton said, they were public servants. They did as they were told.

It crossed her mind, during that minute, that she could

make it a resigning matter. There were issues she would resign over, and for a moment she wondered if this was one. It would free her to make public what had happened. But what, really, would it achieve? A brief satisfaction for her, and then twenty years doing some job that was less important, less relevant, than the one she was doing now. The outcry—as outcry there would be—would not bring Ibn al Siddiq to justice. Its faintest echoes would hardly reach him, safe in his palace near Dhahran. She would suffer; and—not to be too modest—Castlemere would suffer; and public confidence in the British system of justice would suffer; and that would be all.

It wouldn't bring the girls back. It wouldn't bring their killer before the courts. It might embarrass the government, but it had survived worse and would survive this. Nothing would change. It would cite 'wholly exceptional circumstances' and 'the public interest'; and express confidence that the Saudi authorities would deal appropriately with Siddiq back home; and add parenthetically the annual value of British trade with Saudi Arabia and the number of jobs dependent on it; and that would be the end of the matter. There was nothing she could do to affect the outcome, which was that Ibn al Siddiq was going to get away with murder.

But she didn't have to stay in the same building while he did it. She gritted her teeth, and turned with a stamp that she hoped they might hear inside Shapiro's office, and plunged down the stairs again. 'If anybody wants me,' she flung at Sergeant Bolsover in passing, 'I'll be in Peterborough. Trying to explain to Sergeant Donovan that he damn near died for nothing.'

EIGHT

THE DRIVE DID SOMETHING to restore her sense of perspective, even a little grim humour. It was a low ebb, she thought, the day she had to visit her superintendent and her sergeant in different hospitals.

She wasn't sure how Donovan would be. She knew he was on the mend and would be discharged within a day or two. What she was anxious about was his state of mind. It had been a trying week for all of them, but Donovan had been hunted like an animal and then had to watch a murder he was helpless to prevent. Knowing him, knowing how much he invested in his job, Liz understood that his spilt blood was only part of what he'd lost, that the hope of a conviction was about all he'd salvaged from the wreckage. When she took that away too…

She wondered if she should defer telling him. But she didn't want him hearing it elsewhere. If he needed someone to yell at, better her than Hilton or Superintendent Giles. They knew one another well enough, and owed one another enough, that he didn't have to hide his feelings in front of her.

She found him dozing, a blood pack dripping into the back of his hand. He looked pale and thinner than ever, drained and insubstantial under the white sheet. Rather than disturb him she thought she might go and get some coffee; but he stirred, his eyes flickered open and his lips twitched an acknowledgement. So she pulled up the chair and sat down.

'How are you feeling?'

'OK.' She waited for more, and finally it came. 'Sick.'

Liz nodded. 'It'll pass.'

His eyes flared and flicked up at the drip stand. 'I don't mean this!'

'I know what you mean.'

His breathing came ragged and uneven for a moment. Then he said, 'He killed her.'

'Yes.'

'Like—it was nothing. Like switching off a light.'

'A professional,' said Liz. Her expression was tight, her voice acid.

'Twice. He shot her twice. He didn't need to, once was enough, but he was a professional. And it was only a little gun—he had to be sure.' He heard the sob in his voice and stopped abruptly.

'Donovan...'

'I know: it wasn't my fault. I know.'

'So do I.'

For a second his eyes were grateful. Then he shook his head. 'I can't believe I watched somebody kill her.'

'There was nothing more you could do. You couldn't have done any more if he'd decided to kill you.'

'I thought he was going to,' admitted Donovan. 'I don't know why he didn't.'

Liz gave a little shrug. 'Professional respect. He didn't have to, and after the job you'd done he didn't want to.'

'*Respect?*' A shudder ran the length of his body. 'I let her die. I watched her die.'

'You couldn't have saved her. If you need someone to blame, blame me. I didn't take her fears seriously enough, and I told the one man who could stop us what we were doing! The first was an error of judgement, the second was downright stupid. After that an Armed Response Unit wouldn't have got her through. Men with crack bodyguards still get assassinated, it just takes a better mechanic. Siddiq could afford the best.'

Donovan stared at her. 'You know who it was?'

'Ibn al Siddiq,' said Liz, 'some Saudi princeling. It seems two wives back home weren't enough: he wanted to sample the local talent. Kendall fixed him up, and covered for him when it all went horribly wrong.' She told him what she knew, ending short of Siddiq's arrest; in return Donovan told her what Maddie had told him.

'So we've got Kendall.' He looked for some comfort in that, but there was no sense of the anger within him abating. 'It isn't enough. It's like—prosecuting the monkey after the organ-grinder's skipped the country.'

He had to know the truth some time. Liz steeled herself. 'Donovan—no one skipped the country. He should have done, but he was so bloody confident he went on with business as usual, and we got him. Siddiq. And just about now we're losing him.' She told him the rest.

For what seemed a long time Donovan hardly knew how to react. He was too tired to shout up a storm, and nothing less seemed adequate. Distantly, as if from a void, he said, 'I heard the phone. In the car. I was pretty well out of it, but I heard the phone go and I heard him answer it. He just said, "It's too late." I don't remember any more.'

'There wasn't any more,' said Liz. 'I was with Siddiq at the other end. I thought he'd killed you both. It was another hour before we heard you were safe.'

'And now he's on his way home?' He couldn't get his head round it. From the bottom of his reserves he was dredging up enough energy to get angry. 'We know what he did, but we're letting him go? Jesus Christ!—is that what we risk our necks for? To bring down only those who can't afford to buy us off? I got shot! The chief got shot. Why didn't we just stick our hands out at the start and set a price for looking the other way?'

Liz tried to mollify him. It felt like tinkering with the weights on top of a pressure cooker. 'I know: it's a sickener. Frank warned me it might happen. I didn't believe him.'

Donovan shook his head, his breathing rough enough to threaten his stitches. 'So nobody pays for them. Two dead girls, and Wicksy, and nobody pays. Maybe they weren't Citizen of the Year material, but they were worth more than that.

'I wish you'd met her, boss. Maddie Cotterick. She was a nice girl. I don't care what she did for a living, she was a nice girl. Straight, and decent. She was pretty scared most of the time, but she kept going as long as she could and she didn't complain. I liked her.'

He looked at Liz then, surprised, as if he'd just remembered, or just understood, something. 'She could have got away. He was down to this little pop-gun with an accurate range of about a metre and a half, and she was behind the wheel. If she'd put her foot down, he couldn't have stopped her. But he had his pop-gun in my ear, and she wouldn't buy her life with mine. He said he only wanted the car, but she couldn't have believed that. She traded her best chance for my neck, and it cost her her life. And she knew it would.'

These two people had worked together for three years in a business which was occasionally so intense it left them closer than friends, almost like lovers. They had seen one another stripped to the soul. Each had been and would be again a kind of refuge for the other, a place where it was all right to be afraid, to hurt and to heal. They were still what the signs on the doors said they were, a Detective Inspector and her Sergeant; it wasn't a personal relationship.

Yet there were times when they needed contact with another human being who knew how it felt out here in the dark.

Liz touched the back of Donovan's hand with her fingertips, carefully avoiding the catheter. 'What goes around comes around.'

He didn't understand. He looked down at her hand, then at her face with a puzzled frown.

She smiled sombrely. 'Donovan, all the time I've known you you've taken risks for people. You do it so automatically you hardly notice you're doing it at all. But it's rare enough that people notice. That girl can't have known a lot of kindness—the genuine article, that comes with no price tag. It would matter to her that you kept your word: you looked after her, you didn't walk away when the going got tough. You're right, she was a decent person. She wasn't going to do any less for you.'

'I was only doing my job,' objected Donovan.

Liz shook her head. 'The job doesn't ask that much. But you never know when to quit, when to say you've done enough. Then you're surprised when someone wants to return the favour.'

His eyes widened. 'By committing suicide? Yeah, that does tend to make an impression.'

Liz shook her head. 'It wasn't suicide. Either she believed him, that he'd take the car and go, or she thought she was dead anyway but maybe you weren't. Either way, she thought you'd done enough and it was her turn.'

Like most of his countrymen, Donovan had a sentimental soul. Tears pricked his eyes. 'You expect trouble. You expect to get hurt sometimes. But you don't expect to go through all that only to have the sods actually bloody *win*. You watch enough television, you start thinking that right triumphs in the end. Maybe bloody, maybe even a little bowed, but by the time they run the credits the good guys'll have won and the bad guys'll be talking to their lawyers.

'You forget there are people who really are above the law. Who have the money and the connections to do what they like. Who don't care what we find out, because pulling the right strings will get them out from under any consequences. Who can pay for their pleasures, even ones that leave other people dead.

'It's wrong. Three murders, we know who's responsible, we got him—and you're telling me we can't hold on to him? It's not fair. And I don't know what to do about it.'

Liz nodded slowly. 'It *is* wrong, and it isn't fair, and I don't think there's anything we can do about it. I tried to think of something on the way over, and I couldn't. Nothing that would put things right. Maybe it's just one we have to live with. It wasn't our failure, it was a political decision. I don't think there's any point resigning and going public— it's a forty-minute drive,' she said wryly, 'I covered all the options—when the man responsible would still be out of reach. I think we have to take our beating and move on.'

A ward orderly stuck her head round the door. 'Detective Inspector Graham?'

Liz nodded. 'That's me.'

The woman produced a telephone and plugged it in. 'Call for you.'

Liz had obeyed the sign at the front desk and turned off her mobile rather than reset somebody's pacemaker. So she'd been unavailable for half an hour. Somebody must have wanted her quite urgently to route a call through the hospital switchboard.

It was Superintendent Hilton. He didn't waste time on pleasantries. 'Can you get hold of a wireless?' He belonged to the last generation that used the term to distinguish a radio, which operates without physical connection to signal source, from all the other things which do as well.

Liz blinked. 'I suppose so. Can you wait a minute?'

'Let me talk to DS Donovan.'

Donovan took the phone cautiously. A lot had happened since he'd set off for King's Lynn primarily to avoid Edwin Hilton, but the memory of that voice, dry as old bones, and the dislike in the eyes that went with it remained untarnished. And right now he hadn't the heart to continue evasive manoeuvres. If Hilton started on him, there was a strong possibility Donovan would bite back. 'Sir?'

'How are you feeling?'

Donovan sniffed. 'I've felt better.'

'They tell me you're out of danger.'

'Yeah?' Donovan seemed to remember telling Maddie Cotterick the same thing.

Hilton clung to his patience. People had told him Cal Donovan had changed since his days at the Met, had acquired some polish and maturity, but holding a civil conversation with him was still like getting blood out of a stone. 'I just wanted to say, you did a good job. I'm sorry it didn't work out better, but no one could have done more. I wanted to put that on record in case I don't see you before I go.'

Donovan appreciated that. 'You're leaving?'

'My job's done. DI Graham is perfectly capable of running CID in normal circumstances. I was brought in to take over a murder inquiry, one way or another that's wrapped up. I'll be away by the weekend.'

Donovan thought he'd finished; but Hilton added, 'Don't let DI Graham hog that wireless. You'll be interested in the news too.'

Liz found a porter and borrowed his transistor. But when she got back to the side ward Superintendent Hilton had gone. 'What did he want us to listen to?'

Donovan shrugged. Between the horizontal and diagonal stripes of his dressing his bare torso was like the body of a greyhound, just ribs and muscle. 'Something on the news.'

She surfed the airwaves until she found it. The local station had it first because some of the wreckage had landed on their roof.

'...shortly after take-off from Castlemere Airport. Eyewitnesses describe a mid-air explosion followed by a fireball. No other aircraft was involved, so mechanical failure is considered the likeliest explanation. Pilot error was ruled out by expert observers, who say the take-off was normal and the executive jet was climbing towards a thousand feet when the explosion occurred.

'Prince Ibn al Siddiq was a regular visitor to Britain, with both business and pleasure interests in this country. He attended a sales conference held by the Castlemere company Bespoke Engineering before visiting local studs in search of Thoroughbreds for his successful racing string. The tragedy has caused shock throughout the Anglo-Saudi trading community...'

There was more of it but they'd heard enough. They stared at one another in disbelief. When Liz finally found a voice it was to state flatly, 'No one's telling *me* that was an accident.'

Donovan shook his head, stunned. 'He told me. He said he had a plane to meet.'

'What?'

'Dodgson. He said he couldn't waste any more time on me, he had a plane to meet.'

'You think he was on it?'

Donovan looked at her as if she was mad. 'Of course I don't think he was on it! I think he blew it up.'

'With Siddiq on board? The man he was working for?'

It was unclear whether Liz was outraged more by the commission of another murder or the poor after-sales service.

'The man who embarrassed his own government once too often. Siddiq paid for Maddie, someone back home paid for Siddiq.'

'They knew before they freed him.' A note of wonder crept into Liz's voice. 'If Dodgson knew when he was talking to you, the people who arranged Siddiq's release *knew* he wasn't going home. They didn't mean for him to get away with what he'd done, just to avoid a scandal of a trial. A tragic accident was tidier. When Siddiq asked for help with the mess he'd made, they gave Dodgson two contracts. To stop Siddiq being charged; and then to stop him ever putting them in that position again.'

Even after all that had happened Donovan was shocked. Violent death was something he knew about. Expedient death was different, and altogether more chilling. 'Maddie died to keep Siddiq's name out of the papers?'

'It isn't much of a reason, is it?' Liz stood up. 'Donovan, get some rest. It's over. We have Kendall—though Lord knows what we'll charge him with if we've lost the Saudi connection. Maybe he'll make a deal with the CPS and plead to a lesser charge. I don't know. Right now I'm not even sure I care.

'This world they inhabit, where you can do anything and kill anyone as long as ripples don't appear on the surface—it's like an alien planet. Armed robbery, cashing other people's giros, assault with a deadly shovel—these I understand. I've even come across men whose idea of fun is beating some girl to a pulp. But I don't understand a government that thinks its credibility is enhanced by covering up a crime. I don't understand Siddiq's government, and I sure as hell don't understand ours. The only comfort is that Siddiq will never do anything like it again.'

'Dodgson will,' said Donovan grimly. 'Maybe not here, maybe we'll never know where, but he'll do it again. And again.'

'There is no answer to people like Dodgson,' admitted Liz. 'He exists by being better at his job than we are at ours. Maybe one day he'll make a mistake and go up against someone more ruthless than himself. Not a policeman—another mechanic. I can't see anyone else getting the better of him.'

It sounded a counsel of despair, but she was only being realistic. You can't stop a volcano erupting, you can't stop a tidal wave, and it's not much easier to stop someone who's good enough from reaching his target. The best advice to anyone anxious to avoid assassination is only to make poor enemies.

Donovan glanced up at the drip stand. 'I don't know how long I'm going to be here. Will somebody feed my dog?'

Liz nodded. 'I'll see to it.' She didn't say, 'I'll do it,' because she had a sentimental attachment to all her limbs. 'Don't rush back. Tomorrow the reaction will hit you like a train. Get over that before you come back to work.'

'You'll be short-handed.'

She looked surprised. 'Will I?'

'Hilton's going at the end of the week. He thinks you're perfectly capable of running CID in normal circumstances.' He watched slyly for her reaction.

Liz considered. 'Generous of him.'

'What about the chief? When do we get him back? *Do* we get him back?'

'Oh, I think so. It might take time to get everything back in full working order, but I can't see him lying around at home any longer than he has to. Already he's wiggling his toes as if they'd just been invented. By the end of a week he'll be climbing the walls.'

'His wife's back,' volunteered Donovan. 'Maybe she'll stay till he's right.'

'Maybe she will.' He seemed to be getting at something, but Liz didn't know what.

Donovan spelled it out. 'Maybe they'll give the marriage another chance. And since it was the job that split them up, maybe this'll seem a good time for him to retire.'

Liz would have liked to dismiss the idea. But whatever he finally decided, if he had a choice, Shapiro must have considered it. Some time in the next four years he was going to hang up his truncheon: just when was something he must have thought about, even before this. Maybe Donovan was right: for a chance to mend his marriage it would seem a small enough price.

'God, I hope not,' she said fervently. 'No, I don't mean that. If it's what he wants, of course he should go for it. But it'll be a wrench to have him leave.'

'It'll be even more of a wrench to break in someone else,' growled Donovan. He was still watching her, and she still wasn't sure why.

'Maybe Mr Hilton'll come back.'

'Then you'd best think up a couple of years' worth of reasons to keep me out of the office. Or…'

She cocked a quizzical eyebrow at him. 'Or?'

'Or could do the job yourself.'

So that was it. Liz stared incredulously at him. 'As a Detective Inspector?'

'As a Detective Superintendent, Range One. That's what the chief was until last year, and you've been due a promotion at least that long. Find out what's holding it up. Let head office know you're still interested, you're not content to stay the best DI on the force.'

He'd succeeded in knocking the wind out of her. But it

made sense. Before long Castlemere was going to need a new senior detective. Why not her?

'I'll have to give that a bit of thought,' she said, a touch shakily.

'Fine,' said Donovan. 'Do it while there's time.'

'If there is.'

He shook his head impatiently. 'The chief'd come back if he thought you only needed a year to get organized. He cares about Queen's Street and he cares about Castlemere, and there's nothing he'd sooner do for them than leave you in charge. Go for it, boss! Or we could get someone who'll make Hilton look like the Laughing Policeman.'

'I'll think about it,' she said again, firmly. And she did: all the way to the car park. By then she knew it was what she wanted.

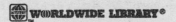

After her husband is killed by a hit-and-run driver, Minnesota police officer Claire Watkins takes her ten-year-old daughter, Meg, and moves to a small town in Wisconsin. Nine months later the crime is still unsolved, but Claire, now working for the local sheriff, is slowly building a new life.

Two things are about to shatter her fragile peace: the murder of her neighbor, and the discovery that Meg has a secret—she saw who killed her father.

Available April 2001 at your favorite retail outlet.

STEVEN F. HAVILL

OUT OF
SEASON

AN UNDERSHERIFF BILL GASTNER MYSTERY

Sheriff Martin Holman didn't like flying. Much less at night,
with bad weather. So why he took a plane ride over a nearby mesa
under those dangerous conditions are questions as disturbing
as why somebody shot the pilot dead from the ground—causing
the plane to crash.

Undersheriff Bill Gastner, just months away from retirement,
now has a murder on his hands. Following his sharp instincts and
a tenacity born of long years as a cop, he uncovers a scheme of
illegal doings and nasty buried secrets. Unfortunately it could
make his biggest case his last.

Available April 2001 at your favorite retail outlet.

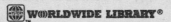

DEAD AND GONE

DOROTHY SIMPSON

AN INSPECTOR LUKE THANET MYSTERY

During a small and decidedly uncomfortable dinner party, Virginia Mintar, wife of a prominent lawyer, disappears, only to be found hours later, stone dead in the garden well of the rustic estate.

Virginia's scandalous behavior had earned her the rage of family, friends and lovers alike. Who had been finally driven to kill her? As Inspector Luke Thanet and his partner, Sergeant Mike Lineham, begin to unravel the tangled threads of dark family secrets, bitter hatred and devious intent, not even they are prepared for the final, ghastly discovery in what emerges as the most poignant and disturbing case of their careers.

Available March 2001 at your favorite retail outlet.

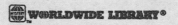

WDS379

JO BANNISTER

Jo Bannister left school at
sixteen and joined the
County Down Spectator, and
worked her way up to editor. In
1988, she left to pursue a career as a
writer. This former award-winning
journalist has written fifteen
mysteries, including the Castlemere
series. Ms. Bannister lives in
Northern Ireland.